AVENUE OF THIEVES

A RYAN LOCK & TY JOHNSON THRILLER

SEAN BLACK

SBD

ABOUT THE BOOK

The winner of the 2018 International Thriller Writers Award returns with one of the must-read thrillers of the summer.

A tense, action-packed novel that shuttles between Russia in the late 1980s, and modern-day New York, where a Russian oligarch is plunged into a living nightmare.

What would you do for a million dollars?

Now what would you do for a billion?

Back in the 1980s, as the Soviet Union collapsed, Dimitri Semenov battled Russia's fearsome mafia, and the KGB, to amass a vast fortune.

Then, as his enemies circled, he fled to America, taking his billions with him.

Now someone wants all that money back, with interest, and they'll go to any lengths to get it.

Sean Black returns with a thriller that's bursting with his trademark mastery of action and suspense.

PRAISE FOR SEAN BLACK

Winner of the 2018 International Thriller Writers Award in New York for *Second Chance*

Nominated for the 2020 International Thriller Writers award for *The Deep Abiding*

"This series is ace. There are deservedly strong Lee Child comparisons as the author is a Brit (Scottish), his novels US-based, his character appealing, and his publisher the same. "
Sarah Broadhurst, *The Bookseller*

"Black drives his hero into the tightest spots with a force and energy that jump off the page. This is a writer, and a hero, to watch."
Geoffrey Wansell, *The Daily Mail*

"Sean Black writes with the pace of Lee Child, and the heart of Harlan Coben. "
Joseph Finder, New York Times Bestselling Author of *Buried Secrets*

Copyright Sean Black 2020

All Rights Reserved

This book is a work of fiction, and except in the case of historical fact, any resemblance to actual persons, living or dead, is coincidental.

1

Togliatti, Samara Oblast, Russia
May 1989

YEARS LATER, long after he'd fled Russia, Dimitri Semenov would discover that Americans had a name for the decision that kickstarted his empire: a choice so blindingly obvious there was no real decision to make, because the likely upside was so vast in comparison to the alternative.

They called such a decision a "no-brainer".

In Russia in 1989 there were tens of thousands, perhaps hundreds of thousands, maybe even millions of business deals that would, by any normal standard, have been considered no-brainers. Some were small. Some were large. Some could make you a year's wages in the space of a few days. Some went far beyond that. These were deals that could make you not just rich but wealthy.

But, as with everything else in life, there was often a snag.

Back then the snag was that no-brainers, deals so extravagantly rewarding that you would have to be a fool to ignore them, attracted plenty of people with no brains but lots of muscle.

That was why you needed a *krysha*, which translated into English as a "roof".

A roof scowled. A roof broke bones. A roof would stab, shoot or throw someone from the top of a building. If required, a roof would murder.

A roof was the person who made sure you could do business. A protector. A criminal to protect you from the other criminals. A shakedown artist who would stop you being shaken down.

The old Communist system had teetered on the edge for decades until, almost overnight, it collapsed. The collapse had offered unimaginable opportunity. Everything was up for grabs. But those opportunities came with risks.

In a regular business deal, as people in America understood it, the greatest risk, the so-called downside, was losing your money. In Russia, it was losing your life.

With the old structures gone, it was a lawless land. People had feared the police and the KGB in a way that most Americans would never understand. As the Soviet system fell apart, those fears evaporated, like a morning mist, replaced with a new, less predictable, force.

Now they feared the *vory*, the hundreds of criminal gangs that had survived the worst the old system had thrown at them. The *vory*: the thieves in law. Men who had no fear of the gulag. No fear of Stalin, a man who had killed tens of millions. No fear of death. Criminals who displayed their contempt for authority on their flesh, in elaborate but lurid tattoos that might depict Lenin buggering Stalin, or something equally obscene.

When he came to America, Dimitri had smiled at what Americans believed constituted rebellion. On television, gangster rappers would curse the police, knowing full well they were protected by the US Constitution. Shout something similar under Stalin or Brezhnev, or any of the old Soviet leaders, and not only might they ship you off to a freezing gulag in Siberia, they could send your entire family along for the ride. To rebel openly when that was the price? That was a *real* gangster.

These were men who, when they attempted an escape from the remote prison camps where they were sent, befriended and took another prisoner, usually a so-called 58er, a political prisoner, with them. If they ran out of food, they would kill and eat their fellow escapee.

The *vory*. Men, and sometimes women, of your worst nightmares. Criminals to be feared.

And nowhere were they feared more than on the Avenue of Thieves, which was where Dimitri now stood, waiting for the delivery of something he knew deep in his bones could transform his life.

2

The Avenue of Thieves was the grand name given to a less than grand alleyway situated close to the end of the Zhiguli assembly line. Zhigulis were at the luxury end of the market. Luxury being a relative term for cars produced in the Soviet Union where quality control, like so many things, was more of an ideal than a reality.

Cars, any kind, were highly sought after, and usually reserved for senior Party officials, union bosses, their families and friends. Even then the average waiting time stretched to years rather than months. Unless, of course, you knew someone. Someone like Dimitri Semenov.

Dimitri had grown up around the factory. His father had come to work there as a supply manager shortly after it had been built in 1967, along with the large town that had been constructed at the same time to house all the workers the factory would need.

Since the collapse of Communism, what had been small-scale corruption, the odd car diverted here, another shipped there, had descended into a violent free-for-all. Criminal gangs roamed the factory floor and the assembly lines, arguing over who would take delivery of each vehicle.

Sometimes the arguments escalated. Full-blown fights would erupt. Fists gave way to bottles. Bottles to knives, and when a gang of *Afghani* (combat veterans fresh from fighting the Taliban) were prevented from taking a shipment they believed earmarked for them, bullets flew.

After that a truce was brokered. The senior *vory*, the *vor v zakone*, sat down and agreed to bring an end to the *razbroki*, as the violent showdowns were known. At least on the assembly line.

Instead, cars whose new ownership was disputed were driven off the line and into the alleyway, where any disputes could be settled without bringing production to a halt. Like everyone else, the *vory* were learning the principles of good business. First production, then distribution.

DIMITRI CHECKED the time on his wristwatch. A little after six in the morning. Still dark and freezing cold. He stamped his feet, trying to drive some warmth into them. He rubbed his hands together, the gloves a present from his mother. Through a friend of his father, he had heard of a number of 'ghost' cars. Vehicles that didn't show on any official or unofficial production schedule. Vehicles that even the *vory* were unaware of. They were produced after the factory was closed for the evening, the assembly lines manned by a second shift of workers who had been promised double their usual pay, and a case of vodka at the end of the month.

The second 'ghost' shift been going on for weeks now without anyone getting wind of it. A minor miracle, helped by the fact that in the evenings most members of the criminal gangs were so drunk in the town's bars that they could barely stand, never mind keep tabs on what was happening inside the vast industrial complex with its twenty-one entrance and exit points.

His father's friend had the cars. But now he needed someone to spirit them out of the plant and sell them on.

The selling part would be easy. Demand outstripped supply by such a huge margin that a car 'bought' with the requisite vouchers, which were required for the paper trail, could be sold on the black market for fifty, a hundred times what had been paid.

The tricky part was getting them out of the Volga plant without any of the vultures knowing about it, and either demanding their cut of the profit or, more likely, simply taking them, with force if necessary.

That was why Dimitri had suggested six o'clock: the ghost shift were leaving, yet it was an hour before most of the day workers would arrive. And a good four or five hours before any hung-over *vory* would appear on the scene to see anything that might pique their interest.

Dimitri hoped that by the time the gangs discovered the subterfuge he would have enough money saved to be able to hire muscle of his own. But he wanted them on a salary rather than shaking him down for an ever-increasing cut of the profits. He planned on asking around, and cherry-picking the most hardened Afghan veterans he could find. Then, once they had scared off the shakedown artists and *vory*, he could begin his expansion. Through his family he already had all the contacts he needed within the vast car plant. What he needed now was what they referred to in the west as working capital, and this morning's car would provide that.

And the best part of all of this? When you lived in a state that had abolished the idea of private property, and that state no longer existed, it wasn't even theft. How could you steal something when no one knew who owned it?

It was like being back in feudal times when whole kingdoms were there for the taking. If you had the nerve.

The throaty rumble of a car engine behind him. He turned to see the manager he'd brokered the deal with behind the wheel of the fresh-from-the-assembly-line car. It had been painted a revolting shade of brown, but that hardly mattered. In Moscow or Leningrad, or anywhere else for that matter, a new car was a new car. No matter how it looked, it symbolized prestige and, most of all, freedom. It would sell.

The car stopped. The manager got out. He held up the ignition key.

Dimitri motioned for him to wait. He walked to the side of the alley, picked up a cardboard box that held six bottles of vodka and handed it to him. "A gesture of my thanks," he said. "Give it to the boys who've been working tonight."

"Of course. They'll appreciate it," said the manager, taking the box and laying it down at his feet.

Dimitri knew the workers inside would never see the vodka. But it was the little dance that people did.

Under the Communist regime you lied to survive. You lied to the Party. To the police. To your family. To your friends. To yourself. Telling the truth would see you dead, sooner or later.

"And the money?" said the manager.

"As soon as I have it. Don't worry, you'll see your cut," Dimitri reassured him. "Keep the cars coming and before you know it you'll be driving one of your own."

The manager gave a curt nod, bent down, picked up the vodka and walked back down the alleyway. Dimitri knew that he'd barricade himself into his office and be blackout drunk by lunchtime.

Dimitri ran his hand over the hood of the car. The paint was still tacky. He opened the driver's door, put the key into the ignition and took a second to savor the grumble of the little engine.

He had already scoped out the exit through which he would drive out. The guard had already been bribed to look the other way. It was all taken care of.

As he pressed down on the clutch pedal and put the car into gear, Dimitri looked up. His stomach lurched.

At the far end of the alleyway stood three men in heavy wool overcoats. The smaller of the three stood in the center, flanked by two younger, larger men.

Dimitri glanced back over his shoulder. The manager was long gone.

Had he informed on him? Or had someone else told them?

It hardly mattered.

The smaller man, the leader, a *vor v zakone*, was familiar to Dimitri. By reputation if nothing else.

Dimitri didn't know his real name, only his *kilchka*, the criminal nickname given to him when he had been granted the official status of a thief in law. He was known to everyone in Tagliotti as the Bitch Killer.

It was a name with rich meaning in the criminal underworld. It referred to a war that had taken place, first in the gulags and then the streets, between the *vory* and the so-called bitches, those inmates and criminals who went against the ancient thieves' code by working with and for the state.

The Bitch Killer was only a few years older than Dimitri, but he had already acquired a reputation for extreme violence and a long memory. He was smart, ruthless and psychotic, in the clinical sense of term.

He stood, staring at Dimitri. Then he did something more unnerving than pulling out a machine-gun.

It was something that almost no one did: a simple act that, in this society, marked someone as either simpleton or lunatic. And the Bitch Killer was very far from a simpleton.

3

The Bitch Killer looked directly at Dimitri through the windshield and smiled. It wouldn't have seemed more threatening if he'd tilted his head back and drawn his finger across his throat.

It hardly mattered whether someone had tipped them off or they had worked out Dimitri's plan another way.

Eventually the Bitch Killer's smile faded. His face could have belonged to someone twenty years older. A few years in the gulag would do that. He stood just over five feet seven inches tall, with penetrating blue eyes and cropped blond hair. His face was a mosaic of blue ink tattoos and scars. There were so many of both that it was hard to tell what was scar and what was artwork.

Dimitri had always been a tough kid. His father had made him box and do martial arts. Both had given him physical confidence and the ability not to shy away from confrontation. This was different. He wasn't afraid of dying. It was what would come before that concerned him.

If the stories were to be believed, the Bitch Killer was beyond sadistic when it came to meting out punishment. He wasn't just creative, he also appeared to be a historian of torture.

One rumor was that he had reintroduced one of the *vory*'s most dramatic, and theatrical punishments: they would place their victim in a box and saw it in half. There was no glamorous assistant, they used a chainsaw rather than a prop, and the gasps were real.

With all that, Dimitri knew that the worst thing he could do now was show fear. Fear was an aphrodisiac to men like the Bitch Killer.

He sat there for a moment, trying to calculate his next move.

The obvious action was to get out, offer his apologies, take a beating, and surrender whatever profit he'd make on the car. They'd let him continue with his scheme. In fact, they'd make sure he did. But he would see a pittance of the revenue.

That was the best-case scenario.

It was just as likely that they'd kill him on the spot or move him somewhere quiet and take their time over it, as a warning to any other dynamic young businesspeople.

Even with his hands trembling as they clutched the heavy steering wheel, and his bladder on the edge of opening, he didn't like the sound of either option.

All his life he'd felt trapped by the system. Now it was gone, the trap felt the same. The only thing that had changed was the uniform of the gangsters.

If only they'd found out a few weeks later, he'd have had time to hire some of his own muscle.

"If," he muttered to himself. "If" never changed anything.

They were walking toward him. The Bitch Killer was gesturing for him to step out of the car.

Dimitri threw it into reverse, praying the night shift had been good enough at their job to install a functioning gear box.

They had. He stepped on the accelerator, reversing back down the alleyway.

The three gangsters stood, arms folded. They knew as well as he did there was no exit in that direction.

But Dimitri didn't plan on fleeing. Far from it.

He wasn't trying to run. He was making sure he had enough of a run-up. These Zhigulis might be slower than a weekend in jail, but they were heavy.

He threw the car into first gear, gunned the engine, then hit the gas pedal.

The Zhiguli barreled down the Avenue of Thieves, picking up speed as Dimitri moved up the gears. Ignoring the two burly heavies, he lasered in on the smaller man.

It would be no use clipping him with the side of the car. He needed to hit him head on.

As the three men realized what he was doing, they either ran back down the alley or made for the walls, pressing themselves in against them.

The Bitch Killer opted for the former. His heels kicking up, he sprinted along the alley, away from the car bearing down on him.

He was fast. But not that fast.

The steering wheel shuddered in Dimitri's hand. He kept his foot jammed down hard on the gas pedal. He aimed straight for his target, his teeth gritted so hard that, he would realize later, he had stripped off some enamel at the moment of impact.

He had no thought for what would come afterwards. Of what the consequences would be. All he knew was that this was the only way. To meet force with force, or skulk back to a life of humiliation and despair.

No. Better to die than live like this. To buckle under the old system was one thing. But to do it when opportunity beckoned? That was unforgivable.

The Zhiguli's metal bumper struck the back of the gangster's knees. He flipped backward, his lower body going in one direction and his torso in the other.

Somersaulting, the top of his skull slammed into the windshield, shattering it on the passenger side. His head and neck protruded through the shattered glass as he lay on top of the still-moving vehicle.

Blood poured from his head and face. His arms flailed back and forth.

He turned his head to look at Dimitri, blood pulsing from a deep cut in his neck. His eyes blinked furiously as he made a gurgling sound.

The car kept moving, speeding down the Avenue of Thieves, the dying man atop the hood, like some kind of hunting trophy.

Between the blood and the shattered windshield, Dimitri couldn't see what lay ahead. Finally, he took his foot off the accelerator, shifted down the gears and brought the car to a stop.

He climbed out, his legs shaking so hard he could barely stand. The gangster's arms had stopped flailing. He lay motionless.

The two heavies were nowhere to be seen. The alleyway was quiet, bizarrely so. Dimitri reached into his pocket for a packet of cigarettes, took one out and, with some effort, managed to steady his hands long enough to light it.

He pulled the smoke deep into his lungs, wishing he'd kept back some of the vodka. He could have used a drink right about now.

Some workers appeared at the far end of the alley. They watched but didn't approach.

Finally, Dimitri managed to compose himself. He waved to the men watching.

"Who wants to make some money?"

They didn't move. They just looked from Dimitri to the man with his head smashed through the windshield.

"Dollars, comrades, not rubles," he added.

One of the men started toward him. A few moments later, the others followed.

4

Thirty years later
Bridgehampton, New York

AT FIRST GLANCE it was like any of the other multimillion-dollar oceanfront estates on Surfside Drive, a long, winding road that hugged the beaches in this part of the Hamptons. Home to Wall Street superstars and the occasional celebrity from the world of entertainment or professional sports. Only the name, Glasnost, a jokey reference to Gorbachev's new openness, which had preceded the collapse of Communism, gave any clue to the origins of its owner.

Like so much high-priced real estate purchased in and near New York, the two separate oceanfront lots on which the home had been built had been paid for via a trust based in the Cayman Islands. Originally untraceable, it was only years later when the house's new name went up on the sign outside that the owner was revealed as the hedge-fund billionaire, Dimitri Semenov.

Dimitri had arrived in the United States in the early 2000s, already a very wealthy man. That was a large part of the reason he had been allowed in. Borders were for poor people. The wealthy were welcomed by most countries.

By the time he'd applied for and been granted his green card, his financial interests back home in Russia were deep and wide. From a chain of automobile dealerships to a steel plant, from financial services interests that included two Moscow-based banks, and on into the real money-makers, gas and oil.

Automobiles had got him started. They had provided him with cash and working capital. The banks had been necessary to allow expansion—back in the 1990s no self-respecting oligarch was without their own bank. But it was the interests he had secured in Russia's vast natural energy resources that had taken him, in under three decades, from poor to obscenely rich to wealthy.

Not that any of this occupied his mind that morning as he showered. It was his experience that the thrill of money was fleeting. And it brought new problems of its own. The biggest being that people wanted you dead.

Dimitri Semenov stepped out of the shower, grabbed a towel, and dried off. Stock prices scrolled over the bottom of the TV in the corner as an earnest business news anchor reported on Apple's upcoming new product launch.

He waved his hand toward the screen and it switched off. He knew what was being announced. He had spent an hour the day before on an investor call with Apple CEO Tim Cook.

Over the past decade he had gradually been shedding his Russian investments and replacing them with others. Many were American, but he also had substantial holdings in the Far and Middle East.

Naked, he walked out into the dressing room. He jumped up, grabbed the bar and busted out five sets of ten pull-ups interspersed with squats, burpees, and push-ups. He prided himself on being in excellent physical shape. Not just for a man of his age, but of any age.

He didn't drink alcohol. Smoking had been tougher. It had taken the birth of his daughter, Anastasia, ten years ago, for him to put that vice to bed. His only real remaining vice, if it could even be called that, was drinking too much coffee. And, of course, women. He was married to Elizabeth, Anastasia's mother, had been for almost fifteen years, but he also kept a series of mistresses and girlfriends, mostly models.

He dressed quickly in his usual uniform of black trousers, expensive leather sneakers, and a cashmere hoodie. He rarely wore a suit. Suits were for millionaires and people who worked for him. He wore what he found comfortable.

He had meetings later, and he was running behind. Usually he would have taken his helicopter into the city, but the new security team had advised against it after the Karchov incident a few months before. Karchov, a Russian oligarch based in London, had perished in a helicopter a few months back. It was widely believed that the crash had been far from accidental, and the result of someone having tampered with the aircraft. Helicopters were sensitive machines. It didn't take much to bring one down.

According to his security team, it was safer, for now, to travel by car. Given that he was paying them almost five thousand dollars a day to keep him alive, the least he could do was take their advice.

5

Three black Cadillac sedans waited out front, engines purring. His designated bodyguard, a former member of British special forces called Neil McLennan, opened the rear door of the middle vehicle.

Dimitri thanked him, got in, and settled himself in the backseat. McLennan closed the door, climbed into the front passenger seat, and the convoy set off. Dimitri settled himself for the long drive into Manhattan, pulled out his iPad, and started on the mountain of reading he had to get through.

His phone chirped as they drove out through the imposing black security gates, installed at the behest of his new head of security. It was his wife, giving him an update on Anastasia. Nothing had changed. She'd had a comfortable night and was resting. They would visit her later.

He said a silent prayer and returned to his reading. He would trade it all, every single dollar he had, to take back what had happened to Anastasia. But there was no taking it back. He had to live with that.

. . .

THE THREE CARS threaded their way through Bridgehampton onto the Southampton bypass, the sedans evenly spaced but not so far apart that another vehicle could get between them. The lead vehicle held two members of the close-protection team, a driver and a passenger. Their role was to scan the road ahead for anything out of the ordinary. The middle one held Dimitri and his designated bodyguard, McLennan. It was McLennan's task to stay with their principal, and directly protect him. That included stepping in front and taking a bullet for him if the need arose. The sedan bringing up the rear had four men inside, a driver and three close-protection operatives. An assortment of British and American former special-forces soldiers, together they made up the counter-attack team. Their job was to engage any threat or threats, giving McLennan and the driver of the middle sedan enough time to get away.

Apart from the President of the United States and visiting heads of state, CA (counter-attack) teams were rarely used in the United States. They were the preserve of high-threat environments, such as parts of Mexico, and areas of ongoing military conflict such as Afghanistan.

The traffic was usually light at this time of year, and they were making good time. With any luck they'd be in Manhattan by eight, and he'd be in the conference room of his office on Avenue of the Americas in SoHo by eight thirty.

He had a lunch booked with the CEO of a tech startup he was considering investing in, then an evening rendezvous with a young Ukrainian model, Ruta Sirka, who was tipped to be on the front cover of the *Sports Illustrated* swimsuit edition. He'd return to his townhouse on the Upper East Side and go with Elizabeth to visit with their daughter Anastasia for a few hours.

The lead sedan slowed as they came up on the Shinnecock Hills golf course. A battered old pickup truck was pulled over on the side of the highway, the hood raised, and steam pouring out. A kid with long hair waved for them to stop.

The two members of the escort inside the lead car looked at each other and chuckled. One of the first rules you learned in this line of work was not to stop, no matter how harmless the person seemed.

The man in the front passenger seat pulled out a cell phone. "I'll call the local LEOs. They can check him out and arrange a tow truck."

"More than I'd do," said the driver.

"Yeah, but I'm a nicer guy than you."

The sedan suddenly accelerated. The man in the passenger seat looked behind them and then at his companion.

"Quit messing around, okay?"

The driver glanced down at the pedals. "I'm not."

"Very funny," said the passenger.

The car picked up speed. A gap was opening up between them and the sedan behind them. The passenger's radio crackled. It was McLennan.

"What the hell do you think you two are playing at?"

Alexei slammed the hood of the pickup shut and got into the cab. On the bench seat was an old Toshiba laptop. Cables ran from it to three display screens mounted on the dash. He brushed hair from his eyes and jabbed two fingers at the laptop's keyboard. A string of barely intelligible mnemonics ran down the screen. He looked from the screens to the laptop display and back.

Up close he was older than his carefully constructed "millennial slacker" outfit suggested. Late twenties rather than early. His skin was ghostly pale, and his eyes bloodshot from a schedule that involved very little sleep.

Still, he was almost there.

They'd promised him a good long break when the job was done. In a few weeks he'd be in Cancún, soaking up the sun and drinking tequila, with ten million tax-free dollars in his bank account.

Now, he had to concentrate. He had done the hard part a few weeks before when he'd installed the new circuit boards. But there had been no real way of beta-testing how it would operate in the real world.

THE DRIVER of the lead car jammed his right foot down on the brake pedal as hard as he could. The car was still accelerating. The digital display swept past fifty miles an hour and kept going.

The passenger was staring down into the footwell. "Why is it speeding up when you don't even have your foot on the gas pedal?"

"How the hell would I know?"

The gas pedal kept inching down into the floor, propelled by some ghost-like force.

The driver wobbled the steering wheel, but the sedan didn't veer off a straight line. Not even by a few inches. He was sitting in the driver's seat, but he might as well have been reclined in back for all the good it was doing him.

DIMITRI UNCLIPPED HIS BELT, grabbed at the back of the seats and pulled himself forward. "What's going on?" he said to McLennan, as the car in front pulled further ahead of them, picking up speed with every second. "I thought they were supposed to stay just in front of us."

"They are," snapped McLennan. "The driver says he's lost control. The pedals aren't working. Nothing is."

"You're sure?" asked Dimitri.

"That's what he's telling me."

"We need to pull over," said Dimitri.

"Sir, as soon as we get you to a safe location, we can debus you––"

Dimitri was thrown forward, between the seats, his head colliding with McLennan's as they were suddenly shunted from the back by the CA team car.

"What the fu––?" said McLennan, shifting side on, trying to get a view out of the rear as to what had just hit them. "Sir, are you okay?"

Dimitri slumped back into his seat. He pulled out a silk handkerchief and dabbed some blood from his hairline. "Yes, yes, it's nothing."

"Sir, please put your seatbelt back on," said McLennan, then keyed the button on his radio.

"What the hell was that?" he barked into the radio.

He released the button and waited for a response.

"We don't know, the vehicle just suddenly accelerated out of nowhere. The brake pedal wasn't responding. Nothing was."

"What about now?" McLennan asked.

"It seems to be back to normal."

There was a muffled conversation as the leader of the CA team checked with the driver.

"Yeah, it's operational now."

McLennan keyed his radio again, using the lead car's call sign. "What about you guys?"

Through the windscreen he could see that the lead vehicle had slowed again, allowing them to catch up. It was two vehicle lengths ahead, matching their speed precisely.

"Everything's working," came the response. "Must have been some kind of temporary glitch."

"You're sure?"

"Positive. We're good."

"Okay, next gas station, let's pull in," instructed McLennan. The last thing they needed was one of the cars losing control in the middle of the Midtown tunnel.

"Roger that."

The driver next to him slammed on the brakes. The car in front had come to a complete stop. The glitch had returned with a vengeance.

An RV's horn blared as it slip-streamed past them in the outside lane.

Then, as quickly as it had stopped, the lead car took off again. Fast. Not just a sudden lurch forward but like someone trying to discover how quickly it could get to sixty miles per hour from cold.

. . .

IN THE LEAD CAR, the driver stamped repeatedly on the brake. The passenger screamed at him as both men were thrown back in their seats by the sudden burst of acceleration.

Up ahead was the bridge that crossed the Shinnecock canal, a crossing point that signaled to summer vacationers they were entering, or leaving, the Hamptons.

They were coming up fast on some other traffic. The driver honked his horn furiously to get people out of his way. If they didn't move, he was going to slam into the back of them.

"Move into the other lane," the passenger shouted.

The driver shook the steering wheel from side to side, the car staying on a straight line. "What do you think I'm trying to do?"

"Let's just hope the airbags on this thing are working."

They were still accelerating, the display showing them inching up past eighty. The driver stayed on the horn, all the while cursing loudly, and planting his foot as hard as he could on the brake pedal.

The steering wheel began to move, turning so hard down to the right that the driver's hands were wrenched from it. The tires squealed, struggling to stay in contact with the road.

A red Mercedes convertible slammed side on into one of the rear doors. The Cadillac kept moving, its nose now pointed straight to the guard rail. The engine revved as it powered through the rail, flipping over in mid-air and landing on its roof in the canal below.

TWO HUNDRED YARDS back the CA team sedan was also picking up speed. It overtook the vehicle with Dimitri, passing so close he could see the panicked faces of the men inside.

It continued onto the bridge as the other cars around it did their best to get out of the way. As it came up on the smashed section of guard rail, it, too, fish-tailed, the back of the vehicle sliding out.

The engine roared afresh, the tires smoking as they spun for a second before it accelerated through the gap.

It took off from the edge of the bridge and hurtled into the air, landing almost flush on top of the first sedan, and pushing it under the green-black water of the canal.

McLennan aimed his handgun square at the dashboard display of the Cadillac. If they couldn't stop whoever or whatever had taken control, he might be able to disable it before they also went over the edge of the bridge.

As he began to squeeze the trigger of his Glock, the car came to a stop. The engine shut off.

McLennan climbed over the seat into the back. He started to reach for the door handle, but his employer was one step ahead of him.

Dimitri yanked open the rear passenger door, ready to get the hell out of the death trap. As he put one foot out, he glanced at the dash display. A message flashed on it in Cyrillic letters.

McLennan looked back too, following Dimitri's gaze.

"What does it say?" he asked Dimitri.

Dimitri didn't answer. Instead, he pulled his foot back inside the car, and closed the door as his bodyguard looked at him like he was crazy.

"Sir, we need to exit this vehicle."

Finally, Dimitri looked at him. "Believe me, if they'd wanted me down there," he said, with a nod in the direction of the water below, "that's where I'd be."

The pickup truck nudged its way slowly through the jam of vehicles that had come to a stop on the bridge. There was the distant noise of sirens and the smell of burning rubber.

People had exited their vehicles and were staring in horror at the two black Cadillac sedans sinking slowly. Some had run to either end of the bridge so they could find a way down to the water below and lend assistance.

Looking up at the truck's dashboard, two of the three screens had gone dark. Only the third remained live.

Reaching down, Alexei snapped the laptop shut, steadied his hands on the wheel, and sped away from the carnage.

Mission completed.

6

Four days later
Manhattan's Upper East Side

Ryan Lock and Ty Johnson shouldered their way through the pack of assembled media gathered behind the crowd control barriers at either end of the block. Two blue and white Ford Fusion police responder sedans were parked nose to nose behind the steel hook barriers. Beyond the vehicles there was a row of more traditional wooden sawhorse barriers.

The six-feet-four-inches tall, 240-pound Marine veteran curled his lip in a show of vague disgust at the shiny new patrol cars as he and Lock approached a patrol officer.

"Cops driving hybrids," said Ty.

"Hey, at least they're American," said Lock, showing the cop his ID, which was then checked off a list of authorized visitors.

"Give me an old-school gas guzzler any day," said Ty.

"With leopard-skin seats and a booming sound system that can rearrange internal organs from a hundred yards?" said Lock, referencing his partner's purple 1966 Lincoln Continental.

Ty was many things. Capable, loyal, as tough as old boots, but shy and unassuming would never appear on any list of his personal qualities. Lock, who'd served in the British Royal Military Police's elite Close Protection Unit, was the classic gray man, who liked to blend into the background. It made them a strange, but also strangely effective, team in the world of high-end close protection.

The cop returned Lock's ID with a brusque "Thank you."

"Exactly," said Ty, digging out his California driver's license and handing it to the cop, who scanned it and waved them both through to the next security check, this one manned by private security personnel who were employed, at least for the time being, by Dimitri Semenov.

Ty turned around to take another look at the patrol cars. "What do you think, Ryan? Level Two?"

"Sure hope not," said Lock, as they made their way onto the block of multimillion-dollar brownstones.

The level referred to the National Highway Traffic Safety Administration's levels of driver assistance technology. They ran all the way from Level 0, cars like Ty's beloved Continental, all the way to Level 5 vehicles, which could drive all by themselves.

The two Cadillac sedans that had been remotely piloted off the bridge and into the Shinnecock canal were Level 2, partially autonomous automobiles that could control functions like steering and acceleration. They were designed to require what was called 'driver engagement', something the hacker had overridden.

Besides killing three bodyguards, two had drowned, and one had died from head trauma, the incident had led to a multibillion-dollar product recall, and a level of security on this particular Manhattan block that was usually reserved for the serving president whose own residence, Trump Tower, was only a stone's throw away. Like many other wealthy Russians, an apartment in Trump Tower had been one of Dimitri's first real-estate purchases when he first relocated to the United States.

From his pre-meeting research, Lock knew these weren't the first of Dimitri's security people to meet a violent end. Over the years more than two dozen people tasked with protecting his life had paid the ultimate price. Most had been killed while the billionaire was back in Russia. Like Mexico, Iraq and Afghanistan, Russia could be a dangerous place to work in high-end security.

This latest incident had been, as far as Lock was aware, the first time Dimitri Semenov had been targeted on American soil. No arrests had been made. A description of a possible suspect who'd been driving a pickup truck had been issued but so far he hadn't been identified, never mind located.

The list of people with a motive to kill or harm Dimitri was a long one. You didn't amass such a vast fortune in such a short time without making your share of enemies. Even those who had inherited huge fortunes had a target on their back. With wealth came violence, or the threat of it. Then there were the run-of-the-mill kidnappers, extortionists and con artists.

An elderly woman walking a tiny dog hustled past them, muttering under her breath.

"Ridiculous. Absolutely ridiculous," she said, loud enough that Ryan and Ty could catch it.

"Guess the neighbors aren't happy," said Ty.

Lock stopped and turned back to take in the circus they'd just navigated. "Can't blame them really, can you? What do you think a house on this block goes for?"

Ty shrugged. "Three, four million."

Lock smiled. "Yeah, twenty years ago maybe."

It was an accepted fact that the Upper East Side, unlike other parts of the island, was where the old money resided. It was quiet, unobtrusive, and that was how the inhabitants liked it, a place to enjoy one's wealth in relative peace, or as peaceful as Manhattan got.

"It'll settle down in a few days," Lock observed.

That was, no doubt, part of why their former client had contacted them. The NPYD would up patrols but they weren't going to maintain this level of security indefinitely.

The period immediately after an attempted assassination or terrorist attack was usually safe. Security was ramped up, and visibly so. It was when things quietened down that you had to worry.

They reached the steps that led up to the front door. Two uniformed patrol officers flanked either side of the steps, looking bored.

"Ryan Lock and Ty Johnson, here to see Mr. Semenov."

One officer checked their IDs again while his partner announced their arrival via his radio.

They were nodded through and climbed the short flight of stone steps. The door opened before they could knock, and they were ushered inside by one of the private security team, who directed them toward an airport-style scanner.

"Talk about locking the barn door," said Ty, unimpressed.

They emptied their pockets into separate gray plastic trays, which were then put through an X-ray scanner, and were patted down by another member of the private security. Finally they were allowed into the main hallway.

The residential security was on point. But guarding a residence was one of the easier aspects of close protection work. Especially during a period of heightened risk. And nothing heightened the attention of focus like the death of your colleagues.

It also explained the stare-downs they'd been getting from the security detail since they'd walked in. The Circuit, as it was known, was a small world, and Lock and Ty were well known within it, if not exactly well loved. Being called upon to review and possibly oversee someone's else's operation was hardly likely to change that.

The company currently tasked with keeping Dimitri and his family safe was Blackfall Group, Inc. Along with the likes of Olive and Armor Group, Blackfall was one of the largest suppliers of private military contractors and high-end private security operators in the world. They recruited mainly former members of the American and British military, including ex-special forces, and had offices in London, New York, Moscow, Frankfurt and Paris, as well as hot spots like Baghdad and Kabul. They were generally well regarded. Lock respected their work and the people they employed.

Lock had asked that immediately after he sat down with Dimitri he meet with the head of the security detail, who would take him through the existing arrangements, and get an idea of what had gone wrong back in the Hamptons. He already had an excellent idea of what that was, but he wanted to assess how honest and open they were prepared to be with him. That would be a good indicator of how well he'd be able to work with them.

The serving head of the team, Neil McLennan, came with an exemplary record. He had been the designated bodyguard on the fateful day. Lock had spoken with a few people who knew McLennan well. To a person they described him as capable and loyal. One had even said that if there was one person he would trust with his life it would be McLennan.

The only negative he'd heard was a report about an incident in Iraq when McLennan had allegedly been involved in the death of an Iraqi prisoner during an escape attempt. The suggestion was that, rather than risk his men chasing after the man, McLennan had given them the go-ahead to shoot him. An investigation had cleared everyone involved and the person who had made the allegation was said to have fallen out with McLennan over a separate matter.

What concerned Lock more was that, from what he had already gathered, there had been nothing in place to prevent the car McLennan and Semenov were in from being driven off the bridge. Or, if the remote carjackers had wanted to, for it to be driven at top speed into a concrete pillar or any other solid object along that route.

The truth was that McLennan hadn't saved his principal's life. Whoever had unleashed all this mayhem had done that.

The cops knew it, the FBI knew it, Dimitri surely knew it, and so would McLennan.

A personal assistant appeared. She was early forties, close to six feet tall, with cropped blonde hair and laser-like blue eyes.

"Madeline Marshowsky," she said, shaking their hands. "Let me show you into the drawing room."

She led them down a mahogany-paneled hallway and into a large room at the front of the property. Bookcases lined the walls. Couches had been pushed back to make way for three desks strewn with papers and computers.

Dimitri Semenov sat at the largest of the desks, peering at several monitors over the top of half-moon reading glasses. He looked more handsome college professor than Russian oligarch. He also, Lock noted, had the appearance of a man who was running on fumes, with dark bags under his eyes and gaunt pinched cheeks.

He looked up at the two assistants manning the other desks and dismissed them with a curt "That'll be all for now."

He pushed back his office chair, rose and stretched. "I'm working from home for the time being," he said, with an airy wave at the chaos. "It's easier."

Lock and Ty walked over to him. He greeted them both warmly, clasping their hands in turn. "Thank you for coming all this way."

"Of course," said Lock.

Dimitri clapped his hands together. "Madeline, can you arrange for someone to bring us coffee?" He turned his attention back to Lock and Ty. "Have you eaten? I can have the housekeeper make you anything you'd like."

"Coffee would be great," said Lock.

He could see Ty thinking about it. He rarely passed up any opportunity to eat. But protocol won out this time.

"Coffee's fine," said Ty.

The assistant exited, closing the door behind her. Dimitri waved them to one of the couches. "Sit. Sit."

One of the things that had struck Lock when working for people from Dimitri's part of the world was how hospitable they were. Rich clients could be hard work, but any Russians he had worked for were the opposite of the grim, unsmiling people presented in the western media during the Cold War.

They sat and Dimitri perched on the edge of another couch, hands clasped together.

"So," said Lock, leading it off. "Tell me what you'd like us to do."

"Review my current security arrangements, obviously."

When they'd been contacted Lock had patiently explained that he wasn't in a position to take over such a large operation. Finding, vetting and putting in place such a team would take weeks if not months. Demand for good people was high. Plus, from his initial assessment, Lock believed that the current team were broadly solid. They'd screwed up somewhere along the line, but that could happen, even with the best will in the world.

"We can absolutely do that," Lock told him. "If you'd like we can also try to ascertain how to prevent a reoccurrence and look at any other possible areas of concern."

"I doubt there will be a reoccurrence of that particular problem," said Dimitri. "But, yes, testing the current arrangements would be helpful."

The room fell silent. Lock sensed an 'and' coming.

"You've both signed the NDA my attorney prepared?" asked Dimitri.

NDAs, or non-disclosure agreements, were standard for anyone working with or for high-net-worth individuals. Despite sections of the media trying to paint these agreements as somehow sinister, and indicators of possible bad behavior, the truth was different. Wealthy people and celebrities were as entitled to their privacy as anyone else. There was a voracious appetite for gossip about them. Hence the need to ensure discretion.

Additionally, the people they employed, such as assistants and housekeepers were often privy to the smallest details of their personal as well as their business lives. And with that access came security issues. Knowing the school a child attended, how they got there, and the name of their teacher would be information that was highly prized by potential kidnappers. And that was only one example.

"Yes, they're all signed off," said Lock.

Dimitri sank back into the couch and closed his eyes for a moment. "That's good. It's been a very stressful time and the media love nothing more than to speculate."

"I can imagine," said Lock.

Dimitri leaned forward again. "Your solemn word that what I'm about to say doesn't leave this room?"

Both men nodded.

"I can't just stay here like a sitting duck waiting for these people to try again."

Lock noted "these people" but didn't say anything. It suggested that Dimitri Semenov had a good idea who had been behind this.

"I need someone who's prepared to be proactive."

Lock stayed quiet. He wasn't sure he liked where this might be going.

"I need you to find the people who arranged this, and I need you to eliminate them."

7

It wasn't the first time Lock had heard that type of request from a client. People whose lives were under threat were understandably emotional. He didn't take it too seriously. At the same time it was important that he make clear what the boundaries were.

There was also the possibility that it was a test. A way of Dimitri working out where the line existed for them.

"Mr. Semenov," he began.

"Please, call me Dimitri."

Lock took a breath. "Okay, Dimitri. We're in the business of protecting human life, not taking it."

Dimitri smiled. "Are you sure about that? I don't wish to be rude, but your track record might suggest otherwise."

That was a fair point. Lock and Ty had both killed people, both while serving in the military and sanctioned to do so by the government, and while working privately.

"I've used lethal force when I've had no other option," said Lock, aware that he wasn't being entirely truthful. "What you would be asking is very different, and it's not something we could agree to."

Lock looked over at Ty for his response.

Ty played dumb. "What were we talking about there? I didn't hear a word of that."

"I expected that to be your answer," said Dimitri, his tone suggesting that he wasn't about to give up on his request.

"Listen, let's take a step back, shall we?" said Lock.

Dimitri nodded.

"We're aware you've always faced a certain level of threat, but when did it ramp up, and why?" said Lock.

Dimitri rose from his seat and paced across to his desk and back as he spoke. "It's been a long time coming. Things are different back home. The agreement before was that people like me would be left alone as long as we didn't interfere in politics."

From his work with wealthy Russian clients, Lock knew exactly what he was talking about. The Russian government resented the wealth of the oligarchs, as those who had built vast fortunes after the fall of Communism had come to be known. The Russian state in general, and one man in particular, Vladimir Putin, saw them as having taken advantage of a chaotic situation to acquire things that weren't theirs.

The oligarchs saw themselves as legitimate businessmen who had spotted opportunities when the country was in a state of transition from one system to another. In the same way the tech billionaires had seen certain technological changes coming and exploited them.

To a degree, both were correct. But only to a degree. Men like Bill Gates had created something that had never existed before. Men like Dimitri, often by using political connections, had been gifted chunks of large, already operating state enterprises. Or they had established their own banks, a guaranteed way of generating wealth.

"You think it's the Russian authorities who were behind this?" Lock asked, pointedly.

"Who else would be capable of something like this?" said Dimitri.

Point taken, thought Lock. The more sophisticated the strike against someone, the more likely a government was involved.

"Of course, proving it is a different matter, and even if I could prove it, then what?" continued Dimitri. "You think anyone would care? The whole point of doing something like this is to make sure that people like me know they can be reached anywhere in the world."

"Well," said Lock, "if your theory is correct, then I'd imagine that whoever did this is long gone by now. Or if they're still here, they're holed up in some embassy or consulate and able to invoke diplomatic immunity, as soon as we or law enforcement get close to them."

Dimitri stopped pacing, his shoulders slumped. "So what do I do? Sit around and wait for them to try again? Give in to their demands?"

Lock traded a look with his partner. This was the first time they'd heard about any demands being made, either publicly or privately. Of course it made perfect sense. They could easily have killed Dimitri back on the bridge. All it would have taken was piloting his car into the water, with the added insurance of a kill team or a sniper waiting for him if he emerged from the water. They had done the difficult part. Posting someone nearby with a rifle and a scope to finish the job was low tech by comparison. Bombing, shooting, stabbing, poisoning, there were many ways of ending someone's life that didn't require the kind of planning and execution that had gone into remotely taking control of several vehicles.

"Demands?" asked Ty.

"You've told the FBI about this?"

"For all the good it will do. Don't get me wrong, they're doing everything they can, and I trust them ..." He trailed off, leaving the inevitable 'but' hanging in the air. When it came to state actors, people from the shadows who were backed by foreign powers, then the FBI was limited. That was more CIA territory, and good luck getting a read on what they would and would not do.

To be fair to the Central Intelligence Agency, their concerns were larger than any one person. While Dimitri Semenov might hold an American passport and was legally regarded as a US citizen, he had been born and raised in Russia. He had made his fortune there. That changed how the US authorities perceived him.

If a foreign government went after, say, Warren Buffett or Mark Zuckerberg they had better prepare themselves for a world of pain.

But try to take down a Russian oligarch who happened to have a US passport and the response depended on how the diplomatic winds were blowing.

It might not be fair. It might not be working to the letter of the law, but it was reality. Just like in Dimitri's old country, everyone might be equal, but some were more equal than others.

"These demands," said Lock. "What are they?"

"They didn't exactly print out a list for me, but the general gist is that they want my fortune. All of it. The money I made back home, and the money I've made since I've been here. They regard it as the proceeds of crime, which is slightly ironic, don't you think?"

"And how did they present this ultimatum?" said Lock.

Dimitri walked to his desk, opened a drawer and pulled out a brown folder. He took out a series of newspaper clippings, and handed them to both men. They were from various Russian newspapers and magazines. English translations were stapled to the front of each article.

Lock quickly scanned the first and moved on to the next. By the third he had the general idea. Only one mentioned Dimitri by name, but they shared the same theme. The oligarchs' fortunes had been stolen from Mother Russia, and now the Kremlin wanted those fortunes returned, with interest.

"First, they required my silence, and now they want everything else," said Dimitri, as Lock traded clippings with Ty.

"This is way above my pay grade, but any way you can negotiate some kind of a settlement?" said Ty.

Lock had been thinking the same thing.

"Oh, I've explored that. I still have friends back home who are in contact with the people behind this. Sadly, they aren't in the mood to bargain. It's all or nothing."

He looked straight at Lock. "This isn't about justice. This is about revenge."

"Revenge for what?" asked Lock.

"That, my friend, is a very long story."

8

Madeline Marshowsky, Dimitri's personal assistant, was waiting for Lock and Ty as they emerged from their meeting. She had a thick bundle of files in her arms, which she handed to Lock: the background and security reports on every person employed by the Semenov family in a personal capacity. In total, and not including private security, the family had a staff of several individuals, including Madeline. Two housekeepers, a nanny, several cleaners, a gardener for the Hamptons property, a chef, a personal trainer/masseuse/yoga instructor, two drivers, an onsite maintenance man, additional personal assistants, all highly paid and all apparently indispensable.

Each person had already been extensively background-checked and security-vetted, but Lock liked to get an idea of who was in daily contact with the family. All of these people were potential threats when it came to keeping a principal safe.

One easy way of bolstering security was to brief domestic staff on the importance of letting the security detail know if they spotted anything or anyone out of place. Domestic staff often knew more about the day-to-day comings and goings in a household than the owners. A change of delivery person, someone loitering outside, someone calling the house to inquire about the family's whereabouts, all of these things could be significant.

"That's great, thank you," said Lock, handing some of the files to Ty.

Madeline hovered.

Lock smiled. "We're going to take a look around. I'll let you know if there's anything else we need."

"Of course," she said, handing Lock a business card. "My cell number is on there if you can't find me."

"Thanks," said Lock, pocketing it, and starting toward the ornate sweep of stairs that led to the upper floors. When it came to reviewing residential security, he liked to start on the roof and work his way down.

Ty fell into step next to him as they climbed the stairs. "So, what do you think?" he asked Ty.

"I think we do our review, make some recommendations, cash the check, and get back to LA." Lock stopped and looked at his partner.

"What?" said Ty.

"I thought you liked a challenge."

"I like breathing too, Ryan. Listen, if he's right and it's the Russian government that wants him dead, there's no amount of security that's going to stop them. The only question is who's going to be standing in front of him when the final bullets start flying. And bullets are what he's gonna get if he's lucky. These are some cold-ass motherfuckers he's up against."

Lock knew precisely what Ty was referring to. In his war on dissidents, or anyone he perceived as an enemy, Putin had been relentless. Once you were firmly in the sights of the Kremlin it was often only a matter of time. It was bold and brazen when it came to assassination, often choosing methods that were guaranteed to draw attention.

It was a strategy that was designed not just to eliminate an opponent but to intimidate and cow anyone else who was thinking about stepping out of line. Not that he would admit it, but Lock had a sneaking admiration for Putin, the former KGB officer. While most governments were busy playing checkers, he had been playing chess.

"That's why I said we'd come in as consultants," said Lock.

"And what was all that other BS about us going on the offensive?" Ty said, in a whisper, as they hung a right and headed for the staircase that would take them up to the next floor.

Lock shrugged. "That's what I'd do if I was him. Otherwise you're just holed up waiting for the other shoe to drop. But no, before you ask, we're not doing that either. We'll take a look, see if we can spot any gaps, and get out of Dodge."

Ty fist-bumped. "Good. Plus it's cold as hell in New York. I miss the sunshine."

THEY ACCESSED the roof via a hatch ladder. Lock went first, Ty following. It was a shared roof space, meaning that anyone could access it from one of the adjoining properties.

Lock walked to the edge and looked down to the street below as Ty paced the perimeter before joining him. Over the years, Lock had found the best way to approach security was to think like a potential threat. If he planned on gaining access, the roof would be his chosen method. Enter one of the neighboring homes or businesses and simply walk across.

Ty joined him at the edge. The end of the block was still thick with cops and media.

"Fire regulations probably won't allow them to secure the hatch, so they need a camera up here. Maybe two. One wide angle, and covering the access," said Lock.

Ty made a note of it. "Motion sensors?" he asked.

"Sure. Why not?"

As they walked back the hatch opened and a man's head appeared. Lock recognized Neil McLennan. He walked over and reached out a hand to help him up. McLennan ignored the gesture and pulled himself up.

"You're the consultant, are you?"

"Ryan Lock," said Lock. "This is Ty Johnson."

Reluctantly, McLennan shook their hands.

"I know the last thing you want is someone second-guessing you, especially now, but it never hurts to have a fresh pair of eyes. I was just saying to Ty, it might be an idea to have a camera up here."

Lock knew there was two ways this could go. Either McLennan would let his ego get in the way, or he would park it and allow them to help him. From his demeanor, it looked like it was going to be the former.

"I suggested a camera up here," said McLennan. "One of the neighbors objected."

"Then don't tell them," said Ty.

McLennan's answer came in the form of a stare.

Lock knew the last thing they needed right now was to get into a pissing contest. "Why don't you take us through the rest of the property?" he said.

McLennan gave a curt nod and they followed him back to the hatch and down the ladder.

"How long have you been running the detail for them?" Lock asked, as they made their way down.

"About two years give or take," said McLennan.

"Any serious breaches before this one?" Lock inquired, as they made their way into the plush carpeted hallway on the top floor.

"These are all bedrooms," said McLennan, opening a door while ignoring the question. He pointed up into the corners of the hallway. "Motion sensors there, there, and that corner over there. In fact, they're in all the public areas. We have cameras front and back, including ones that cover as far as the end of the block, and in areas where staff work. Those are monitored twenty-four hours. There's also an alarm that connects directly to the nineteenth station precinct."

McLennan stopped and opened a door that led into a plushly appointed bedroom with a king-size four-poster bed. As they followed him, he continued his run down. "Every visitor and every staff member, including the CP team, is searched upon entry and exit."

He walked over to the windows, which faced out onto the street.

"All the externally facing doors and windows are blast and bullet proof up to level three. I suggested we go to level eight, but the client's wife wouldn't agree for aesthetic reasons. But I did persuade them to add reflective material so no one can see in to get a clear shot, without of course blocking light entry. It's the same at the house in the Hamptons, and the mansion they have in Barbados."

He turned back to face Lock and Ty. "If there's anything else you think we could add, I'm all ears."

Lock had expected that kind of reaction and McLennan hadn't disappointed. Ty leaned into him. "Wonder who chose those dumbass cars?" he whispered, *sotto voce*.

McLennan started toward him, hands raised. "I lost three of my best mates on that bridge so you might want to keep your smartass comments to yourself."

Ty dead-eyed him. "Listen, buddy, everyone in this room has lost people, so if you think we're going to tiptoe around shit because you might get triggered then you're in the wrong game."

"No one's questioning your professionalism, McLennan," said Lock, hoping to calm things down.

"Your mate just did," said McLennan, stalking past them and out of the room.

Ty looked at Lock. "Touchy."

THEY FINISHED the rest of their tour without McLennan, who didn't reappear after he'd stormed off. There was no sign of either Dimitri's wife or his daughter. Lock wanted to drill down into their security details, assuming they had them. If they didn't he would recommend that Dimitri added additional protection for them, at least while they were at this heightened threat level.

Other than that, all the arrangements McLennan had outlined were in place. Besides a few minor tweaks, Lock didn't have much to suggest to Dimitri. He guessed the meat of the conversation would revolve around the steps they could take to augment any police investigation into who was behind the attack in the Hamptons.

Lock would suggest that law enforcement were best placed to conduct any investigation. That said, sometimes people were more likely to share information with someone who wasn't official law enforcement. Understandably, the FBI spooked people, especially those who might have something to hide, and people on the edge of criminality were often the most useful when it came to gathering intelligence.

The locks on the door at the rear entrance could have used an upgrade, and he'd suggest to Mrs. Semenov that she rethink the upgrade on the windows. Level 3 would stop a bullet from a handgun, but snipers weren't noted for using handguns, so it was as much decorative as protective, as far as Lock was concerned.

One thing niggled at Lock, though: Ty's question about who had selected those particular sedans for close protection duties. It was, at best, an odd choice. Not that Cadillacs weren't good vehicles, they were, and Lock loved an Escalade as much as the next man, but cars at the forefront of new tech were vulnerable. In general, smart security people favored the tried and tested, whether that was a firearm or transport.

As they came back into the hallway, the blonde PA was waiting for them. She seemed to have the knack of being there only when required, a good skill to have when you catered to the super-wealthy.

"Is there anything else you need, gentlemen?"

"Just a few moments with Mr. Semenov, if he's available."

"I'll find out," she said, disappearing into the temporary office.

Lock turned to Ty.

"What do you think?"

Ty tilted his head back and pivoted around, taking in the foyer. "Security's solid. If anyone's going to have another pop at him, I doubt it'll be here. And not with a bunch of New York's finest posted at the end of the block."

Lock agreed. As was usually the case, static locations were often the safest place. Problems came when a principal moved to an unfamiliar location or was in transit. You could remain safe if you never left home, but barring the occasional eccentric recluse, people went out, and that was where problems arose.

Madeline returned. "Mr. Semenov will see you now."

They walked inside to find Dimitri standing by the window, a disconcerting habit for a man whose life was under threat. The oligarch motioned for them to sit down.

"So?" said Dimitri. "What's your assessment?"

Lock decided to circle back to the question of vehicle selection. And he'd go easy on McLennan. The guy's back was up. Understandably so.

"I think, barring what happened, you have a good security detail, and that apart from some minor tweaks residential security in this property is about as good as it gets."

"So there's nothing to worry about?" said Dimitri, unable to keep a hint of sarcasm out of his voice.

Lock didn't take the bait. Like McLennan, he knew that Dimitri's stress levels had to be off the charts. Part of his and Ty's job right now was to offer some kind of reassurance. "I wouldn't say nothing, risk is always present, but on the residential level you're fairly well squared away. It wouldn't be a major area of concern."

The central cold hard fact of bodyguarding was that if a person or persons wanted your principal dead the real deciding factors were resources, and the level of determination present on both sides. If what Dimitri had told them was correct, and these threats were being supported by the Russian regime, the chances were that sooner or later they would get lucky. It was a matter of when rather than if. But that was the case for everyone on the planet. Little comfort to the man standing in front of them.

"So what should concern me?"

"There are two main areas of vulnerability that apply to most principals—when you're out of the residence, either in transit or in a location with less robust measures. That's one for sure."

"And the others?"

"The second thing, always a concern, is the people around you. Both in terms of safeguarding loved ones and making sure that staff and visitors have been properly vetted. You have a wife and daughter?"

"Yes."

"Any other family here?"

"My wife has, but my mother and father are both dead and I was an only child. I have an ex-wife back in Russia but, as you can imagine, she's hardly someone they would target."

"Not on good terms?" asked Ty.

Dimitri shrugged. "She was there when I was building the business and we divorced shortly before I left to come to America, so she's a little bitter that she never really enjoyed the fruits of my labor. I gave her a handsome settlement, enough money to keep her for the rest of her life, but that hasn't stopped her attacking me," He paused. "In the press. They've gone to her every time they need a quote that places me in a bad light."

"Okay, then I guess we can cross her off the list," said Lock. "You're currently married to Elizabeth, with a daughter, Anastasia, who's ten years old."

Dimitri's features darkened, and he turned back to the window.

Lock glanced over at Ty. He'd also picked up on it.

"We didn't see them when we were taking a look around," said Ty.

Dimitri cleared his throat before turning back to face them. "My daughter has some health problems at the moment. My wife is visiting with her in hospital. I don't want to say any more than that. It's why I have to be here."

There had been nothing in any of the reports Lock had read about his daughter being ill or hospitalized. He hadn't had time to go through all the logs of everyone's movements yet, but it was strange that such a significant thing hadn't been flagged.

"Okay," said Lock. "Is someone assigned to be with them?"

"Of course, yes. Someone is with Anastasia around the clock, and my wife also has someone assigned to her when she goes out."

"Which hospital?"

"Sinai."

"We'll take a look there too, if you don't mind."

Dimitri seemed to hesitate. "Speak to McLennan. I'm sure he can organize it."

"And your wife?" said Lock. "Besides hospital visits, what's her routine?"

"The usual," said Dimitri, almost dismissively. "Pilates. Lunch with her friends. She runs in Central Park most mornings but there's always someone with her."

"Okay, if you don't mind we'll speak to her about perhaps varying her routine. It's never a good idea to be too predictable with your movements when you have an ongoing threat."

"I understand."

"Ty, could you give us a moment?" Lock said to his partner.

Ty didn't question him. They had already discussed how they'd handle the next part of their briefing with Dimitri. It was going to be delicate, and even though Lock would share the details, he wanted Dimitri to know that he understood the need for discretion.

Ty got up, walked to the door, and closed it softly behind him.

"I've looked after a lot of people over the years. Often the high-net-worth individuals, and those who've been very successful in whatever field, can have quite complicated personal lives," said Lock, launching into the standard speech he used when broaching the subject. "It's not my job to judge these complications, but I have to be aware of them."

Dimitri seemed to relax. He even smiled again. It was one of the things Lock actually enjoyed when working with self-made business-people. They were smart, fast on the uptake. Rarely did you have to draw them a picture and that saved time.

"I don't drink. I don't take drugs. Never really have. But I do like women," said Dimitri.

"Like I just said, none of my business, but it would be helpful to have a name or names of anyone you might currently be seeing socially, as well as where you meet them. Assuming, of course, that McLennan doesn't already have that information."

"I always have someone with me but, no, I haven't shared details.

You know what staff can be like. One person confides in another and suddenly everyone knows."

"I get it. You won't have that problem. I'll share with Tyrone, but that's where it stops."

"How good are you at remembering names without writing them down?" said Dimitri.

9

Ruta Sirka tilted her head, allowing her long blonde hair to cascade over her shoulders. She arched her back, pushing her breasts forward as the photographer moved around her.

"Beautiful. Now give me more sex."

She narrowed her eyes, adjusting her head position fractionally so that the light caught the angular slice of her high cheekbones.

"Yes. Yes, baby. Give me it all."

She tried hard not to laugh. Fashion photographers were ridiculous. Especially the men, and they were mostly men. They talked about sex this, sexy that, when the people who bought *Vogue* and other fashion magazines were women.

Off to one side, her iPhone chirped. It had been a gift from Dimitri. The very latest one, given to her before they had even gone on sale in the stores.

The photographer, an old Italian, who looked to Ruta like a cross between a walnut and a prune, lowered his camera, and glared at the iPhone. "Didn't I tell everyone to switch off their phones?" he shouted, at the small army of make-up, hair and other assistants, who were cowering at the nearby tables.

As well as giving ridiculous directions, this particular photographer was notorious for his bad temper. He would throw things, shout, scream, and even strike the people working for him. Ruta thought it made him an asshole. But in the upside-down world of high fashion everyone else saw it as confirmation of his genius.

"It's mine," said Ruta, saving everyone else the rest of the harangue.

He wouldn't strike her. Almost everyone knew that she was dating Dimitri Semenov, and what would happen if she turned up to see him with a black eye, or even so much as hinted that someone had upset her.

No amount of genius would save them. Dimitri was a gentle soul, a gentle lover too, if a little clumsy and rushed. But he had an edge to him that people feared. No one came from where he had without being capable of looking after themselves.

"Okay, okay, take your damn call," said the photographer.

"It's okay. They can leave a message," said Ruta.

The chirping stopped. It went to voicemail.

The photographer was pacing up and down. He threw up his hands. "It's ruined. The moment. The ambience. It's ruined."

And models were supposed to be the divas, thought Ruta.

"Take a break, everyone," said the photographer, stalking out of the studio.

Ruta reached down, took off her high heels and wiggled her toes. Someone brought her a chair and passed her the phone. Someone else brought her a bottle of Evian water. She checked the screen. The number showed as private. She tapped the screen and hit the icon to check her voicemail.

"Hello, Ruta. It's your Russian admirer."

It was Dimitri's voice. She smiled. She would tell him later about the hissy fit his call had caused. She would find a way to tell it so that he found it funny. He needed laughter and fun with everything that was happening to him.

"I'll see you tonight at the usual place. But maybe we can try something different," Dimitri's message went on.

She frowned as she listened to rest of the message with its detailed instructions about when she should arrive, what would be in the room for her, and what he wanted her to do.

It didn't seem like him. So far when they'd been intimate he'd been so vanilla, and this seemed kind of kinky. Not that she minded. It was just odd, that was all.

She thought about trying to call him back, but he really didn't like her doing that. If she called him while his wife was there it would be awkward. He had told her that she should only call if it was an emergency, and this was hardly that.

She could speak with him about it tonight.

10

Lock walked down the steps to the sidewalk where Ty was waiting for him.

"So?" said Ty.

"Mistress and a couple of girlfriends," said Lock, as they walked back down the block.

"No, not that, the general situation."

"Honestly? If what he's telling us is true, about the Russians wanting him to magically hand them his fortune, I think he's screwed. Unless he can make it difficult enough for them that they're prepared to cut some kind of a deal."

"What? Like give them half so they leave him alone?"

"Something along those lines," said Lock. "But I don't see it."

"And if it's not them?" asked Ty. "I mean, there's nothing that says for sure it is, and they're hardly going to come right out and admit it's them."

They reached the barriers, thanked the cop who'd checked their IDs on the way in, then shouldered their way back through the knot of media and onto 76th Street and Madison Avenue.

Outside the cordoned-off area, New York life went on as per usual. Ty didn't like it, but Lock missed the energy of the place, even if the memories it held weren't always the best. The streets held ghosts for him, but so did those of Los Angeles. Here, though, the gray concrete canyons made them seem somehow more vivid.

Ty had a point. Everything pointed to Russian state involvement, especially the high-tech nature of the carjacking, but drawing conclusions without overwhelming evidence was a dangerous strategy.

Ty stepped to the edge of the sidewalk and stuck out his arm to hail a cab. Two went whizzing past him.

Lock moved past him. "Here, allow me to leverage my white privilege." He laughed as the first cab he hailed cut across two lanes to pick him up.

Ty shook his head, chuckling, as they got in.

"Where to?" asked the cab driver.

"101st and 5th."

"Sinai?" said Ty.

"Yeah, I want to know why he was so cagey about the kid," said Lock.

"I feel you. That was kind of strange. What about the vehicles? You ask him who okayed them?"

Lock nodded. "He did."

"And no one thought to mention that a Level Two vehicle might not be the best idea in the world?"

"Doesn't look like it, but the PA is going to send me through all the information. Apparently there was a shortlist, but the final call was his."

THE CAB DRIVER let them out on the corner, and they walked up to the main entrance of Mount-Sinai. Using the pretext they needed to take a look at the security measures that were in place, Lock had cleared their visit while they were still in transit.

He hadn't said anything to Ty, but he'd decided that once they'd completed their review he'd submit a report with recommendations. They didn't have the resources to take over this size of security detail, and he didn't know where they'd even start when it came to tracking down those who were out to get Dimitri.

As they made their way to the entrance, Ty side-eyed him. "Guy in the black leather jacket and jeans about a half-block behind us."

"Good looking out," said Lock, checking him without being obvious. He was about six feet tall, late twenties, with a blond crewcut and Slavic features. "Where'd you pick him up?"

"He was hanging out when we jumped the cab. Got into one and tailed us up here. Should we talk to him now or wait?"

"Talk?"

"You know what I mean," said the six-foot-four Marine.

Lock did. "Too many people. If he's surveilling us we can grab him when we're somewhere a little more private."

"Then I can talk to him?"

"Exactly," said Lock.

ANASTASIA SEMENOV WAS in a private corner room on the top floor of the building. A bored-looking hospital security guard was posted at the end of the corridor that led to her room. One of McLennan's men stood outside it. Dimitri's PA had already called ahead to let him know that Lock and Ty would be visiting.

"I'll let Mrs. Semenov know you're here," he said, disappearing inside, and firmly closing the door on them.

"Maybe we should have left this until she's better," said Ty, looking around. Hospitals set him on edge. It was something the two men had in common. Lock wasn't much of a fan either. As he'd been known to comment, "I try to avoid those places. People die in them."

Moments and then minutes ticked by. Lock started to second-guess his intrusion. He reminded himself that sometimes being intrusive came with the territory.

As soon as they had established the proper security protocols were in place and spoken with Mrs. Semenov they'd leave her and her daughter in peace.

Apart from anything else, tweens and teens, especially girls, needed to be informed of the importance of taking care with what they posted on social media. Sites like Instagram could be the bane of a private security detail's life. Kids happily shared all kinds of things, including where they were, or where they were headed, without a second thought. It was a criminal's dream.

The bodyguard reappeared. "She'll be with you in a moment."

Ty had wandered off down the corridor and was studying something on the wall, a poster or a sign of some kind, Lock couldn't quite see what.

"Anastasia is resting."

Elizabeth Semenov closed the door behind her and stood there with her back to it.

Lock introduced himself and explained that he was conducting a review of security for her husband. Ty wandered back along the corridor. "This is my partner, Ty Johnson."

Elizabeth Semenov didn't say anything to that. Lock was beginning to think this was a bad idea. The woman looked completely washed out.

"Your husband never mentioned what was wrong with your daughter," said Lock, addressing the elephant in the room.

"I bet he didn't. I'm sure there's a lot of things he didn't tell you." She moved so that her back was to the door.

"I'm not going to go in there without your or Anastasia's permission," said Lock, "but if we're to help keep you both safe then we have to make sure that everyone is taking the correct steps."

"It's a little late for that," said Elizabeth Semenov, reaching behind her, opening the door, and pushing it open so that they could see past her and into the private room.

Anastasia Semenov lay on a hospital bed, surrounded by IV stands and monitoring equipment. Lines and tubes ran in and out of her. An oxygen mask sat snug over her mouth and nose. The little girl was ghostly pale, her eyes closed, hands down by her sides. The long blonde flowing hair that Lock and Ty had seen in the happy family portraits in the townhouse was completely absent. She had no hair left at all. She looked exactly like someone in the middle of chemotherapy for cancer, which was what Lock assumed this was. A child with cancer who was struggling to stay alive.

"Cancer?" Lock asked Elizabeth Semenov.

"Acute myelogenous leukemia. Thankfully we caught it early, but the chemo has been hard on her."

"I'm sorry," said Ty. "Can't be easy. Especially not with everything else that's going on."

"It hasn't been, but she's a fighter. She gets that from her father."

"How much longer are they saying she'll be in here?" said Lock.

"I was hoping to have her home soon, but maybe she'd be safer here for now."

11

The two veterans walked out of the hospital entrance without saying a word to each other. They were both still coming to terms with what they'd seen.

Ty's expression was that of a gathering storm, his brown eyes somehow obsidian black, his jaw set. As they passed through the shoals on the sidewalk, people got out of his way, sensing the quiet menace that emanated from him.

"So, how come Dimitri didn't mention this little detail?" Lock said to his partner.

"I don't know, Ryan. I mean it's not exactly something that would slip your mind, a kid in hospital like that."

"And we've both signed the NDA. It's not like either of us would go running to the press."

"Maybe he wanted the reaction," said Ty. "I mean we were both thinking we'd bail on this at the first possible opportunity."

"And now we're not ..." said Lock.

It made a kind of sense. Dimitri wanted them on board, and he would have gathered enough information on them to know that they were rarely motivated purely by money. The more Lock thought about it, the more it made sense.

Ty nudged Lock's elbow. "Check it out. Ten o'clock."

Lock glanced over to see the guy with the blond crewcut and black leather jacket who'd been following them before they went inside.

"You want to grab me a pack of gum?" said Lock.

It took Ty a second to catch on. "Oh, yeah, sure. That store right over there?" he said, pointing across the street.

"That's the one," said Lock.

Ty peeled off, quickening his pace, and dodging across the street. Lock kept walking.

Crewcut seemed torn, uncertain as to whom he should follow, Ty or Lock. It was a good indicator that he was alone and not part of a team. Lock walked back to the other end of the block and waited at the crossing. Crewcut went with him.

On the other side of the street, Ty disappeared inside the store.

Lock crossed and headed back down the block, heading for the store. He'd lost direct sight of Crewcut. Glancing into a gleaming storefront, he glimpsed him about twenty feet behind him.

He kept walking, picking up his pace a little. Another glance confirmed that Crewcut was still behind him, not matching Lock's pace, but keeping up.

Passing the storefront, Lock kept walking, blowing past the entrance.

TY STOOD to one side of the store entrance, partially obscured by a magazine stand. He watched as Lock walked past, neither of them acknowledging the other.

A few seconds later Crewcut appeared. Ty ducked deeper into the store then walked briskly out and onto the sidewalk.

He came up behind Crewcut as he walked past the alley. Ty threw a massive arm around the man's shoulders.

"Oh, man, I thought it was you," said Ty, smiling.

Crewcut looked shocked. He tried to wriggle free, but Ty's hand clasped his shoulder hard. His other arm came up and crossed the man's chest as he felt for a shoulder holster. Handguns were highly illegal in New York, but no one seemed to have told the criminals.

It was clear. All the guy had under his arm was a serious case of body odor. Ty's hand dropped to the man's waist. Also clear.

"What are you doing this far uptown" Ty continued, propelling the man off the street and into the mouth of the alleyway.

"I don't know you," Crewcut said, with an unmistakably Russian accent.

He went to push away, but it was too late.

"Sure you do," said Ty, manhandling him further into the alleyway.

As the man broke free, Ty shoved him hard with both hands into a Dumpster. Crewcut stumbled back, slamming into it as Lock strode toward them.

"You can't do this," said Crewcut. "You're not the police."

"Yeah, and neither are you, asshole," said Lock. "Now, who are you, and why are you keeping tabs on us?"

Lock didn't expect him to cough up any answers to either question. Etiquette demanded that he was at least afforded the opportunity.

"I don't know what you're talking about."

A standard response. He didn't look like a guy who'd be overly troubled by a few broken ribs or a black eye. Beating information out of someone could work. Beating accurate information out of them was harder. And in the end it all came down to the individual.

Thankfully, there was a more direct route that Lock had employed over the years.

He gave Ty the nod. Ty grabbed the man's wrists, pulled his arms behind his back and spun him round so that he was facing down the alley. Lock reached over and frisked him, coming up with a wallet.

Crewcut began to struggle, which kind of gave the game away. Ty let go with one arm and dug a hard left hook into the man's liver. The Russian doubled over with a groan.

Lock flipped open the wallet, looking for ID. He came up with a driver's license, a bank card, American Express, and a work ID. Whipping out his phone, Lock took a quick snap of the driver's license, put it back into the wallet, which he returned to Grigor Novak's pocket.

He grabbed the scruff of Novak's jacket, pulled him upright and fished inside. From a pocket he pulled out a green and gold passport. Lock recognized it immediately.

He flipped it open. The name matched everything else.

Lock held up the passport for Ty. "Diplomatic."

"No kidding," said Ty, sarcastically. "What are the odds, huh?"

Lock handed it back to Novak. Embassies and consulates were rife with spies and intelligence officers. Diplomatic immunity gave them almost completely free rein to conduct business. If they were caught, the worst that could happen was that they were expelled.

"Go tell your bosses that Dimitri Semenov and his family are off limits from now on. Oh, and this," said Lock, dangling the passport in front of his face. "It won't save you if we meet again. We're not the government, and we don't give a shit about creating a diplomatic incident."

Novak's expression didn't shift. He straightened, still clutching his side.

Lock doubted very much that he would file a police report. The only people he'd be reporting this incident to were his superiors, and even then that wasn't guaranteed. Spies tended not to admit they'd been spotted, dragged into an alley, beaten up, and given up their identity.

"Hey, wait a minute," said Ty, staring hard at Novak and moving around him to get a better angle on something.

Ty pulled the leather jacket from his shoulder. Grabbing his shirt collar, he yanked hard, exposing his neck.

Inked on Novak's neck from just above his shoulder was a single eight-pointed star. Etched in blue ink, it was solid.

"How many diplomats you know rocking tats, these days?" said Ty.

The comment drew a smirk from Novak, but he kept his own counsel.

The passport looked real enough, but Lock figured it might be a very good fake. But why would someone following them, presumably working for the Russian government, go to the trouble of carrying a faked diplomatic passport?

Passing yourself off as someone representing the Russian government was a serious offense. If you were working for them while living here, you'd almost certainly have one.

"Take off your jacket," Ty ordered Novak.

He did as he was told. Lock watched as, at Ty's order, he stripped off to the waist, revealing several more crudely rendered but weirdly ornate tattoos. The main one, spread across his chest, depicted what looked to Lock like a three-domed Russian Orthodox church.

Ty had been right. Something was off about this guy, thought Lock.

A solitary star was something you might just get away with. No doubt, like here, some spies came from the military. But this guy had a lot of ink.

Lock whipped out his phone and took pictures. A couple of the smaller tattoos were words written in Russian Cyrillic script.

"What's the deal, Grigor? Who you with? Because I ain't buying this diplomat bullshit."

Still smiling, Novak reached out a hand to take his shirt back as the sharp whoop of a siren at the mouth of the alleyway announced the arrival of an NYPD patrol car.

Ty handed the man his shirt as Lock braced himself to explain the situation to the two cops who were walking toward them, hands resting on the grips of their Glock 19s.

12

Stepping into the vast hotel suite, Ruta Sirka felt like a princess in a fairytale. Dimitri had pushed the boat out this time. The hotels where they met were always five-star, always beautiful, with every possible amenity, but this was on another level entirely.

She checked the time on her phone. She had an hour to prepare herself. Plenty of time. She had kept her hair and make-up on from the day's photo shoot, and she would be lying naked on the bed when he arrived, so she didn't have to worry about what to wear when he appeared.

On a small side table, a bottle of freshly opened champagne stood in an ice bucket. Next to it were two crystal flutes.

It had been a long day. She poured some champagne into a glass and took several sips. She walked into the white marbled bathroom with its claw-foot tub. She ran a bath, and sipped champagne as she watched the bath fill.

Walking back into the bedroom area of the suite, she crossed to the window. She took off her clothes and stood naked by the window drinking in the view across Central Park.

It was hard to imagine that less than eighteen months ago she had been a struggling student back home in Kiev. Now here she was in a hotel suite bigger than her parents' apartment, about to spend the evening, if not the night, with one of the wealthiest men in the world.

Some of the American models she worked with looked down on things like this. They said they would never sleep with a man because of his money. Ruta smiled to herself when she heard them make these comments. All it proved to her was that they had no idea what it was like to be properly poor.

In any case, the boys her age were just that, boys. Not men. Okay, so they might have flat stomachs and muscles, but a man like Dimitri Semenov offered more than just money. He had been around. He knew how the world operated. He had wisdom.

And usually all she had to do was pleasure him for a few minutes. He rarely lasted longer than that. Another thing to be grateful for, as far as Ruta saw it. Young men approached sex like some kind of athletic challenge, leaving her tired and sore.

Stepping back into the bathroom, she put her glass on the side of the tub and slowly submerged herself in the hot water. After standing around all day in those preposterous shoes they made her wear, it was bliss.

Her mind drifted to the message from Dimitri. He had sounded different than normal, but she couldn't decide how exactly. Maybe disconnected, a little out of it. He had said something about his daughter being sick, so maybe that was it. And, of course, there had been that business with his bodyguards, which had been all over the news.

From the other men she knew, though, she suspected it was something else. When they talked about sex some men just sounded different. Their voice changed. She suspected that was it.

After twenty minutes in the tub, she got out. She didn't want her skin to go all wrinkly. She used some body lotion she found in a basket next to the sink. It smelled of lavender. As she applied it, she padded back into the suite and refilled her glass. She hadn't eaten and was feeling a little lightheaded.

In the bedroom, she rearranged the pillows on the king-size bed looking for the blindfold Dimitri had told her would be there. It was made of black silk. She put it on and lay down, sinking into the plush mattress.

Without even being aware of it, she drifted into a light sleep.

THE MAIN DOOR into the suite opening and closing woke her. She panicked for a second when it was still pitch-black. Then she remembered the blindfold and giggled to herself.

She called out to Dimitri. He didn't reply, but she heard soft footsteps as someone entered the bedroom and walked over to the bed.

For a moment she worried that maybe it was a member of staff. Then she caught the faint trail of the cologne he always wore, Tuscan Leather by Tom Ford, and relaxed. She bit down on her lower lip, stopping herself smiling. Men, especially older ones, could get mad if you laughed when they were trying to be sexy or romantic.

His fingertips touched the top of her thigh. She startled a little then tried to relax. This was so funny. There was obviously more to him than met the eye.

His hand ran up and down the inside of her legs. It moved up over her flat stomach to her breasts, fingertips circling her nipples.

Yes, there was definitely more to this Russian than she had realized. A lot more.

Hands reached under her at the knees, and the neck, strong arms scooping her up from the bed. He was still dressed. She could feel the material of his clothing as he carried her, still blindfolded, across the room.

Ruta shivered as a sudden blast of cold air swept across her body. He was carrying her, but she didn't know where. The cold intensified. At first she'd thought it was the air-con, but it wasn't. It felt like the whip of wind from an open window.

What was he doing? Where was he taking her?

"Dimitri?" she said, shivering.

He had told her not to speak when he came into the room. To put the blindfold on, and lie there, naked.

He didn't respond. Without thinking, she reached up to touch his face. His hand grabbed her wrist.

"No," he said.

A sudden fear surged through her. It wasn't Dimitri's voice.

Somehow she managed to free her wrist from his grip. Pulling the blindfold up, she looked around. Drapes whipped into the air at the open window. Her eyes flashed from it to the face of the man carrying her toward it. He had piercing blue eyes, and his hair was clipped close to his scalp. She screamed as loudly as she could, kicking, arms flailing as she tried to scratch at his face with long nails.

Eyes wide, she looked to the billowing drapes as he carried her to the window. Her mouth dried. Her vision tunneled until all she could see was the top of a small tattooed star on his neck as he tightened his grip on her.

As she struggled, he took three final steps to the window. He rolled her out of his arms like a carpet. Her hands grabbed for him, trying to hold on.

Limbs flailing, she fell, tumbling through the air and down toward the sidewalk below.

13

Grigor Novak got out of his car and walked to the edge of the stand of trees. This place was only an hour and thirty minutes outside Manhattan, but it might as well have been way up in farthest Michigan. It was pin-drop quiet.

He paced anxiously back and forth and rubbed at the stubble on his chin. He should have shaved. Dimitri Semenov was always clean-shaven.

That tiny detail had almost screwed up the whole thing. It had only occurred to him when the girl had reached up to touch his face. That was when he'd panicked and grabbed her wrist.

She was stronger than she had looked. Skin and bones, but strong. For a second in the hotel suite, just as he was dropping her out of the window, she had almost grabbed him and taken him with her.

It had been close.

He wouldn't mention it to Ninel. He would keep that little detail to himself. He was worried about her reaction to him having been caught by the two guys he'd been tailing. He didn't think she knew anything about it, but he couldn't be sure. That was why, when the cops had shown up, he'd played dumb until they grew exasperated and let everyone go.

The sound of a car engine snapped him back to the present. He watched as an ancient Cadillac sedan trundled over the rutted ground. Ninel was in the passenger seat. Alexei was driving. No computer-controlled cars for them, thought Novak. You might be able to cut the brake cables, but no one was hacking this vehicle, not even the kid driving.

Since Ninel had begun spending more time around this kid Alexei, Novak had noticed that she was increasingly paranoid about technology, especially anything that could be connected to the internet, either by wireless or using a Bluetooth connection. Messages were typed or handwritten and delivered using old-fashioned dead drops. The most crucial meetings and debriefs were conducted face to face.

NINEL TARASOV GOT out of the car and slammed the door. She was a plain-looking woman in her early fifties with short, spiky black hair and almond-shaped brown eyes. About thirty pounds overweight, she stood a little over five feet six inches tall. She wore jeans, sneakers and a brown turtle-neck sweater. Physically she was in every way the opposite of the young Ukrainian model whose death she had rubber-stamped.

Ninel had a brusque, businesslike way of dealing with people that reminded her fellow Russians of an old-style Soviet bureaucrat. It was fitting because her parents had both been senior Communist Party apparatchiks. Ninel was Lenin spelled backward, and she had never really shaken off the manner of someone who had been born thirty years later than she should have been.

She shared one other characteristic with the old Soviet Party bureaucrats. She loved her country, and she could easily separate her personal feelings from what were, as she saw them, her professional duties.

She hadn't always been like this. Certainly she had always had a steely inner core, but bitter life experience, and certain disappointments, especially when it came to matters of the heart, had hardened her.

With Alexei trotting behind her, she made her way across to Novak. As she walked she scanned the nearby tree line. Beyond it, hidden by the sycamore and ash trees, was an old water-filled quarry. "Tell me," she said to him, skipping the formalities.

He shrugged. "There's not much to tell. It went to plan. No one saw me enter the room. I left immediately and no one saw me then either."

Ninel closed the distance between them. "Is that a scratch on your face?" she asked, reaching up to touch his face.

This time he didn't bat away the hand but let her trace over his face.

She inspired fear in him. Scaring men like Grigor Novak was perhaps her greatest gift. It was a gift she had honed over the years until it was razor sharp. Her reputation preceded her among the *vory*. It had been built over decades.

Men like this were useful. But they had their limitations. They were like dogs. Biddable, eager to please their master, but sometimes not as clever as dogs.

"It's nothing," said Novak, taking a step back. "She was struggling. It's only a scratch. It'll be gone by next week."

Ninel didn't say anything to that. There was no point in explaining DNA trapped under a fingernail to him. He had messed up, not once but twice. His work was good, but sloppy. Surveillance required a knowledge of counter-surveillance.

"What about the two men with Dimitri? The security operators?"

"I haven't had time to finish my report, but I don't think there's anything to concern us. They visited with him, then with the girl at the hospital. That's all."

The girl at the hospital. The one part of this that Ninel felt bad about. An innocent among thieves. Ninel could only pray that she made a full recovery. The orders had been clear that no one from their side should threaten her in any way. She was to be left out of this. This was between them and Semenov. Sure, they might use family and friends, like this young mistress, as leverage, but children were strictly out of bounds. Even in the darkest days Ninel had held to that rule.

Ninel said nothing to his comment. What was the point in confronting him with the truth? It was easier to let it go. Or appear to let it go.

She turned back to the old sedan without another word. Alexei followed her.

"What now?" Novak called after her.

She opened the car door. That was the signal for the sniper posted in the trees.

There was the briefest crack, like a branch snapping, and Novak fell forward, clutching his chest as blood blossomed from it.

She looked across at Alexei. His mouth was open, and she could hear the faint splash of urine as his bladder opened with fright.

The sniper and another man appeared from the trees. They were dressed like hunters, appropriate under the circumstances. One rolled out a plastic ground sheet.

The sniper grabbed the body by the shoulders and dragged it onto the sheet. The two men rolled it up.

Alexei was still rooted to the spot. He looked down.

"Don't feel bad," said Ninel. "I did something like that the first time I saw someone shot."

It was a lie. But she didn't want Alexei to feel too bad. It was better to offer him reassurance now rather than spelling out what they both knew. The message had been delivered. Mess up and you'll meet the same fate.

So far Alexei had exceeded her expectations. People threw around the word "genius," but this kid with his savant-level hacking skills came close. Not only had he managed to hack the sedans, he was also an expert in so-called deep fakes.

That was how they had found him. He had staged one of the first deep fake robberies. Capturing the voice of a Russian CEO, he had used sophisticated artificial intelligence software to mimic the man's voice in a call to his bank, which had released several million dollars into an account Alexei had set up in the CEO's name. The money had been quickly whisked offshore. The FSB had found him but decided it would be a waste to let him rot in jail when he could be working for them.

"Are you hungry?" Ninel asked Alexei, as she got into the car.

"Huh?"

"We could go to a drive-thru. Save you getting you out of the car in those pants," she said.

"Oh, yeah," he stuttered.

They got in and she lowered the window. It didn't smell too bad now, but it would.

"At least you didn't have asparagus," she said, sniffing the air.

"What?"

"Never mind," said Ninel.

She watched through the windshield as the sniper and his spotter picked up the groundsheet with Grigor, and carried him to the trees, headed for the quarry.

14

Togliatti, Samara Oblast, Russia
March 1990

THE BAD NEWS was that the Bitch Killer was still alive. He had suffered serious injuries but, week by week, month by month, slowly but surely, he was recovering. Perhaps not well enough to do something himself, but well enough that he could have someone else exact revenge on his behalf. The *vory* were fiercely tribal. That was why they had survived for so long.

It was a lesson that would be reinforced in Dimitri's mind over the years. Bad people didn't just survive, they thrived. You knocked them down, and somehow they popped up stronger than before.

The good news was that by running him over, Dimitri had bought himself the time he needed to make some money and marshal his forces. He now had a dozen security personnel, all battle-hardened former military *Afghani*.

He made sure they were paid well, and on time. "Well paid" being a relative term: what was considered starvation wages in the West was a king's ransom in Russia.

And the money Dimitri was making selling the cars from the plant? Even in the West those were unimaginable sums. He had even refined his scheme. He paid several factory managers and other local bureaucrats to falsify export orders, then had the cars driven to Moscow where they were sold not for vouchers but for cash. Hard currency. Mostly American dollars. Even with the economy on the verge of collapse, enough people in the cities were making money on the black market to be able to pay for a car.

Within a matter of weeks, and with Dimitri having secured a reputation as someone not to be messed with, he was moving dozens of vehicles from Togliatti to Moscow. On the return journey he had his drivers use the money they were being paid to buy all manner of goods that were only easily available in Moscow. That way he could double, and in some cases triple, what was already a colossal profit.

He reinvested most of the money, at the same time making sure it wasn't just his bodyguards who were properly compensated. Everyone made money, from the men who came in to work the night shift to those who opened the gates and studied the newspaper while the cars were spirited out of the factory.

Then, just as he was beginning to worry that it was all too perfect, too easy, it happened.

15

Ninel had been deemed not sufficiently attractive to be sent to State School 4. Even if she had been there was no way on earth that her father would have allowed it. State School 4 was for the so-called swallows, young female KGB operators who were trained to seduce, establish relationships with, and in some cases marry men the state deemed important.

Instead she had undergone training at the famed Dzerzhinsky Higher School of the KGB located on Michurinsky Prospekt in Moscow. One of only two women in her class, she had graduated just ahead of the collapse and the academy's temporary closure before it became the main training center for the KGB's replacement, the FSB.

It was by pure chance that she had been assigned as a young officer in Togliatti. The vast Avtovaz car plant was seen as a strategic asset. It was also, as it turned out, the best place to go if you wanted to learn the ways of the *vory*. Since *perestroika*, the old enemies of the state had infested the surrounding area like cockroaches. They understood the black market better than most.

Then there were men like Dimitri Semenov. Not *vory*, but hardly law-abiding. Not so much corrupt as corrupters. He, and those like him, saw themselves as vanguards of the free market.

Where many saw chaos, Ninel saw a conundrum. If under the old system all property was owned, in theory, by everyone, then now, with the reforms, no one could claim ownership, which men like Semenov took to mean that they could.

And what was happening here was repeated across the land. In Moscow the theft was off the charts. It was a pure kleptocracy, a government of thieves, by thieves, and for thieves. Entire state enterprises were being taken over wholesale and carved up by the politicians and their cronies.

Like a good KGB officer, Ninel kept her own counsel. She waited, she watched, observing the shifting sands, and when the opportunity arose, she took it, with both hands.

16

Dimitri was smoking a cigarette and making Turkish coffee in a copper *cezve* on the tiny gas stove when he heard the knock at the door. The power was out for the third time that week. The apartment was a tiny one-bed in a crumbling tower block that had been hastily thrown up to house factory workers.

He'd been so busy that he hadn't got around to finding somewhere new. In any case, he was hardly ever there. Life kept him working, either here or in Moscow, or on the road between the two. That was how he liked it. He'd quickly found that wheeling and dealing was something he never got bored of. It had become like a drug.

Whoever it was knocked again. None of the *Afghanis* were here. They usually collected him and escorted him to work. During the night one of them was posted outside keeping watch. As an extra measure they had given him a pistol and shown him how to use it. Now he wished he'd paid more attention but, truth be told, he'd always had a Russian's fatalistic view when it came to his own death.

If his number was up, it was up.

He picked up the pistol from a table in the living room as he made his way to the front door. He knew it didn't have a safety and that it was loaded so he presumed it would simply be a matter of pointing it and pulling the trigger.

The knocking came again. This time it was a lot more insistent.

"Police!" shouted a man on the other side of the door. "Open up!"

Dimitri's hand was shaking. Either way this couldn't be good. There was a decades-old fear of the police coming to your door. And if it was *vory* pretending to be police, which was one of their new tricks, it was even worse.

For the most part, the police were easy to bribe. They were paid even worse than the factory workers. But usually when they wanted to shake someone down so they could buy vodka you were stopped on the street or, in Dimitri's case, pulled over in your car. That was a weekly occurrence.

On the off-chance it was the police, Dimitri wasn't going to open the door to them waving a gun. He stood back.

"If you're with the police then push your ID under the door and I'll open up."

On the other side of the door there was a hushed conversation between two men. "Open up right now, or this will be a lot worse for you, Comrade."

Comrade, thought Dimitri. People still used that term. It was ironic: here they were, fighting like rats in the bottom of a barrel, as they had been for years, but still everyone spoke like they were brothers in arms.

He walked over to the table, grabbed his wallet, pulled out a fistful of rubles, and slid them under the door. The money was grabbed before it had even fully cleared the other side.

More hushed discussions in the corridor, then two ID cards appeared. Dimitri picked them up and studied them. The longer this went on the less likely they were *vory*, who were not noted for their patience. They would have kicked the door in by this point, or at least made the attempt.

He picked up the IDs and studied them. They looked genuine enough. If they were forgeries they were good ones.

Quickly he hid the gun under a cushion, walked back, opened the door and hoped he'd made the right decision.

17

As the two police officers escorted him to their car, Dimitri glimpsed the *Afghani* who'd been posted outside being released from his handcuffs by two other cops. He kept his eyes down but looked sheepish. Dimitri didn't blame him. He would speak with the head of his security later and make sure he knew this kid had no alternative. Assuming there was a later.

They put him into the back of their car. It reeked of stale smoke and even staler urine. They had cuffed his hands in front of him so he could get to his cigarettes. He lit one, using the fresh smoke to cover the noxious odor.

They pulled out onto Leninskiy Prospekt. They drove for a mile, the vast car plant on their left. The main regional police station was on Frunze Past, but they drove by the turn for it and kept going.

Dimitri tried not to show the panic bubbling inside him as they kept moving, making a right turn onto Yubileinaya Street and a left onto Primorskiy Boulevard. Finally they stopped outside a large gray building near the local government offices.

Everyone in Tagliotti knew and feared this place. People avoided it like the plague. If they had to walk down this section of the street they usually crossed to the opposite side and picked up their pace, lest some invisible force would draw them inside, and they'd never be seen again.

This was the local headquarters of the Komitet Gosudarstvennoy Bezopasnosti, the KGB, Russia's less than secret police. A metal gate was pulled open and the police car bounced down a ramp, and into an underground car park.

Dimitri closed his eyes and took a drag on a freshly lit Ziganov cigarette as the gate clanged ominously behind them. Now he was firmly inside the belly of the beast.

It wasn't the same fearsome beast that it had been before. Like every other part of the state it had been weakened by economic collapse. But, like a badly injured animal, this was when an organization such as this could be at its most dangerous—when it was in its death throes.

They pulled into a parking space near an elevator. The two regular police officers got out. They both looked nervous. Dimitri didn't blame them. Normal cops were terrified of the KGB, and with good reason. Corruption was endemic. You might not be the most corrupt, but you were likely guilty of something, and that was all the KGB needed.

He noticed there was no call button on the elevator. It opened automatically and they all shuffled inside. The door closed, again with no one touching any buttons, and they began their ascent.

The doors opened into a windowless corridor. The walls were bare. No pictures. Every door looked the same. None was numbered.

Dimitri was led down the corridor until they stopped at a door that had a sign outside. One word: Interrogation.

The cops hesitated at the door until one said, "Go on. Open it."

"Why don't you?" said his partner.

"Let him," said the first cop, reaching down, and unlocking the cuffs. "Go on," he said, with a nod to the door handle.

Dimitri turned it. The door opened into a large room, twenty feet long by twelve wide. No windows. Tiled flooring that was easy to wipe blood from. In Russia, floor coverings were usually a good indicator of how bad things might get. No one beat the hell out of someone in an office with a carpet.

There was a bench that ran along one wall. In the middle of the room, a metal table had been fixed to the floor. Two chairs on either side were also bolted in.

The cops led him to one of the chairs, pushed him onto it, and cuffed him to the leg of the table. Like he would have been able to go anywhere anyway.

So far the most unnerving part of this was the absence of anyone else, the lack of natural light, and the almost total silence. He assumed the place was soundproofed, not so much to exclude noise from elsewhere as to make sure that no one outside could hear the screams coming from within. That was the local wisdom.

"Let's get out of here," said the cop.

"My handcuffs?"

"Okay, you stay with him, then."

That did the trick. They walked out of the room, closing the door behind them.

Dimitri was alone. Cuffed to the table. He tried to run through what he could say if they asked him about his operation. There really wasn't anything. The paperwork gave the appearance of order, but that was about all.

He could deny, but it wouldn't work. It might buy him some time, but no more than that. He would have to resort to the classic solution in a situation like this. Bribery. Even the KGB had their price, especially in these straitened times when inflation was rampant and a public servant's salary had been barely enough to live on before.

THE WAIT SEEMED to go on endlessly. He was grateful for his wristwatch, a Czech Pobeda chronograph that his parents had bought him as a high-school graduation present. He had a half packet of cigarettes left, and a lighter.

He was thirsty, his mouth dry. He should have slugged down some of that coffee before he had opened the door at home.

Minutes went by. Then an hour.

He tried to make some calculations as to how much it would take to pay them off. Would a one-off payment be enough?

Unlikely.

A single bribe would get you out of a speeding ticket, but not something like this. It would have to be an ongoing arrangement.

That meant thinking about two things. How much he could get away with paying them, and establishing what they could provide in return.

Not beating him to death was hardly adding value to his business.

This would have to be a negotiation like any other. That was how he would have to approach it. He could give them something, but they would have to provide something in return.

Having focused on his predicament in this way, he immediately felt better. He lit a fresh cigarette and took a puff as the door finally opened and two people walked in. One was a middle-aged man with a big belly and a red face, and the other, to Dimitri's surprise, a plain-looking mouse of a girl around his age.

She had greasy brown hair, cut short, and was wearing a long gray skirt, white blouse, and gray jacket. Under her arm she held a series of files. She didn't look at him as she took a seat opposite. Instead, she arranged the files next to her in a neat pile, took one from the top and began to flip through it.

He couldn't think of anyone who looked less like a KGB officer. Which made what happened in the next few hours all the more surprising.

18

The man introduced himself as a colonel. The woman didn't say anything. Her mousy appearance belied an unflinching gaze that, on first viewing, didn't seem to fit with the rest of her. She looked directly across the table at Dimitri, eyes narrowed, as if studying something under a microscope.

It was a stare that didn't seek to intimidate. Dimitri found that made it all the more unnerving.

"We have some questions for you," said the colonel.

Dimitri's response was a curt nod.

The woman passed the first file to the colonel, who opened it to reveal a set of black-and-white photographs. He placed them on the table and slid them one by one over the surface to Dimitri.

The first print showed Dimitri with the manager who'd been supervising the night shift. They were standing in the alleyway, a crate of vodka at Dimitri's feet.

Dimitri moved through the photographs looking at each one turn. He said nothing.

"This is you," said the colonel.

"Yes," said Dimitri.

There was no pleading the fifth amendment. No invoking one's right to remain silent. No demanding that one have a lawyer present.

The first two didn't exist, and the third wouldn't help. Even now, with all the reforms, the KGB had sweeping powers. There was only one way out of this, money, and it was way too early in the game to play that hand.

With his blood pounding in his ears, he did his best to stay calm.

"Who is this?" said the colonel jabbing a meaty finger at the manager.

Dimitri gave them the man's name.

"Why are you giving him vodka?"

"He's a friend of mine. I don't drink very much. He does," said Dimitri.

The colonel nodded. The woman gathered up the photographs from the table, tamped them into a neat pile, the edges lined up, and put them back in the file. She moved that file off to one side and continued with the show-and-tell.

File after file, photograph by photograph, purchase order by purchase order, Dimitri's scheme was laid out in front of him in meticulous detail. It was impressive. They had pieces of paper that even Dimitri hadn't been aware of.

On and on it went. They had more than enough evidence to bury him several times over. A half-hour in, he gave up any denials. There was no point. The only thing it would have achieved was aggravating them.

One last file remained, unopened. Dimitri couldn't help but look at it. The woman pointedly ignored it as she gathered the files he had already seen.

She and the colonel pushed back their chairs and got up.

"It's lunchtime," said the colonel. "Ninel here will bring you something to eat later."

They walked to the door, leaving the unopened file lying on the table, easily within Dimitri's reach.

A mind game.

Did they want him to open it? Did they not? Did it matter?

He left it where it was and lit another cigarette. He should have asked them for a fresh pack. He was almost out. Maybe he'd ask the woman when she brought him food. Not that he had an appetite.

His gaze drifted back to the file.

Just over thirty minutes later the door opened again. The woman came in with a plate of cold meat and sliced beetroot. She put it down in front of him.

She picked up the file. "You didn't open it," she said.

It wasn't phrased as a question. They'd been watching him. He'd assumed they would be.

"It's not mine," he said.

"And the cars you've been taking? Were they yours?"

He shrugged. "No, but they weren't anyone else's either. If I didn't sell them then someone else would have. No one is obeying the rules. Why pretend that they are?"

It was the most he had said at any one time since he had got here. While she unnerved him, he also felt he could be honest with her in a way that he couldn't with her boss.

"That's true," she said. "But if you're caught stealing bread it's not much of a defense that you just happened to steal it before anyone else could."

He didn't respond to that. She was right. He was finished. If they wanted, they could send him to prison for the next twenty years. Unless he could bribe them.

She picked up the file and opened it. A single sheet of blank paper fluttered out and onto the table. "Your friend, the Bitch Killer, didn't do so well. He opened it as soon as we left the room," she said.

This time Dimitri knew his expression had given him away. There was no way he'd kept his surprise from registering on his face.

He kept his own counsel. She would be expecting him to ask a million questions, but he stayed silent.

"We also know that you tried to kill him," she added.

"He was going to kill me."

"Again, not much of a defense, is it?"

"So what happens now?" he asked.

She paced to the back of the room, walking behind him. It was suitably unnerving. "Fifty per cent of what you make," she said.

"You're full of surprises."

"Times are hard. Even among my comrades in this building. People have mouths to feed."

"And what do I get in return?"

"You need a roof," she said.

"I have security."

"Bodyguards are not the same as a *krysha*. We can make sure that you are left alone. Not just by the *vory* but by everyone. One payment to us is a lot simpler than death by a thousand cuts."

"Do I have a choice?" asked Dimitri.

She appeared at his side. She dug into a pocket, pulled out keys, and removed his cuffs. She motioned for him to stand.

He took his time. His left leg had fallen asleep from sitting in the same position. He rubbed at his wrists, then reached down to massage the pins and needles from his calf.

She walked to the door and held it open.

"I'm free to go?" he asked.

"Not exactly. I want to show you something."

He followed her out of the room and into the corridor. As they walked he asked her how she knew which room was which. She ignored the question.

They got into an elevator. This one, he guessed, was for staff. It had buttons.

They rode down to the basement. Dimitri did his best to look calm. If local folklore was to be believed, this was where the worst abuses by the KGB took place. Underground, where it was harder to hear you scream. Not that anyone would have done anything if they had.

The elevator doors opened, and she walked him through a guarded entry port and into a corridor of cells. Most were empty, the doors left open to reveal bare concrete rooms with only a toilet, sink, and a bench to sleep on.

He followed her to the end of the corridor where they stopped at a closed cell door. She produced a key and stood there for a moment.

"You'll still need a *vory v zakone*, at least for now, someone the other *vory* acknowledge. Think of it like a rubber stamp, a simple authorization."

Now that the terms of the deal had been outlined, Dimitri felt in a better position. Suddenly he had ground under his feet, something to use for purchase. He'd calculated that as it was a split of net profits he could likely bump up his end by inflating and, if need be, inventing expenses that he would keep.

"You want to meet yours?" she asked him.

She was enjoying this part. He could tell. She stood at the cell door like a magician about to reveal their latest trick.

Dimitri really didn't care. He'd wanted to avoid any partners, and now it looked like he was going to be lumped with not just one but two.

He was reconciled to it. But that didn't mean he had to like it.

She opened the cell door. In the far corner of the room sat a man. He was curled into a ball, his knees pulled up into his chest. His head was tilted down, his chin tucked in.

"We picked this one up a few days ago." She turned to Dimitri. "He's still not in the best physical shape. Someone ran him over with a car, apparently. But he wouldn't tell the police who it was."

As she spoke Dimitri slowly picked out the man's outline and matched it in his mind with the picture he had of the Bitch Killer.

"Hey," she shouted at the prisoner.

Slowly, the Bitch Killer looked up at them. The expression in his eyes was more frightening than anything Dimitri had ever seen. It was one of pure, unmitigated terror. He looked broken, a shell of a man. Someone whose will had been sucked out of him.

Part of Dimitri wanted to know how this had been achieved. Part of him, the greater part, hoped he would never find out.

"Don't worry," she said. "His reward for this is being allowed to live."

The Bitch Killer's eyes were wet. He muttered some kind of apology to Dimitri. He would do what needed to be done. He wouldn't interfere in the business, other than to make sure that the other *vory* stayed clear.

"We have an agreement?" the woman said to Dimitri.

He nodded, his eyes still glued to the man huddled in the corner of the cell. "Yes, we have an agreement."

"Good," she said, pleasantly, closing the cell door and escorting him back toward the elevator.

"That wasn't so bad, was it?" she said to him. "There's not even a scratch on you."

"No, there's not."

She looked him in the eye. "Breaking a man's body is no great achievement. But breaking a man's mind …"

19

"Several weeks ago an audacious assassination attempt left several of his security team dead in their vehicles and now tonight authorities are questioning Russian billionaire Dimitri Semenov about the death of a young Ukrainian model apparently thrown from the Presidential Suite of the Plaza hotel. Over to our reporter Price Phillips, who's down at One Police Plaza. Price, what can you tell us?"

Lock and Ty stood next to Elizabeth Semenov in the living room of the Upper East Side townhouse and watched as the TV news report continued. They had headed back here to brief Dimitri, only for events to overtake them. Lock had been in the middle of some shit storms in his time, both while serving and in the private sector, but this was moving faster than most.

As soon as they seemed to get a handle on one assassination attempt or threat, another shoe seemed to drop.

Back on screen the male reporter was doing an earnest piece to camera. "Authorities here are saying that while no arrest has been made a voicemail apparently found on the victim's phone was from Dimitri Semenov, and allegedly it's him arranging a rendezvous with her at the hotel room of what is now being treated as a murder scene.

And homicide investigators are hinting that this appeared, at best, to be a bizarre sex game gone wrong."

Elizabeth paced in front of the huge screen. Lock felt for her. Not only was her daughter ill in hospital but now she was having to face public humiliation.

Back on screen the reporter went on: "But the attorney for Mr. Semenov is fighting back tonight and saying that their client has a cast-iron alibi, and that this is part of a plot to destabilize Dimitri Semenov's business interests, a plot they claim is being engineered back in Moscow. However, one thing they're not denying is that that their client knew and had met with the victim previously. Only one thing is certain. This story is going to run for some time."

Humiliation complete, Elizabeth grabbed the remote, clicked off the TV, and threw the control across the room as hard as she could.

The reporter had nailed one thing, thought Lock. Money, sex and scandal were ingredients that would absolutely guarantee Dimitri Semenov stayed in the public eye. Whether that was a good or a bad thing remained to be seen.

Usually, the higher the profile the safer someone was. But so far whoever was out to ruin Dimitri's life hadn't seemed particularly concerned about attracting unwanted attention. In fact, quite the opposite. They seemed to be using the increasing chaos to ramp up the pressure on him.

On the domestic front, at least, it appeared to be working. Elizabeth was incandescent with rage, so full of anger her hands were shaking.

"I'm going to divorce the selfish bastard. That's what I'm going to do. Take my half of the money before it's all gone. His daughter is in hospital and he still can't stop himself whoring around."

Ty nudged Lock. "Maybe we should get out of here."

"Let's see what the security arrangements for tonight are first," said Lock.

A principal being questioned by the cops would be a drain on resources. Once he was released they'd need a PES (personal escort section) to bring him home. Three, four, maybe even more men would have to be assigned, leaving the rest of the detail short.

There was also the matter of Anastasia Semenov. Seeing her had personalized this for both of them. Ty in particular had reacted badly, as he always did when he saw the young or vulnerable under threat. The Russian tailing them earlier had been lucky the cops had arrived when they had.

It had also been telling that he hadn't used the cops' arrival to have them arrested, even though it was a fairly open and shut case of unlawful detention. It confirmed to Lock, if confirmation had been needed, that the Russians were knee deep in all of this. It looked like Dimitri's belief that this was a shakedown by the Russian state wasn't as far-fetched as it might have seemed.

"Have you seen McLennan?" Lock asked his partner, as Elizabeth paced back and forth, continuing her expletive-laden rant.

Ty shook his head. "He'll probably be with Dimitri, right?"

Lock nodded. That was how something like this usually went.

"So what do you think?" Ty asked him, looking at the TV screen. "You think he did it? I mean, the guy's under a lot of pressure. She says something. He loses it."

"No," said Lock. "I'm not buying it."

"Me either, seems too much of an almighty coincidence, but we hardly know him."

"It's not a question of knowing him or not, Tyrone. People are capable of doing all kinds of crazy things, including slamming that self-destruct button and blowing themselves up when it seems like the least rational thing to do in the world. But think about the mechanics of tossing someone out of that window."

"You kidding me?" said Ty. "I've had pit bulls that weighed more than some of those models do. Dimitri's a big enough guy, and that's if she was fighting him. He could have drugged her, tied her up. They said it was some kinky stuff."

"All true," said Lock. "But you're missing something."

"Oh, yeah?"

"Windows in skyscrapers don't just open like a regular window in a regular two-story house. If they did, people would be hitting the sidewalk every week for one reason or another," explained Lock. "They have limiters in place so you can only crack them. Even a super-thin model isn't going to squeeze through that kind of a gap. And especially not if she's fighting."

Ty nodded slowly. "So someone would have had to throw her through it?"

"Which is a hell of a lot tougher than it looks. She'd just have bounced off. That's why they use sugar glass in movies. I mean, have you ever tried to throw someone *through* a window?"

Ty smiled.

"Yeah, maybe don't answer that," said Lock as, out of the corner of his eye, he saw Elizabeth pour herself a treble Scotch on the rocks and throw it back like it was lemonade.

"No," Lock continued. "Someone would have had to deal with the window first. Make sure it would open wide enough *before* they picked her up and tossed her out. They would have had to have the tools and the know-how."

"So pre-meditated?" said Ty.

"Exactly. Dimitri Semenov may be an asshole, but he's not dumb, and I doubt very much he's capable of a stunt like this. Losing his temper? Sure, I could see that. It's within the realms of possibility. But going in ahead of time, and jimmying a window while the champagne's chilling, knowing he's going to throw her out of it later? That's one hell of a leap."

"Leap?" said Ty.

Lock held up a hand. "No pun intended."

OVER BY THE BAR, Elizabeth was refreshing her drink, although this was more of a home-pour double than a treble. One more and she'd be completely trashed.

Lock knew better than to tell her to take it easy, or even suggest it. He didn't doubt she was under an immense amount of pressure, and the booze was self-medication. But alcohol was not a drug that helped people in tough times.

"Elizabeth, could Tyrone and I speak with you for a moment?" said Lock.

"Elizabeth" seemed overly familiar, but he didn't know her maiden name and calling her Mrs. Semenov might not be the best idea right about now.

She waved her glass in the air. "Sure. What is it?"

He figured that as long as she was talking or otherwise occupied, she wouldn't be throwing back Scotch like it was water.

"Who do you have working security in the house at the moment?" said Lock.

She reeled off two names from McLennan's team.

"And with your daughter?"

"There's always someone with her. Twenty-four seven. I make sure of it."

"Okay. Ty and I are going to swing by the hospital, just to make doubly sure everything there is watertight."

"You don't think anyone would—"

Lock cut her off. "No, I don't, but right now I'm guessing peace of mind is going to be very valuable for you both. If you could let them know we're stopping by that would be helpful. If your husband returns here this evening, let us know."

She tilted her glass back and took a sip, leaving a smear of lipstick on the rim. "You know something, I don't even like Scotch."

"It's a difficult time," said Ty. "We understand that."

"Are either of you married?" Elizabeth asked.

"In a long-term relationship, but no," said Lock.

"Confirmed bachelor," said Ty.

She eyed up Ty. "Maybe you could take over . . . What's the proper term? Residential security."

This was where Lock knew you had to take a firm hand with clients. "We're going to do everything in our power to keep you, your daughter and everyone else safe. Like I said, if you could let the hospital know we're on the way that would be very helpful."

. . .

At the end of the block the media were out in even bigger numbers than they had been before. Dimitri Semenov was in for one hell of a welcome. Once he'd run the gauntlet of reporters and TV cameras, his home was hardly going to be an oasis of calm.

Ty must have been thinking along the same lines as Lock because as they walked past the cordon, he said: "Dude's going to need a bodyguard to save him from her."

"Roger that," said Lock. "She may be more of an immediate threat than the Kremlin."

"Maybe he can go stay at a hotel."

Lock glanced at his partner. Ty smiled. "Joke most definitely intended."

One of the reasons they got on so well was that they shared the dark humor that military people utilized to get them through the tough times.

Ty slid into a doorway. "I'll hang here while you hail that cab. But I'd like to make a stop on the way."

"Where?" said Lock.

"5th Avenue and 49th Street."

Lock recognized the address immediately. "You're a big softy, Tyrone."

Ty grinned back. "Yeah but keep that shit on the down low. Oh, and we'd better tell the cabbie to step on it. We have like ten minutes before they close."

20

Carrying two large FAO Schwarz toy-store bags, Ty and Lock climbed out of the cab.

"She's probably sleeping," said Lock.

"Then it'll be like Christmas morning when she wakes up." Ty grinned.

"You're a piece of work, you know that?"

Ty looked around. "No one following us this time. Have to admit, I'm kind of disappointed. I thought old Novak had more to him than to give up so easily."

"Oh, I'm sure he'll be back."

"I look forward to it," said Ty.

"I don't doubt it."

They walked in through the entrance of Sinai.

"So, speaking of our friendly neighborhood shadow, I had someone look into the tattoos for us," said Lock.

"Let me guess, they're not usually associated with a Russian consular official?"

"I was thinking that maybe at a stretch they were military. Some of those guys get moved over into espionage."

"Military guys don't just get military ink. I saw dudes with all kinds of dumbass tats when I was in the Corp from before they enlisted," said Ty.

"Yeah, but these aren't military, and they aren't general stuff either. Remember when we were both in the Bay?" said Lock. He was referring to Pelican Bay Supermax Prison, where he and Ty had been placed undercover to guard an inmate.

"Hardly likely to forget it."

"Okay, remember how the Aryan Brotherhood gang members all had that shamrock on their knuckle."

"Yeah, tipping the rock. Wasn't that what they called it?"

"That's the one. It was the way they identified another AB member. They were the only ones allowed to have that tattoo. So that star you noticed? Solid, eight points, placed high up like that? It means you're a *vory*."

"Say what?"

"It's a tattoo that identifies a *vory v zakone*, a member of the Russian Mafia. They've been deep into getting tattoos from way back."

"So what was he doing running around with that passport? Had to be a forgery, right?"

"I don't know," said Lock. "Looked real enough to me, but I'm hardly an expert."

"I dunno, brother. There's a whole bunch of stuff that seems off here."

"Such as?"

"The big one?" said Ty. "I don't get why a government would be going so hard against one guy. If he was involved in politics, opposing them, trying to bring them down, that I'd understand."

Lock had to concede it was a fair point. But there was a counter to it.

"How hard would you go up against someone if you thought they'd cough up several billion?" he asked Ty.

"I feel ya," said Ty. "But it still feels like we're not getting the full story here."

. . .

As they got out of the elevator, Lock dug into a bag and pulled out one of the toys Ty had purchased for Anastasia. Ty was generous, and warmhearted, especially when it came to kids, but any excuse to visit the world Mecca of toy stores when they were in New York and Ty took it. Watching the six-foot-four Marine wait his turn to play on the store's giant electronic piano was forever etched on Lock's memory.

Lock held up the Booty Shaking Plastic Llama and shook his head at his partner. "Really?"

"What did the lady say? This is the hot-ticket toy at the moment."

It was true. It had been the salesperson's recommendation. Not that Ty had appeared to need much persuading.

"Come on, dude. A dancing llama. Way better than that singing Billy Bass shit all you white folks lost your minds over a few years back."

They headed inside and took the elevator up to Anastasia Semenov's room. The bodyguard was posted on the door. He stood up from his chair as they walked down the corridor.

Lock hoped that Elizabeth hadn't been so soused she'd forgotten to let him know they were dropping by. He held up the bags as a signal that they came in peace.

"Her father's in there with her," said the bodyguard.

"That's good. We need to speak with him," said Lock. "And in the meantime we need to speak with you about the arrangements here."

"We brought her some toys," said Ty, holding up the bags from FAO Schwarz.

The bodyguard peered into the bags and shot Ty a look. Ty stared him down.

"I'll let Mr. Semenov know you're here."

"Where's McLennan? In fact, where's the rest of the personal escort team?"

"Side room," said the bodyguard, with a nod to a nearby door.

Fat lot of good they were doing in there, thought Lock. Someone could have strolled out of the elevator, taken out this guy, and been in the room with the principal and his daughter before the others could do anything about it.

An assassin didn't approach with a big arrow over their head. They were usually blending in. All it would take was some kind of uniform and a cleaning cart.

"Ty, take this door," said Lock. "I'm going to have a word with McLennan."

"Got you," said Ty, moving in front of the door as the bodyguard went to inform Semenov they were there.

As Lock pushed the door open, one of the security detail jumped to his feet, hand moving to his gun. McLennan saw it was Lock and waved for him to sit back down. "Relax, he's one of ours," said McLennan.

"Didn't mean to interrupt your break," said Lock.

McLennan put his hands on the table and levered himself up. He had dark bags under his eyes, and looked exhausted. "I'll come out there."

Lock held the door open and they stepped out into the corridor. "So what's the deal? You have your principal in a room guarded by one guy who's standing in an unsecured corridor."

"It's been secured," snapped McLennan.

"When?"

"When we got here."

"And since then we walked in here with no one stopping us," said Lock.

"Listen, pal," said McLennan. "I've been on this job for months now, and every time I think it can't get any crazier it does. Maybe if Semenov could keep his dick in his pants for longer than a few minutes at a time we might actually be able to regroup for long enough to get a handle on this."

Lock wasn't buying it. Crazy clients and crazier principals came with the territory, especially at the wealthier end of the scale. Close protection was about dealing with and managing chaos.

In any case it was hardly a minimum-wage mall-cop gig. McLennan and his team were being extremely well remunerated. Six months on a gig like this would make them what it would have taken ten years of active service to pull down.

"So why don't you quit?" said Lock.

"That what this is really about? You suggesting we should be replaced so you and your buddy can take over?"

"The only thing I want to see is that the job gets done properly. If it's you doing it, or me, makes no difference. Now, if you think our boy here is taking unnecessary risks then man the hell up and go tell him."

"You think I haven't tried? I'm just the hired help, and so are you if you stick around."

"Fine," said Lock. "Then do the job. Go get one of your guys and post him next to that elevator and have another stand at the end of that corridor. And whoever you have left, put them on transport duty downstairs."

"You're giving the orders now?" said McLennan.

"I guess I am," said Lock.

McLennan turned on his heel and disappeared back inside the room. Lock heard him dishing out the same commands he'd just been given.

The door into Anastasia's room opened and Dimitri appeared just in time to see his PES move into the positions they should have been taking this whole time.

Rather than staying angry at their slacking, Lock was pleased. Whatever his personal moral failings, Dimitri Semenov didn't need any additional worries at the moment.

"We're going to need to find a backup team for when these guys walk," Lock said to his partner.

"You think they will?" Ty asked him.

"I think they were mentally checking out as soon as those cars took off over that bridge. Even if they hang around for the cash we're going to need some fresh bodies in here."

"Ryan, we don't have the time to do that and work out what the hell's going on."

"We don't have to," said Lock. "He has a whole office full of people. I'm sure he can spare us a couple of folks to work on sourcing some new close protection operators. Probably best to go with one of the big companies. That way it's plug in and play."

"Full replacement?"

"Absolutely. In the meantime we can gather enough information to deal with the handover."

Ty nodded as Dimitri headed over to speak with them.

"You're right," said Ty. "Fresh team is what this needs."

Lock would have to be careful how he broached the subject with Dimitri. It probably wasn't a discussion for tonight. He'd wait until he'd had some sleep and was a little fresher.

Dimitri shook their hand. "Thanks for being here, and for the gifts. Anastasia loves them, especially the bracelet."

"Yeah, some of my cousins' kids have those bracelets," said Ty. "They never take them off."

"Oh, and that little dancing animal," said Dimitri. "That seems to be her favorite."

"Told you," Ty said to Lock.

"The bracelet contains a tracking chip," said Lock. "We thought it was a good precautionary measure. I cleared it with Elizabeth before we collected it."

"You think she's a kidnap threat?" said Dimitri.

"You don't?" said Ty.

"A bracelet can be removed, though," said Dimitri.

"It could," said Lock. "There are subcutaneous chips that can be inserted under the skin, but those can be removed by kidnappers too, only that's a lot more traumatic."

Wincing a little, Dimitri nodded to Lock to continue.

"So with kids we usually recommend something unobtrusive that they would wear anyway."

"The bracelet's regular. We fitted the tracker chip. It's not one of the commercial tracking devices on the market that someone's going to toss as soon as they see it," said Ty.

"And the other toys?" asked Dimitri.

"All regular stuff," said Ty.

"Distraction strategy," said Lock. "You sit down with a girl that age and go through why she has to wear a tracker, it's not good, it only creates more anxiety. This way, she slips it on, and she's so busy playing with the other stuff that it barely registers."

"If she starts taking it off we can have the conversation," said Ty.

The oligarch tilted his head back and stared up at the ceiling. "What a way to live."

"It won't last forever," said Lock.

"I hope not, because right now I don't see any end to this madness."

"There's always an end. The important thing is that we put in place all the measures now to make sure that we can get there safely," Lock told him.

"You're right. It's just . . . I know it may not seem like it to you, or anyone else, but Elizabeth and Anastasia mean everything to me. Someone harming me is one thing, but harming them?"

"I understand," said Lock, meaning it. He knew the intense pain of losing people close to him. It never left you and, in a strange way, you didn't want it to leave you.

"So how are you holding up?" Lock asked Dimitri.

"I'll tell you when I get home," he said, a smile appearing briefly on his face.

"Yeah, you might want to take a raincheck on that," said Ty, earning a look from Lock.

"It's fine," said Dimitri. "It's important to retain your sense of humor in times like these. Sadly, I don't think there are many hotels in the city that would be delighted to have me as a guest right now."

Lock had to hand it to him. Dimitri was made of tough stuff. By now, most men would have folded under this kind of pressure. Certainly Lock had walked in on a bunch of men who should have been way more capable of a healthy degree of forbearance, only to find them seemingly contemplating their escape.

Former special forces personnel could often be excellent close protection operators, but they sometimes struggled with the reactive nature of the job. They were used to being on the front foot rather than waiting for a threat that might or might not come. That was what Lock suspected was going on here.

The job had once been described to him back in the Royal Military Police as consisting of 'hours of boredom, and moments of terror'. SF guys were trained to deal with the moments-of-terror part. The stress of being, as they saw it, sitting ducks was something else. Sure they were used to downtime, but not this kind of downtime.

"How's Elizabeth?" said Dimitri. "I tried calling her, but she hung up. Not that I blame her."

"You want the polite answer or the truth?" said Lock.

"That good, huh? Maybe I'll sleep at the office."

"No," said Lock. "The fewer locations these guys need to cover the better. We can't afford to be spread too thinly over the ground right now. You have a spare bedroom, right?"

"One or two." Dimitri smiled.

"That's good," said Lock, hesitating. "There's something else. Ty and I both think that you may want to consider replacing your current security team. Not immediately, but these things take time so the sooner we get started on sourcing a replacement, the better."

"Replace them?" said Dimitri. "Why? I thought they've been doing everything they should be, give or take one or two slip-ups."

Like choosing one of the few vehicles in North America that could be hacked to the point where it could be driven at high speed off a bridge, Lock thought, but didn't say. "They're a solid team," said Lock. "And I'm not questioning their integrity or the work they've done for you so far. But at the very least they need to be rotated out for a while, given the opportunity to decompress. The military do it all the time. You can't leave someone on constant deployment in high-stress situations."

"Could have fooled me," Ty said under his breath. During his time in the Marine Corps he had been constantly deployed and redeployed as normal cycles had been set aside after 9/11, and the stop-loss policy had extended his service.

Dimitri was quiet. "I don't like. I show loyalty to those who show it to me."

"Okay. Then keep them on some kind of retainer and let them take some time off."

From his expression, it didn't look like Dimitri was buying into the idea. "Anastasia is used to seeing the same faces. It's comforting for a child, especially when they're sick."

"It's usually the same couple of guys with her at the hospital?" said Ty.

"Yes."

"Then keep them on for the time being," said Lock. "How long before she's able to come home?"

"They won't say. It depends on how this new round of treatment goes, but maybe another week and she can have some time with us."

"Okay, switch them out then," said Lock. "She'll be so happy to be home that she probably won't notice."

Dimitri sighed. "That would work. So are you going to tell them, or will I?"

"We can break the news. We're already the bad guys anyway," said Ty.

"They may be pissed, but I think they may also be relieved," said Lock.

"They should be happy," said Dimitri.

"How's that?" asked Lock.

"They get a break. I don't."

"Like I said before, this will pass."

"I hope you're right, Mr. Lock. I really do."

21

Lock had pressed McLennan to double up the men on duty at the hospital. There would be a man directly outside Anastasia's room, and another posted further down the corridor. The second would be able to liaise with the hospital's existing security without the bodyguard on the door having to leave his post. In the morning they would switch with two others.

Meanwhile Lock and Ty had accompanied Dimitri and his PES back to the townhouse. As they walked him inside, Ty nudged Lock.

"If anyone in the world needs a bodyguard right now . . ." said Ty.

"No kidding."

"So what's the protocol for a wife attacking the principal?"

Lock took a moment. Ty was joking, but it was a good question.

"Reasonable restraint," said Lock. "The last thing we need is anyone taking a trip to the hospital. Or any more fresh meat for the vultures standing outside with TV cameras."

"Roger that," said Ty, as they followed Dimitri into an eerily quiet living room.

A housekeeper appeared.

"Mrs. Semenov has gone to bed," she told them diplomatically.

Lock guessed that with the way she'd been pounding down the Scotch she'd eventually passed out and been taken to bed.

"Thank you," said Dimitri. "Are all the guest rooms prepared?"

"Yes, Mr. Semenov."

"You guys don't mind staying over, do you?" he asked Lock and Ty.

"I was going to head back to Sinai," said Ty. "Couple of things I want to check. If that's okay with you?"

"Of course," said Dimitri.

On the journey back Ty had expressed some concerns to Lock about some of the existing security, especially the apparent lack of checks on access to the elevator. Even though they had two men there, he'd told Lock he'd feel better if he was there personally.

"Okay," said Ty. "I'm out."

He fist-bumped Lock and headed from the room.

"Come on," Dimitri said to Lock. "I'm going to make some coffee."

He must have picked up on the slightly puzzled expression on Lock's face.

"I wasn't always a billionaire," he said. "There was a time when I had to do everything for myself."

Lock followed him out of the room, along a corridor and into the kitchen, as McLennan and the others made themselves scarce. He had a feeling he was in for a late-night therapy session, with Dimitri being the patient and him in the role of therapist.

"Mr. Semenov, would you give me one second? I just have to make a quick call."

LOCK'S GIRLFRIEND, Carmen Lazaro, picked up his call. She was at home in the up-scale apartment they shared on Wilshire Boulevard in Los Angeles.

"Hey, sweetie, it's me. I meant to call earlier but it's been kind of hectic."

"So I've seen from the news."

"You caught that, huh?" he said.

"Pretty juicy story," she said. "Not every day that a supermodel's tossed from the window of a five-star hotel by a billionaire Russian."

"He has an alibi, and lots of witnesses," said Lock.

"Just as well. So how is it?" Carmen asked.

He sensed what was behind the question. What she really wanted to know was when he'd be home. "It's going to take a little longer than I thought."

She laughed. "I had a feeling you were going to say that."

"I'm sorry," he said. "Why don't we go up to Napa for the weekend when I get back?"

"Sounds good. Ryan?"

"Yeah?"

"Just be careful, okay? These Russians, they don't play."

"Hey, neither do I."

Lock walked into the cavernous kitchen to find Dimitri hunched over a long-handled copper pot on the stove.

"A *cezve*?" said Lock.

"You're the first American I've met who knows the proper name."

"Half American, half Brit," said Lock. "Plus one of the benefits of overseas service is you get to see the world."

"Travel the world, meet new people, and kill them. Isn't that how the saying goes?" said Dimitri.

"Something like that."

Dimitri opened a cupboard and pulled out two espresso-sized cups. "I used to live on this stuff when I was getting started building my business. Even after I moved to New York. Some took cocaine, but I always stuck to coffee, black as mud."

"Probably saved yourself a lot of money."

"For all the good it's done me."

"Oh, come on, you can't resent all this, can you?"

He started to decant the sludgy, sweet coffee into the cups. He handed one to Lock. "Thanks."

"Ask me a year ago, and I would have said no, but now it seems like all it's done is put a big target on my back."

Lock took a sip. Damn, that was some strong coffee. He saw an opportunity here to ask Dimitri about Grigor Novak. He hadn't had the opportunity to raise it with him before now. Maybe he would have some insight into why a guy carrying a Russian diplomatic passport also had a tattoo that signified membership of Russian organized crime.

When Lock had finished telling him a moderately edited version, Dimitri put his tiny coffee cup down on the marble countertop next to the stove. He had seemed almost amused by the story and Lock's questions.

"So what do you think?" asked Lock.

"I think people here are very naive. They hear 'Russian spy' and they think about maybe some cartoon or something."

"What about the passport?"

"It was probably genuine," Dimitri said casually.

Lock was a little taken aback. He couldn't imagine a scenario where a member of, say, the Italian mob or the Aryan Brotherhood would be given a genuine diplomatic passport. Used as informants, that was totally credible, but this was on another level. "You think it was the real deal?"

"I don't know. I would have to see it."

Lock pulled out his phone and showed Dimitri the pictures they had taken.

He studied them for a moment. "Genuine. I'd bet a million dollars on it."

"That's like me betting a buck."

"Okay, a hundred million."

"Why are you so sure?"

"Apart from the fact it looks real and not a forgery?"

"It could be a good forgery."

Dimitri looked Lock in the eye. "You don't go around with a forged diplomatic passport from the Russian government over here if you value your life."

"But the tattoos indicate he's Mafia. What do they care?"

"That's a good point, and that was true for many decades in Russia."

"It's changed?" asked Lock.

"The government and the *vory* came to an arrangement. That's not to say they don't step on each other's toes from time to time. But they're both gangsters, and the Kremlin has no problem using them when they need to. If you don't believe me, go look at who controls some of the Caucasus," said Dimitri, referring to some of the further, and more lawless, outposts of the post-Soviet Russian empire.

"So a gangster working for the government?"

"They're all gangsters, my friend. It's just that some don't have the obvious marks," said Dimitri, pulling at his shirt collar to show a neck free of tattoos. He held up one finger. "That's not quite true. There are patriots too. But they are even more dangerous than the gangsters."

"You think that was who threw Ruta out of the window?" said Lock.

"No, that would have been a gangster. But the person who ordered them to do it? That might well have been a patriot."

"We should forward Novak's details to the NYPD. Make sure he's properly on their radar."

"I'll pass them to my attorney. That way you can stay out of it," said Dimitri.

Lock leaned against the edge of a kitchen counter. He needed to ask Dimitri about the murder of the young model, but he wasn't entirely sure how to broach the subject.

"You want to know if I killed her, don't you?"

It was Lock's turn to smile. "Is it that obvious?"

"It's what everyone will want to ask me. It's what people will associate with me from now on. That was why they did it. It's one more turn of the screw."

"Well, the cops couldn't have thought you did it or you wouldn't be back here. You weren't even formally arrested, were you? Just questioned?" said Lock.

"When it happened I was in my office, surrounded by other people, including people who don't work for me and would have no reason to lie. My alibi was cast iron."

"Not much of a frame-up job, then," Lock said. "That was a lot of trouble to go to for something that didn't even get you arrested."

"Maybe they got their timings wrong."

"What do you mean?"

"I was supposed to be there, but I had some business to deal with."

Lock was confused. "So the voice message they were talking about on the news?"

"I'd left her a message, but it wasn't the one they found on Ruta's phone. Poor Ruta."

Now Lock was even more lost than he had been even a second ago. "How is that possible?"

"You tell me," said Dimitri, pulling out his cell phone, tapping the screen, and handing it to Lock. "One of my attorneys used to be a prosecutor. He has excellent contacts in law enforcement and the District Attorney's office. He managed to get hold of the message the cops found on her phone. The one I left must have been deleted. They're speaking with the phone company to see if it can be retrieved. Anyway, this is the one they found," he said, jabbing a finger at an audio file on the screen.

Tapping the play icon, Lock held the phone to his ear so he could hear the message without having to ramp up the volume. As he listened he could feel Dimitri's eyes on him, studying his reaction to what he was hearing.

When the message finished, he lowered the phone. "I'm no expert, but that sounds exactly like you," he told him.

Dimitri laughed. "It does. It sounds so like me even I was confused. I started to wonder if maybe I'd left that message and forgotten about it. But I hadn't. That's something else they're very good at. Gas lighting. Making you doubt your own sanity."

Lock held up the phone. "Could you forward me a copy of that?"

Dimitri shrugged. "Sure, but why?"

"It might be nothing, but I'd like to run it past a couple of people. Confidentially, of course. They'll also be under an NDA before I give it to them." Lock moved the coffee cups into the dishwasher. "You should get some sleep. I'm going to crash in one of the other bedrooms if that's okay with you."

"Worried about someone breaking in to kill me?"

"No, I think the person that's most likely to do that is already in the house, don't you?"

22

The bodyguard stepped out of the hospital-room door as Ty came down the corridor.

"She's awake if you want to say hello," said the bodyguard. "She wanted to thank you before for the stuff you got her, but you'd split."

Ty glanced back down the corridor to where a hospital security guard was busy playing on his phone.

"Listen, if you want to go use the bathroom, grab something to eat, I can hold the fort here for a few minutes while I say hi," said Ty.

"That'd be great. Appreciate it."

"No problem."

Ty pushed the door open and stuck his head around. Anastasia Semenov was sitting up in bed. She looked a perkier than the first time they had seen her. Her cheeks had a little more color.

"How's the dancing llama?" Ty asked.

Her face lit up. "I love it."

"Yeah, that's what the lady in the store said. You mind if I come in?"

"No."

Ty walked into the room. "I'm Tyrone, but most everyone just calls me Ty."

"I'm Anastasia, and people call me Anastasia," she said, deadpan, then laughed.

"You're funny."

"And brave. I get called that a lot," said Anastasia.

"Well, you are."

"I don't see why lying in bed all day being sick makes you brave."

"Do you complain?"

Her head tilted to one side as she thought about it. "Not really. It's not like it'll change things."

"Then that makes you brave, especially compared to most grown-ups."

"You think?"

"You mind if I sit down?" said Ty, pointing to the very edge of the bed.

She shrugged. "I don't mind."

"Thanks. Yeah, most grown-ups like to complain about every little thing, so you're definitely braver than them."

"I guess. So do you work for my dad?"

"At the moment I do."

"You're a bodyguard?"

"I prefer close protection specialist, but bodyguard works too."

"What's the difference?" asked Anastasia.

Ty decided not to give her the usual smartass answer he reserved for people who asked that question, which was 'About five thousand dollars a week.' Instead he said, "Bodyguards are all about muscles, and close protection is all about using your brain."

The answer seemed to satisfy her. "Okay."

"So how come you're not asleep?"

"The medicine they give me, sometimes it messes up my sleep."

She propped herself up on her elbow, her chin cupped in her hand. "So how come you can't sleep?"

"I used to be in the Marines. Marines don't sleep."

Anastasia took her time thinking it over. "That's not true. Everyone sleeps." Her brow furrowed with concentration. "Even owls."

"Okay, we don't sleep *much*. Hey, I have a question for you. Are you wearing the bracelet we put in with the toys?"

She held up her other arm. It was fastened around her wrist. "Yeah. I like it. It's cute."

"That's good, because we're going to need you to keep it on."

Ty had always believed that, when it came to security, it was better to level with kids, and be honest. The trick was doing it without scaring them, which was a tough line to walk sometimes.

"Why do I have to keep it on?"

"Let me show you something," said Ty, leaning over.

"You just told me not to take it off."

"Just for a second."

She took it off and handed it to him. He turned it inside out, finding the section where they had inserted the tiny tracker, and held it up.

"See this little silver part? That's a tracking device. It means that your dad, and your mom, will know where you are. As long as you're wearing it."

Anastasia eye-rolled him. "But I'm always here. It's not like I get to go anywhere."

Ty handed it to her, watching as she rolled it back over her hand and onto her wrist. "Good point. But when you get out of here, and you will get out of here," he said, emphasizing the last part, "it's important that we know where you are. Not that you can't go visit friends, and stuff like that, but we need to know where we can find you."

"Okay." There was a long pause, like she was building up to saying something, but she wasn't sure how to say it.

"Ty? Can I ask you something?"

"You can ask me anything, anything at all."

Her brow furrowed. "Are you scared of dying?"

Ty had always thought that honesty was the best policy when it came to talking to kids, especially about big stuff. Besides anything else, kids had a way better BS detector than adults. If you lied to them, they picked up on it.

There was an extra responsibility here too. For most kids—hell, for most people—this question was abstract. For Anastasia Semenov, he guessed, it was all too real. She was already facing her own mortality.

One of the joys of childhood, as Ty saw it anyway, was that you were free from these big questions. You got to live in the present. It was only with adulthood that that was stripped away.

"I guess I'm scared of not seeing the people I love anymore. Not for a while anyway," said Ty. "That part scares me. But I've tried not to be too scared."

"Why?" asked Anastasia.

"The way I see it, if you go through your whole life being scared of it being over then you're not really living. You're just walking around worrying about something that hasn't happened."

The little girl fiddled absentmindedly with her bracelet. "You think you'll go to Heaven?"

"I hope so," said Ty. "But it's not really my call."

"I get scared," she said. "I try not to let Mom and Dad know, but I do. Sometimes I cry."

"I wouldn't worry about letting them know how you're feeling. They'll understand."

"I know, but Daddy has so much that he's worried about. There are some people who don't like him. People from where he used to live before he came to America and met Mommy."

Kids always knew what was going on, thought Ty. Especially bright ones like Anastasia.

"That's definitely not something to worry about," Ty told her. "Me and my partner, Ryan, we got that covered. No one's going to hurt your family while we're around."

"You promise?"

"I promise."

She yawned.

Ty patted the bed. "You should get some sleep."

She lay back, her head sinking into her pillows. Ty stayed there until she drifted off.

23

An hour had passed, and Anastasia's designated bodyguard still hadn't returned. Ty was happy to sit with her all night, if he had to, but this was turning into one long coffee break.

Finally, he pulled out his phone and dropped Lock a text asking him to see if someone there could raise the guy. A text pinged back from Lock almost immediately: *On it.*

Opening the door, Ty checked the corridor. It was empty. He didn't want to call out in case he woke Anastasia. The kid needed her sleep.

A minute later a fresh text came in from Lock. This one read: *They can't raise him.*

Ty muttered something under his breath that he definitely didn't want the kid to hear. He prowled back to the door and took a step into the corridor. A nurse came around the corner. Ty waved her across.

"Excuse me, Miss. Have you seen the man who's usually with Anastasia?"

"No, sorry. Is everything okay?"

"Yeah, fine. It's just that he went on a break and now no one can raise him."

"You want me to speak with security?" the nurse asked.

"No, you're good, I can do that. I just thought maybe you'd seen him."

"If I see him, I'll let him know you're looking for him."

"Appreciate it."

He watched her walk back down the corridor. Then she stopped directly outside a storeroom. For a second Ty thought she was going to check inside. That struck him as strange, unless, of course, she'd seen the bodyguard hole up in there before when he was taking a break.

She looked down at her shoe with a puzzled expression. She lifted her heel, balancing on one leg. It was like she had stepped in something, but Ty was too far away to see what.

Reaching down she touched whatever it was. Her hand came back up, the fingertips red.

She startled, almost losing her balance. She looked down to the floor.

The red liquid that had been on her shoe was seeping out from under the door. Ty knew blood when he saw it. He guessed from her expression that she did too.

She took a step back and looked back down the corridor to him.

Ty didn't move. He stayed exactly where he was. In the doorway of the room, his body side on so that he could see what was happening out there and have eyes on Anastasia at the same time.

He didn't plan on moving either. Not for anything. One hand went to his SIG Sauer P226. The other fumbled for his phone.

As he called Lock, he started calculating how he could extract Anastasia from the room if he had to. She was hooked up to at least one drip. The bag was on a stand, and the liquid was clear, not blood.

She wasn't on a ventilator. That was good. The other connections looked to him like basic monitoring such as heartrate.

He decided that if they needed to move her, he would disconnect the cannula, pick her up and move her like that.

Back down the corridor, the nurse opened the storeroom door. Ty edged a little further out of the door.

"Leave it," he called, doing his best not to shout and wake Anastasia.

It was too late. She opened the door, and stepped back, horrified.

Ty said a silent prayer of thanks that she hadn't screamed.

She turned to Ty, freaked out.

Lock picked up his call. "We haven't located him yet. They tried calling him but he's not answering."

"Try again. Right now."

"Ty? What's going on?"

"Forget the radio. Call his cell," said Ty.

The nurse backed out of the storeroom, her shoes slick with blood. Ty didn't have an angle to see inside and there was no way he was moving any more than six feet from Anastasia.

He muted his end of the call.

"What is it?" he said to the nurse.

There was the trill of a cell phone ringing from inside the storeroom.

"He's shot himself."

"You're sure?"

"I think so," she said. "He's still holding the gun."

Ty hit the mute icon again. "Ryan, I need Sinai security and the NYPD up here ASAP."

"You got it," said Lock.

Ty could hear Lock barking orders to someone in the background. Ty scanned the corridor in either direction, ready to draw his weapon. Behind him the girl roused a little.

"What's going on?"

"Someone spilled something in the corridor, that's all. Go back to sleep."

Ty tensed as the elevator at the far end of the corridor opened. The other private security operator ran out. Ty's hand closed around his SIG.

Right now he wasn't prepared to trust anyone.

"What the hell's going on?" yelled the guy, rushing to the storeroom.

He skidded to a halt, almost losing his footing as he hit the blood. His face went pale.

"Get on comms," barked Ty. "Get security up here and take up your post down there until they get here."

The guy ignored him, rushing past the nurse and into the storeroom to take a look at his buddy. Ty seethed quietly. Their primary task was to make sure Anastasia remained safe. That included shielding her, as much as possible, from the gory details of whatever had just happened. Everything else came second.

A few seconds later the guy reappeared. His clothes were covered with blood.

Ty stared him down as he walked along the corridor.

"It doesn't make sense. I just saw him like an hour ago."

"You see anyone else?" asked Ty.

"No."

Ty lowered his voice. He fixed his gaze on him. "Good. Now go do your job and secure that end of the corridor until we have backup. Your buddy in there is gone and nothing's going to change that so follow my orders. I'm not going to tell you again."

24

Two hours later

NYPD PATROL OFFICERS were posted at either end of the corridor, securing the scene. A team from the Crime Scene Unit, part of the force's Forensics Investigations Division, moved back and forth from the storeroom, collecting evidence.

Outside the room containing Anastasia Semenov, Ty stood guard in front of the door, arms crossed. The patrol cops had asked him to move, only to be met with a snarl. They had swiftly backed off, then contradicted themselves, telling him he shouldn't leave until he had provided a statement.

Lock threaded his way through the melee with Dimitri and Elizabeth Semenov, a frosty detente having seemingly been arrived at since they had taken the call about the latest horrific development.

Ty opened the door for them and stepped aside. Elizabeth pushed past her husband and into the room, where a nurse was busy doing a routine check on Anastasia. Dimitri shot Lock and Ty an apologetic look and followed his wife inside.

"How's the kid?" Lock asked his partner.

"She figured out pretty quickly something was up, so I told her there had been an accident, but I stayed light on details. Made sure she knew it was nothing for her to worry about."

"You hear anything?" asked Lock.

"No, that's the weirdest part. I was in here with Anastasia, the door was closed, but I'd have thought I'd hear *something*. First thing I knew was when the nurse opened the door to that storeroom. This is some twisted shit, Ryan."

"The cops are saying it's a suicide."

Ty looked incredulous. "Say what? Come on, dude."

Lock shrugged and looked at Ty with a that's-all-I-know expression. "They checked the cameras. No one saw him go into the storeroom, but they picked him up getting into the elevator and he was on his own. No one came up after him, apart from medical staff, and their stories all seem to be checking out."

"And what about before?" asked Ty.

"They're still checking, but it doesn't look like anyone was roaming the corridors up on this floor who shouldn't have been here," said Lock. "I guess someone could have been already in there, waiting—it's a big enough space that they could have concealed themselves—but the position of everything else is suggesting he killed himself."

"How many bodyguards you know who've offed themselves?"

Lock started to answer before Ty cut him off.

"On the job. We both know plenty who've eaten a gun when they've been back home sitting with their demons."

"On the job? I can't think of any," said Lock. "But that doesn't mean anything. The guy saw his buddies drown. He waits until you take over, gets some fresh air, makes his decision, comes back in, holes up in there and does it as quietly as he can."

"How is shooting yourself in the head quiet?"

"Noise suppressor on the gun. Plus they're saying he had a pillow between the hot end and his head. Smallish caliber. That door closed. This door closed. Not surprising you didn't hear anything."

"I don't buy it," said Ty. "Model gets tossed out of a window and now a bodyguard kills himself, all in under twenty-four hours."

"I'm not saying I do either, but that's how it's looking. They'll have a better idea when they've done the autopsy. That should give them the angle, how close it was, all that good stuff."

A fifty-something guy with white hair, wearing a gray suit, walked up to them. He flashed his shield and introduced himself as an NYPD detective. "I just need to take a quick statement from the kid."

Lock put his hand on Ty's arm, a pre-emptive gesture intended to damp down what he guessed would be his partner's reaction. It didn't work.

"She didn't see anything," said Ty. "She was in the room the whole time, door closed."

"Maybe he said something to her, then. Either way I need to speak with her."

Lock stepped between the cop and Ty. He could feel Ty's rage building. "She's a pretty sick little girl, we don't want to do anything that might upset her. I'm sure you understand that, Detective."

"I have to speak with everyone who was here. I can get a female officer to do it, if that makes you guys feel any better."

Ty stared at the cop. "The answer is no, unless her parents say otherwise, which I very much doubt they will."

The cop went to move past Ty. "I'll ask them."

Ty's arm shot out, almost clothes-lining the detective's neck in the process. "We'll ask them."

Lock ducked under and into the room as Ty death-stared the cop. He reappeared less than five seconds later.

"It's a no," said Lock.

"You didn't have time to ask anyone anything," the cop protested.

Ty took a half-step in. His chest was against the smaller man's head. He glowered down at him. "We're done here," said Ty. "Conversation is over."

The detective stepped back, returning Ty's glare before about-turning and heading back down the corridor.

"We're going to have to decide what we do," said Lock.

"What do you mean?"

"I spoke with the Semenovs on the way down here."

"Bet that was a fun car ride," said Ty.

"Oh, yeah," said Lock. "Anyway, they think she can continue her treatment at home. They only kept her here because it was more of a controlled environment and they didn't want her seeing the circus outside the family home."

"And now not so much."

"Exactly," said Lock. "The physicians say she can return home if she has private nursing, which isn't an issue. She can come back in as and when required."

Ty nodded. "Kid would probably be happier at home. In her own bedroom."

"That was what I was thinking."

"Plus, what is it you always say about hospitals?"

"People die in them," said Lock.

"No kidding," said Ty, looking back down the corridor to the storeroom. "So when we thinking about moving her?"

"Let's wait until they're done here," said Lock. "You want to supervise the transfer?"

"Well, I'm not letting any of these clowns do it."

25

Dimitri's PA, Madeline, laid out the papers in front of Lock. They were standing in the kitchen, which seemed to have become an informal hub in the house as everyone hunkered down, waiting for the next unwelcome development.

"This is the purchase order for the sedans," she told Lock. "And this is the shortlist that was drawn up prior to the purchase decision being made."

Lock picked up the shortlist document. It was six pages in total. There was a cover sheet, one page for each of the recommended vehicles, of which there had been four, and a final summary page.

"Mr. Semenov made the final decision on the purchase."

Marveling at the detail involved, Lock flicked through the details of the four possible contenders. "That's great, thank you."

"Will there be anything else?"

"I want to talk to you about rerunning background checks. I want the report on everyone who works directly for Mr. Semenov, and I'll need to know when the report was conducted. But first I'll take a look at this."

"Of course, I'll get on that. I'll just be through in the office if you need anything else," she said.

"Oh," he said, calling her back. "Who drew up this shortlist?"

"I did. I mean, I wrote it up. Mr. McLennan gave me the names of the vehicles that might be most suitable."

He settled in at the kitchen table, pulling out his phone so he could run his own search of the vehicle details. He was looking for one thing in particular.

A call came in from Ty.

"What's the situation?" Lock asked.

"Corridor's clear, body's out, she's going to be moved to an ambulance. Should be with you in about twenty-five. The equipment set up in her bedroom?"

"Nursing-agency people are here getting it done."

Being around the ultra-wealthy, Lock was still amazed, not by the houses and cars and other obvious symbols of money, but by how quickly they could solve everyday problems with the wave of dollar bills.

Dimitri had handed off his daughter's care to staff and in no time they had secured not only private nursing and medical support but all the equipment to go with it. This was the real power of money, the ability to solve almost instantly issues that regular people struggled with.

Lock didn't harbor any resentment about it. Not when a child was involved. But it did make him wonder about how the world was set up when kids died every day from a lack of clean water.

"What about outside?" said Ty.

"It's a mess. Let me know when you're in transit and I'll deal with any sidewalk static."

"Roger that."

"How's she doing?"

"I don't know. She's kind of quiet. She knows something's up, but no one's told her exactly what happened yet. I'd like to keep it that way for now, but that's her parents' call. Tell you one thing, though, the kid's a trouper, man."

"That's good," said Lock.

The call over, he went back to checking the vehicle details. Out of the four possible vehicles, three of them, including the Cadillac that had been selected, were classified as Level 2 when it came to driver assistance technology. That meant they were all potentially hackable to the point where control could be taken over from the driver.

None of the other two had any known security flaws, but then neither had the Cadillacs before they had been remotely piloted off the bridge. That left one other manufacturer and model on the list, the BMW 7 series, which had Level 1 driver assistance technology.

Lock looked at the prices to see if that gave any clues. The BMW would have been more expensive, but the difference was relatively marginal, especially given Dimitri's net worth.

Maybe it was just a matter of personal preference. He would ask him.

Lock got up, grabbed a mug and poured some coffee from the Krups machine on the counter. Next to the Turkish coffee it tasted weak, but he needed the caffeine jolt.

Once they had Anastasia safely inside, Dimitri wanted Lock to accompany him to his offices. He and Ty had come in as consultants: slowly but surely they were being pulled into more direct roles.

The sooner he could help source a replacement security team, the better. One thing had become abundantly clear to Lock over the past twenty-four hours. If Dimitri and his family were going to make it out of this unscathed, they needed to get off defense and onto offense. Easier said than done. Especially with how fast new problems were coming at them. But, as far as Lock saw it, offense wasn't just their best shot, it might be their only shot.

26

Ty sat in the passenger seat of the car behind the ambulance that contained Anastasia. One hand was on the butt of his SIG, the other rested on the door handle, ready for a fast debus from the vehicle.

Traffic along Fifth Avenue was heavy. The NYPD had declined a request for a patrol car to accompany the transfer. After the last twenty-four hours their attitude toward the Semenov family had cooled.

Shifting nervously in his seat, Ty scanned the traffic and people on the sidewalks. Nothing jumped out at him. He doubted they would encounter any problems. Attacking an ambulance carrying a sick kid in the middle of Manhattan, with people all around, didn't strike him as all that likely.

Then again, he wouldn't have imagined that a bodyguard would hole up in a store cupboard and shoot himself in the head. Or that someone would launch a model from a hotel window for no other reason than to mess with a billionaire.

Traffic slowed, even though the light up ahead was green. A few seconds later it came to a complete halt.

Ty popped the door open and hopped out. He walked through

traffic, staying tight to the edge of the ambulance.

Up ahead, what looked like a minor fender-bender had escalated. Both drivers were out of their cars, screaming at each other while behind them other drivers honked their horns to get them to move. It was about as New York a scene as you could get, neither man wanting to back down.

Still scanning the surrounding area, and wary that it could always be what was known in the close protection trade as a 'come-on', Ty jogged over to them.

"Hey, assholes, I got a sick kid in that ambulance. Now get back in your vehicles and pull over to the side if you want to continue this."

One started to say something. Ty cut him off with a look. Wisely, the guy thought better of it.

As they got into their cars, Ty jogged back to the ambulance. He tapped on the driver's door. The driver lowered his window. "What's the matter?" Ty said. "You don't have a siren fitted to this thing?"

"We're only supposed to use it if it's an emergency," explained the driver.

"Listen, this kid's family are under threat. That counts as an emergency in my book."

"Okay, okay," said the driver. "Tell you what, if the traffic gets snarled again by a couple of assholes, I'll blast it."

"Thank you."

Ty got back into the car and called Lock to give him their ETA.

THE AMBULANCE ROLLED onto the block. Ty hung his head out of the car's passenger window and cursed under his breath as he saw that the NYPD had withdrawn the barriers at the end of the block, allowing traffic and pedestrians to flow freely. Now, rather than being contained at the end of the block, the media were camped directly outside the townhouse. Ty told his driver to pull over at the curb. He jumped out, jogging alongside the ambulance.

Lock was outside, standing at the top of the steps with McLennan and another member of the residential security team. When

McLennan didn't move, Lock came down the steps and began speaking to the press of media.

No doubt he was explaining the situation. No doubt, thought Ty, the reporters would ignore him to get their shot for the news that night. He only hoped that they had persuaded the Semenovs to stay inside while they brought Anastasia from the ambulance into the house. Dimitri or Elizabeth appearing would be like throwing chum into shark-infested waters.

The ambulance was four hundred yards from the steps. Lock had them facing him, keeping their eyes in the other direction. Then the front door opened, and the reporters' heads went on a swivel as Elizabeth Semenov appeared. A couple of reporters rushed the steps, only for McLennan, Lock, and the other security guy to push them back.

Ty knew he had to act quickly. He picked up his pace, running so that he was in line with the front cab of the ambulance. He signaled for the driver to lower the window.

"What's up?" he asked Ty.

"You have some earplugs back there, some cotton wool, anything you can put in the kid's ears?"

"What?"

Ty repeated his question.

"Yeah, we'll have something. I don't know about earplugs, but we have cotton wool for sure. Why?"

"I'm going to need you to use that siren, that's why."

"The siren? We're almost there, bro."

TY TOOK up position at the rear of the ambulance as it stopped at the curb. Lock was at the bottom of the steps, doing his best, along with McLennan, to establish some kind of reporter-free space.

A couple of patrol cops had reluctantly joined the melee. They stood between the media and Elizabeth Semenov, who was ignoring Lock's repeated request to go back inside her home. Lock had no idea if she was just so eager to see her daughter that she couldn't wait an additional few minutes, or whether this display of parental concern was for the cameras. If he'd had to guess he would have gone with the latter.

The back doors of the ambulance opened. As they began to move the gurney, Ty saw that Anastasia was wearing a spare EMT headset they must have found in back.

They lowered, then pushed the gurney out before re-extending the trolley mechanism. Ty walked in front of them, clearing the way to the bottom of the steps.

Elizabeth rushed to be at her daughter's side, Anastasia looked scared by the press of people. Ty made sure she could see him. He took up position on the other side from Elizabeth, who held her daughter's hand.

Looking up, Ty signaled for the driver to hit the siren as the reporters began to pepper Elizabeth with questions.

"Were you aware that your husband was having an affair with Ruta?"

"Is it true that you've hired a divorce attorney?"

Lying on the gurney, the headset tucked over her ears, the siren wailing loudly enough to wake the dead, Anastasia Semenov heard none of them.

They moved the gurney up the steps. The front door opened. Between them Ty, Lock, the other bodyguards and the two cops managed to keep the reporters and a gathering crowd of onlookers at bay.

At the front door Dimitri Semenov joined his wife. The frenzy of questions ramped up a notch. He and Elizabeth stepped to one side as the EMTs moved the gurney through the door, leaving themselves momentarily together at the top of the stone steps.

Dimitri went to take his wife's hand, a gesture of solidarity no doubt intended to redirect the story looming behind the machine-gun staccato of the questions that continued to pour in. Elizabeth shook him off as the driver cut the siren, and a final question came that seemed to catch everyone off guard.

"Mr. Semenov, are you aware that Interpol just issued a Red Notice for your extradition back to Moscow?"

27

An Interpol Red Notice wasn't exactly an international arrest warrant, but it was pretty damn close. Interpol, which was the shorthand name for the International Criminal Police Organization, was a kind of bureaucratic United Nations for law enforcement. It didn't have any detectives or police officers of its own. Instead it acted as a kind of central clearing house where different countries could share information as well as seeking and receiving information from police forces in other countries.

A Red Notice was a communiqué issued by Interpol, which asked law enforcement in every member state to look out for and detain whoever was the subject of the notice. In any given month as many as five to ten thousand Red Notices would be active. They were usually reserved for the most dangerous criminals, particularly terrorists.

In recent years they had also been open to abuse, mostly by totalitarian regimes who used them to track down and harass dissidents and other opponents who had fled overseas. Interpol often turned them down, but occasionally one would slip through.

Dimitri Semenov sat at the head of a long mahogany conference table in the office of his hedge fund, surrounded by attorneys, and stared down at the Red Notice with his name on it. One side of him sat Madeline Marshowsky, his personal assistant, on the other Ryan Lock.

Dimitri took off a pair of reading glasses and looked down the table at his main criminal defense attorney, Richard Bauer, a man with long, slicked-back white hair and over-sized tortoiseshell glasses.

"Should I be worried?" he asked Bauer.

"Yeah, you should be worried," said Bauer. "But not by this. There's no way you'll be detained on American soil for this piece of crap. I'm just amazed that Interpol are still letting Russia get away with this kind of horseshit."

One of Bauer's younger associates chipped in: "They apply for maybe a hundred of these every year against people like you."

"People like me?" said Dimitri.

"Dissidents, people they don't like. Once in a while one slips through and gets issued as a Red Notice. Don't worry, we'll crush it."

"But for the time being, be careful with international travel," said Bauer. "Uncle Sam isn't going to act on it, but that doesn't mean some other country won't."

"That's not a concern," said Dimitri. "I don't have any travel plans. But there is one thing."

"What's that?" said Bauer.

"The indictment back in Russia, I'd like to know who's behind it."

Down the conference table, Bauer sighed. "That won't be easy. I can make some calls, but I'd imagine whoever's pulling the strings on this is pretty well concealed."

Dimitri drummed his fingers on the table. "Anyone have any other good news for me?"

"It's not good news, but it's news," said Lock.

"Go ahead, Ryan."

"This Red Notice being issued could make replacing your security team more difficult. A lot of the big companies aren't going to want to be seen to be working for someone with an active Red Notice against them, bullshit or not."

"Okay," said Dimitri. "Then I'll offer them more money."

"You're paying top dollar as it is," said Lock. "That might not do it. It's reputational. A lot of these companies' work comes from places like Russia and Saudi."

"The two countries who abuse the Red Notice system more than any others," said Bauer.

"Okay," said Dimitri. "Then you and your partner stay with me until the stink lifts and I can hire someone else in. And I keep McLennan on as well. That should be enough, right?"

"It's not ideal in terms of numbers, but we can make do and mend."

"Anything else we should be doing on the security side, Mr. Lock?" asked Madeline.

"Just what I've already raised. I'd like to background-check everyone again. Once we're confident that everyone's solid on the inside, that takes away a lot of concern."

"You think we have someone who's working for them?" asked Dimitri.

"Anything's possible," said Lock. "When you have a government involved, especially a government like Russia's, the tools at its disposal can be a lot more sophisticated."

"I still don't get why they're going to all this trouble," said Bauer.

"You don't get why someone would go to all this effort for billions of dollars?" said Dimitri.

"Frankly, no. Wait, let me clarify that. I get why a criminal outfit would. Risk and reward, right? In this case the reward is huge. But there's no way someone is just going to sign over that kind of money and bankrupt themselves because of all this, no matter how unpleasant it might be."

"Then," said Dimitri, "you don't understand the Russian mentality. I've already explained this to Ryan. This isn't just about money, it's about revenge. I'm the one who got away, with the money."

He slammed his hands down on the table. "Now, are we done?"

There were nods and rumbles of agreement around the table.

"Good. Now you can go justify the enormous retainers and salaries I pay you all."

28

At first Ninel Tarasov had hated every second of it. The heat. How, within minutes, her clothing and hair were soaked with her own sweat. The ridiculous contortions she was expected to perform. The faux-mysticism spouted by the instructor.

And, above all else, she hated the beautiful young gamine girls and entitled trophy wives who surrounded her in the class. These were women who had, for the most part, won the genetic lottery. They had been born to be slim and attractive but had somehow convinced themselves that it was the magical result of what the Americans euphemistically called "lifestyle choices".

They confused beauty with virtue, and appearance with morality, and Ninel hated them for their stupidity. There was only one person in the class, currently lying on a mat a few feet from her, that Ninel had any time for.

After the first few months of attending the hot yoga class in the studio on the Upper West Side, Ninel had found one part of it that she had come to enjoy. The last section. The part where they would lie quietly, eyes shut, and focus on their breathing, on being in the present.

She found these precious few minutes soothing. Not that she

cleared her mind, far from it. Instead she used this time to think through where they were with Dimitri Semenov.

The past few months had been frantic. She worried that they had overplayed their hand. The hacking of the vehicles, the killing of Ruta Sirka, and then the Red Notice. Had it been too much? Would it bring too much attention from the Americans?

The Red Notice hadn't even been her idea. That had been put into motion by someone back in Moscow, an overzealous member of the FSB who had thought he was helping. When Ninel had first learned of the application she had done her best to have it withdrawn.

As a way of bringing extra pressure to bear on Semenov it had, she explained, two drawbacks. The first was that it was never likely to be acted upon by the Americans. Even if they had wanted to, and there were some in New York and Washington who would gladly have been rid of Semenov, detaining him would look bad. The press would spin it as cooperating with the Russians, and that was something politicians didn't want to be seen to do.

The second reason she opposed it was that it showed their hand. It came too closely on the heels of the Ruta Sirka murder. Instead of maintaining the pressure on their target, it defused it. Suspicion was now on them rather than him.

She had comforted herself with the understanding that it was unlikely to be granted, and then, out of the blue, it had been.

Thankfully, it didn't appear to have done much damage. Rather than having people rally around Dimitri Semenov it had served to isolate him further. It had served the beauty of the strategy. Sow confusion. Let chaos reign. Put in motion so many conflicting strands that you create an atmosphere so paranoid and poisonous that all people want is to be rid of this oligarch.

If it looked haphazard and anarchic to the outside world then so much the better. That was the point.

Now lying here in this rare moment of personal calm she reminded herself that, like a great symphony, the beats of silence were as important as the notes. They had thrown several rocks into the water and now was the time to watch the ripples. Those would dictate the next move.

A bell chimed, and the yoga instructor signaled an end to the class. All around her people slowly got to their feet, rolling up their mats, sipping water, and heading for the showers.

Ninel lay there, watching as Madeline Marshowsky walked past her, neither of them acknowledging the other. This was their routine. They attended the class three times a week. Some weeks they made only small-talk, two women from similar backgrounds who had forged what appeared to be a perfectly casual friendship.

Other times, when Ninel initiated it, they stayed back a little longer. They waited until the other women were gone, and Ninel gathered what she needed.

No paper trail. No electronic trail. No surreptitious meetings in public places that might be picked up by Semenov or American intelligence. Just good old-fashioned spy work. Locate your target. Study their routine. Insert yourself into their life. Befriend them. Gain some level of trust. Then wait for the moment to present itself.

In this case it had come a year ago when, having attended the class at the same time for months, Ninel had noticed Madeline crying. She had asked her what was wrong. She already knew what it was, but that was hardly the point.

Not satisfied with his wife, mistress and girlfriends, Dimitri had engaged in a short affair with Madeline, only to end it abruptly and badly. Ninel had come by this information by more conventional means, namely Madeline's personal email account, which Alexei had hacked into. He had laughed at the simplicity of the task. It was, he'd told Ninel, like asking a PhD student in applied mathematics to recite their twelve times table.

Madeline's emails had been to a friend, detailing the affair, and how, although she was still deeply in love with Dimitri Semenov, and planned on keeping her job, he had shattered her heart. Like an addict, she still wanted to be around the very thing that had caused her so much pain.

As soon as Ninel had asked her what was wrong, the floodgates had opened. Of course Ninel hadn't shown her hand then. That would have been stupid. She had waited, listened, gauged, and then, when the moment had presented itself, she had made her approach.

There were few intelligence assets that were more motivated than a woman scorned. Blackmail, bribery were superficial. But a woman who had been used and then discarded? That was pure gold. And Ninel had more reason than most to understand that.

29

The President Hotel
Moscow
March 1995

WITH A YOUNG FEMALE companion either side of him, Dimitri Semenov sat in the bar of the President, a bottle of Taittinger champagne in an ice bucket next to him, the table laid with the finest Caspian caviar.

As the two young models, recent arrivals in Moscow from the provinces, sipped champagne, Dimitri sorted through a file of paperwork. He dug out a small pocket calculator from one of two briefcases at his feet and set to work checking some totals at the bottom of a spreadsheet.

Later he would take one of the two young women up to his suite, but for now he had work to do and a guest to wait for. She was running late.

He returned his attention to his spreadsheets. Each detailed the shares he held in various agricultural, manufacturing and service companies. Recently he had started to discover discrepancies between the shares he'd purchased and his total holdings. Several of his employees thought they could shave a little here and a little there, and he wouldn't notice. Or if he did, he would let it slide.

They were very wrong.

Thanks to Yeltsin's new economic reforms, Dimitri had become a very rich man. It was only a few years ago, but the deals he had done back in the Avenue of Thieves days seemed like something from a past life. Now he didn't just sell the cars from the production lines, he owned large chunks of the factory, and dozens like it all across the old Soviet Union.

When the government had brought in the "vouchers for shares" scheme, which gave millions of people almost free vouchers they could use to buy a share in the places they worked, Dimitri had spotted the opportunity. He either bought the vouchers from people who were desperate for his rubles or paid them in vodka and cigarettes.

It was, he explained to his mother and father on a trip home, like waking up one morning and finding discarded, but winning, lottery tickets littering the streets, like leaves after a late September storm. With no idea of what a share even was, but a keen appreciation of their empty bellies, his countrymen were happy to part with what they saw as worthless pieces of paper.

Dimitri, and the other oligarchs, gratefully scooped them up. Of course he kept his car-trading business. That gave him the cash he needed. But he had expanded it. Rather than sell Russian models, he imported cars from the West, first second-hand and finally new Mercedes.

With the money he made, he bought his shares in all these companies. He barely concerned himself with picking which company to invest in. He knew that even if half of them were terribly run, riddled with old Soviet inefficiencies, half would return his investment ten-, maybe twenty-fold.

He felt a tap on his shoulder. He startled, turning to see Ninel standing behind him.

"How—" he started to ask, then stopped. He had been glancing up at the bar's entrance and hadn't seen her come in until she was directly behind him.

His bodyguard, a burly Cossack, began to lumber across from his seat at the bar. Dimitri waved him away and equally curtly told the two models to go find something to amuse themselves.

Ninel took one of their seats next to him.

"Do you enjoy sneaking up on people?" he said.

"Old habits, Dimitri." She nodded toward the Cossack. "You should replace him."

"Replace?"

"Yes. Fire him and hire someone else." She looked at the ice bucket. "Have you been drinking more than champagne?"

He smiled. In a country where people went blind and sometimes died from drinking homemade vodka, champagne, wine and beer were regarded as soft drinks. It was common to see workers drinking beer on the Moscow subway on their way to work.

Like so many of her old KGB counterparts, Ninel had a way of using terms like "replace" when what she really meant was "kill". Their language was so opaque that it was often hard to tell what she was suggesting. Dimitri did not believe that was a mistake either.

"I thought you meant replace him like you replaced the Bitch Killer."

She didn't say anything to that. She had never so much as hinted that she'd had anything to do with his death a year ago, but he was positive she had either killed him or, more likely, had him killed.

Six months before, he had been found riddled with bullets in the front seat of his Italian sports car. Ninel had mentioned to Dimitri that the old system was moving so quickly that he no longer had any need for a roof. As Gorbachev and then Yeltsin had liberalized the economy, the need for secrecy and the fear of law enforcement had begun to evaporate.

Over time, the *vory*—or, rather, certain of their functions—had become surplus to requirements. They had been squeezed out by the oligarchs on one side, and the old KGB on the other. They still had their fiefdoms, and they still had their uses, mainly revolving around the dirtiest of dirty work, but obeying the old criminal niceties now seemed as much of an anachronism as the bronze statues of Lenin that had been torn down all over the country.

"I had nothing to do with that," said Ninel, sharply. "Why did you want to see me?"

"I've heard something from one of my contacts here in Moscow."

"What?" she said. "Spit it out."

"The loans for shares scheme that people are talking about," he said. "Is it real?"

"I don't know what you mean," she said, sinking back into the chair.

"Oh, come on, you expect me to believe that someone like you hasn't heard about it?"

Since their original meeting back in Tagliotti, Dimitri hadn't been the only one whose star had risen. The money she had received as her cut of his deals, she had carefully disbursed to her superiors and even some of those below her in rank, as well as numerous former Party functionaries. As a result, Ninel's career had rocketed. Most cops and KGB officers kept their dirty money to themselves. But not Ninel.

Already established as a capable intelligence officer, almost overnight she had become a strange mixture of Robin Hood and Santa Claus and, as a result, she was now based in the Lubyanka building, the old KGB headquarters near the Kremlin.

Just as Dimitri had taken the money from the sales of the first ghost cars and reinvested it in vouchers that he could trade for shares, so Ninel had invested in buying influence far beyond her lowly rank. Every ruble she handed over gained interest over the months and years, interest she could reclaim in the form of favors.

"I've heard about it, yes," said Ninel. "Yeltsin needs money, and fast. Another few months of this and we won't be able to pay salaries, pensions, anything."

Dimitri noted how she said "we." Even with all her wheeling and dealing, she was still a child of the old regime, still tied to the old idea that they were somehow part of a collective. He saw it differently. He saw rats running around inside a barrel, either eating each other, or trying to find a way out.

It wasn't new information. Everyone in Moscow with even the vaguest connections to the government had heard the same rumors. They were on the brink of a new collapse with a drunk at the helm.

What only a few people had heard, though, was that there was a rescue plan, of sorts. Some Kremlin insiders and businessmen who had already made fortunes from the free market reforms were planning on lending the country money in return for the right to buy shares in the larger state enterprises.

Of course, everyone knew there would be no way to repay the loans. At that point they would be able to exercise their right to buy the shares. Coal, oil, natural gas, mining, all of these would be up for grabs at a fraction of their true value. But not everyone would be allowed in on the deal. That was why he needed Ninel and her connections.

"I want to do my duty by the country," Dimitri told her. "I'll lend as much as I can to help out."

"And what has brought about this sudden patriotism, Dimitri?"

"Russia needs me."

She wagged a finger at him. "You should be a politician."

"Maybe I will. I'm still a young man."

"What they're talking about, I don't have the kind of connections to get someone into those meetings."

"Then cultivate them. You're very popular, everyone knows that."

"Such charm. Yes, maybe you will end up in politics." She stood up. "I'll see what I can do. But I make no promises. And, of course, if I do manage by some miracle to introduce you to the right people, I'll expect that—"

He cut her off. "Don't worry, I'll make sure you're taken care of."

She leaned in, standing over him. "On the same terms."

He was going to argue, but now was not the time. He couldn't gain access to this without her. They both knew it. Fifty percent was one hell of a cut for getting him into a room with the right people. But what if she did? This would make the vouchers scheme that had earned him so much money look small-time.

This was the big league. They both knew it.

He could deal with Ninel and her part of the deal later. For now he would promise what he had to.

30

Ninel and Madeline retreated to a juice bar downstairs from the yoga studio. They took a table in the rear so no one would be able to see them from the street. Usually they talked in the locker room, but a change to the studio's schedule meant another class was about to begin, and it was too crowded.

Ninel usually kept these conversations light and gossipy. There were two reasons for that. The first was to avoid suspicion, if anyone, including someone surveilling Madeline, overheard them. The second was that she had found, over the years, you could glean more useful intelligence that way, which made the asset feel they weren't directly betraying anyone.

"You look tired," said Ninel.

"I'm exhausted. There's been so much going on."

"Are you sleeping?"

"How can I sleep?" Madeline took a sip of the juice Ninel had ordered for her. "I'm not sure I can keep doing this," she said, eyes darting from the tabletop to Ninel and back to the tabletop.

Ninel had already explained that Madeline would have to stay where she was for as long as she was needed. "You're a strong, capable woman," she said. "You'll find a way."

Madeline looked up and this time she didn't glance away. "I'm not sure I will. You don't know what it's like. Being around him. Being around his wife. And then all this. That girl who was thrown out of the—"

Ninel moved her hand so that it rested on Madeline, a signal that she needed to quieten down. "You must, and you will. Don't worry, it won't be for much longer."

As soon as Ninel had said it she knew she had made a mistake.

"What does that mean? What are you going to do?"

Ninel tightened her hand around Madeline's. She had an exceptionally strong grip, the result of years practicing judo, first as part of her KGB training, and later as recreation. "No one is going to do anything, Madeline."

"I don't believe you."

This was spinning out of control and fast.

A waitress came over. "Is everything okay, ladies?" she asked.

"It's fine, thank you," said Ninel. She waited until the waitress had left.

"I promise you. No one is going to do anything."

"What about the bodyguard? Anastasia's bodyguard?"

"What about him? He killed himself. Not even the police believe anything else."

"Yes, but why?" said Madeline.

"Who knows what goes on inside someone's mind? He was a veteran. Maybe he had PTSD. Psychological problems. People commit suicide for all kinds of reasons. Being a bodyguard is a very stressful job."

That seemed to calm her.

"Have some more juice," said Ninel, pushing her glass toward Madeline. "I always get so thirsty after yoga."

Madeline pushed the glass back. "I'm fine, thank you."

"How are the new hires doing?"

"The new hires?"

"Mr. Lock and Mr. . . . . What's his name?"

"Johnson."

"Yes, Johnson. So, how are they fitting in?" said Ninel.

"That's not what you're asking me, is it?"

Madeline's tone was starting to concern Ninel. She'd been an excellent asset so far, but maybe her time would be drawing to a close soon. Ninel hoped not. She liked her, and in many ways she related to her. A capable woman in a man's world who had sacrificed her personal life for her career. It was a trade-off that no man had to make. "No, it's not."

"So what do you want to know?"

Ninel spread her hands on the table. "Is there anything we should be concerned about?"

"They're asking about the cars. Who recommended them, what the process was for the tendering."

"And?"

"I told them there was a shortlist and that Mr. Semenov made the final decision."

"That's good. Have they asked who chose the shortlist?"

"Yes. I gave them the document we talked about before."

"Good," said Ninel. "That's good. Anything else?"

"Yes," said Madeline. "They're having everyone background-checked again."

"Just background?"

"That's what Lock asked for."

That wasn't a concern for Ninel. Nothing would show for Madeline. She was a perfectly clean skin. She had never had any involvement with Russia before. Not until Ninel had cultivated her, and even then the only time they crossed paths was here. There was no electronic trail to link them together. That was the beauty of old-fashioned informant meetings such as this.

"What happens next?" asked Madeline.

Ninel didn't like the question. Madeline had never asked anything like it before. It had to be handled carefully. "That depends on Dimitri. If he repays what he owes then this all goes away."

"And if he doesn't?"

Ninel got up from the table. "That was a great class." She picked up the check. "I have this. Oh, and I left you something under the table. There seems to be a problem with your old one."

As Ninel went to pay the cashier behind the juice bar, Madeline looked down to see a bag. She peered into it.

Inside was a brand new, latest-model iPhone.

THE TWO MEN sitting in the blue Ford Edge SUV watched as first Ninel, then Madeline left two minutes apart. The driver tapped his phone screen, activating one of three cameras mounted at various points on the car.

Only a dope actually lifted a camera or a phone to their eye, these days. Everything was automated.

The passenger watched Madeline with a more than professional interest.

"She's in pretty good shape for a woman her age," he said to his partner.

"Like you're picky," said the driver.

The passenger laughed. "Quantity over quality, that's my motto."

"I know, I've seen some of 'em."

The driver looked down at the photos they'd taken of the two women. They knew who one was, Madeline Marshowsky, personal assistant to Dimitri Semenov. They had no idea about the other.

"So, what do you think?" said the driver, tilting the phone screen.

"I already told you. I like the tall blonde one."

"Not that, you moron. You think this means anything?"

"I think it looks like two ladies who do yoga and gossip, but what do I know?" said the passenger.

31

Ty gently closed Anastasia's bedroom door and stepped out into the hallway. Since he had got home he had assumed the role of *de facto* head of residential security with special responsibility for ensuring she was cocooned from as much of the craziness as possible.

Meanwhile, Lock had assumed the role of designated bodyguard to Dimitri, shepherding him from the house to the office. McLennan seemed to have accepted the changes. Mentally, the guy seemed to have checked out. It would have been better to have him out there, but according to Lock, the Red Notice from Interpol was making it even more difficult to get good-quality replacements in post that would allow them to step back from their current babysitting duties.

His shoes sinking into the deep pile of the carpet, Ty walked down the hallway, heading for the stairs. As he passed the master suite, Elizabeth Semenov called to him from inside.

"Hey, Tyrone, can you spare me a second?"

He about-turned. The door into the master suite was cracked open. He couldn't see Elizabeth, but he could hear her.

"What's up?"

"Come on in."

He pushed the door open and walked into a master suite that he guessed was three times as big as many people's Manhattan apartments. A huge antique four-poster bed dominated the high-ceilinged room. Separate walk-in closets and his and hers en-suite bathrooms were located on either side of the bedroom.

One of the bathroom doors was open, and he could hear water running into the tub. Elizabeth appeared with her hair pulled back into a ponytail. She was wearing a thigh-high silk camisole and an equally short silk robe.

"What can I do for you, Mrs. Semenov?" Ty said, businesslike.

"Call me Elizabeth, please. Mrs. Semenov makes me sound old. You know I'm only thirty-two."

That was a lie. Ty knew from all the background reports that she was thirty-seven. Not that it mattered to him either way.

She bent down to pick up a discarded item of clothing and throw it into a laundry hamper. He made a point of keeping his eyes elsewhere. This was one distraction he mostly definitely did not need.

"What can I do for you?" he repeated.

"I just wanted to thank you for looking after Anastasia."

"You're very welcome but I'm just doing my job," he said, turning back toward the door.

"Except it's more than a job to you," she said.

It was like she was determined to keep him here, talking. He had a good idea why, too.

"I mean," she continued, "I see how you are with her. And I see how she is with you. She likes you."

"I like her too. She's a good kid." He made another move toward the bedroom door.

"Stay and talk to me," she said. "Please."

"I have things I need to be doing," he said.

"Five minutes. There's no one I can talk to around here."

"I thought that was what therapists were for," said Ty.

Her eyes flashed with anger. She hadn't liked that comment.

"Everyone thinks that just because I have all of this I should be happy to accept all the other things," she said, her arms taking in the plush surroundings. "But it hurts. It hurts to be married to a man who behaves like he does."

Ty really didn't want to get drawn any further into this, but he sensed her pain was real. He knew what she was saying. Money could solve some problems, but not all of them. Some it only made worse.

"I'm an attractive woman, right?"

"Mrs. Semenov …"

"Elizabeth."

She let the robe slip from her shoulders and puddle on the carpet.

"I used to model. I'd like to think I still have the figure for it. God only knows I do enough dieting and Pilates. What do you think?"

Shimmying out of her camisole, she stood there, naked. Ty stepped toward her. He was standing next to the bed. He held eye contact with her as he reached down to the bed.

His hand felt for a blanket at the foot. He picked it up and tossed it the few feet to her.

"If you want to keep talking to me then cover yourself up," he said, his voice firm. "This isn't a game, and I'm not here for your or anyone else's personal entertainment. You have a bad marriage or you're unhappy? Go speak to your husband or get yourself a divorce lawyer. Either way it's none of my business."

She took the blanket and tucked it around her torso. "I didn't mean to—"

"Lady," said Ty. "If some Russian assassin comes through your daughter's window at three in the morning, I'm prepared to take a bullet to stop him hurting her, or you for that matter. But don't go twisting that into me doing anything else for you."

"I'm sorry. I feel stupid."

"I'm not asking for an apology, or for you to feel anything. This isn't a game to these people. The quicker you wake up to that, the better."

He stalked to the door and this time she didn't attempt to stop him or call him back. He walked out into the corridor, pulling the bedroom door closed. He stopped for a moment, leaning against the wall and closing his eyes. "Man, save me from crazy rich people."

32

Along with McLennan, Lock escorted Dimitri up the stone steps leaving the two patrol cops to handle the reporters on the sidewalk. Ty opened the door, scanning the people outside as they stepped in.

"How are you, Tyrone?" asked Dimitri.

"I'm good."

If Ty's encounter with a naked Mrs. Semenov had left him feeling uncomfortable, greeting her returning husband at the door wasn't helping. He pulled Lock to one side as Dimitri went to see his daughter. "How'd it go?" Ty asked in an undertone.

"The attorneys think there's no chance of the US doing anything with the Red Notice, so that's good. We're back in one piece. And no one else got killed today as far as I know. How were things here?"

"I'll tell you later," said Ty, as McLennan headed over to speak with them.

"Listen, I was down to have the evening off. Jeff'll take the night watch. You mind if I get out of here?"

"No, of course not. We got you. Ty and I can stay here tonight. Give your guy the night off," said Lock.

"Really?" said McLennan, apparently taken aback by Lock's largesse.

"Sure. When did you last have some time off?" said Lock.

"Weeks ago," said McLennan, sounding as weary as he looked.

"Take tomorrow as well. Check back in tomorrow night. I'd rather have people fresh."

McLennan took a step back, like he was seeing Lock for the first time. Or, at least, seeing this version for the first time. Ty also seemed caught off guard by Lock's generosity.

"That'd be great. I appreciate it."

"No problem," said Lock.

Ty waited until McLennan had headed back outside. "What? You're best buds all of a sudden?"

Lock walked down the hallway, headed for the kitchen. "The Red Notice isn't going to be an issue in terms of any kind of arrest or extradition," he explained. "But it's scaring off the big private security companies."

"So we'd better start being nice to the men we do have?"

"Precisely," said Lock. "So what was it you were going to tell me later?"

"Mrs. Semenov."

"What about her?"

"Let's just say her husband isn't the only one who has a wandering eye."

Lock smiled.

"Don't laugh, man. Shit ain't funny."

Lock did his best to look serious. "What happened?"

Ty leaned in so he wouldn't be overheard. None of the house staff had been party to Elizabeth's little show and he wanted to keep it that way.

"She calls me into the bedroom and dropped her drawers. And, no, before you say anything else, nothing happened. I'm just keeping you in the loop."

"Hey, the woman's not made of stone, is she?"

"Very funny," said Ty. "Listen, the last thing we need in the middle of this shit show is the lady of the house chasing around after me. That kid up there is sick. The grown-ups around here need to step up and start behaving accordingly.'

"You want me to speak with her?" said Lock.

"No. Definitely not," said Ty. "Like I said, I just wanted to give you a heads up."

"Okay. I'll try and make sure she's not left alone with you."

"Any more word from the cops about the model? Or the bodyguard?" Ty asked.

"Nope, and they don't seem to be in a particularly sharing mood with our principal either."

"Maybe he could make a donation," suggested Ty. "NYPD must have some kind of benevolent fund and, not to stereotype or anything, it's not like a little bit of bribery would be an alien concept where he's from."

"I'll mention it to him. Never hurts to support local law enforcement. How's the kid?"

"Checked in on her an hour ago. She seems a lot perkier. I think she's just happy to be home."

"That's good," said Lock.

"Maybe things are starting to settle down," said Ty.

"Either that, or this is the calm before the storm."

Dimitri walked back down the stairs. He clapped Ty on the shoulder. "That's the best Anastasia has looked in weeks. Whatever it is you're doing, keep doing it. Perhaps you can see if you can cheer up that wife of mine while you're at it. What do you say?"

Ty gave a nervous smile as Lock studied the carpet at his feet.

"In fact, why don't you both join us for dinner?"

"That's not really how it works," said Lock, stepping in to save Ty any further embarrassment.

"I insist."

33

Ty pulled Lock to one side as they made their way into the dining room.

"Can't you make an excuse for me?" said Ty.

"What am I, your mom?"

"Come on, man. This is going to be awkward as all hell."

Lock wasn't going to lie. He found Ty's discomfort a rare ray of entertainment among all this chaos. "I thought nothing happened."

"It didn't," Ty protested.

"So what's the issue?"

Dimitri and Elizabeth walked down the stairs together and into the hallway. Elizabeth had changed into a figure-hugging dress and had put on make-up. She looked every inch the glamorous wife of one of New York's wealthiest men. A snapshot taken right now would have made their life seem perfect to many people, Lock reflected. Dimitri Semenov seemed to have it all.

"Problem?" said Dimitri, as he spotted the two bodyguards' conspiratorial huddle.

Ty saw his chance to extract himself. "No problem, but someone should probably keep an eye on the camera feeds."

"We have one of McLennan's men on that," said Lock. "You can take over after dinner."

Ty shot Lock a death-stare as Elizabeth bore down on them.

"You know what they say?" she said, linking her arm through the African American Marine's arm.

"What's that?" said Ty.

"All work and no play. Now why don't we have ourselves a little pre-dinner cocktail?"

"Not for me," said Ty. "I'm still on duty."

"Yes, you are," said Elizabeth, sounding like she'd already had a drink.

Behind them, Dimitri caught Lock's eye and shrugged. "This is my wife's way of punishing me for my many indiscretions. She likes to humiliate me in public."

"You don't look humiliated."

"Oh, I'm not," said Dimitri. "She just looks ridiculous."

"I heard that," Elizabeth shouted over her shoulder. "Now can I get anyone else a drink?"

Lock was starting to think that Ty might have had a point. They should have found some pretext to duck out of this. There were few things Lock enjoyed less than being trapped in the middle of someone else's domestic drama. Unfortunately it was often part of the job. For some reason bodyguards were often seen as substitute therapists. And, unsurprisingly, being hit on or propositioned also seemed to come with the territory.

Lock watched as Elizabeth poured herself and Dimitri drinks. She handed one to her husband. The body language between them was weird. Lock was no psychologist, but it was if all the sniping was for the benefit of the evening's audience.

Madeline walked into the drawing room. "Sorry I'm late," she said. "I had to finish up a few things at the office."

"I asked Madeline to join us," said Dimitri.

"Oh, good," said Elizabeth, her tone layered with a faint hint of sarcasm. "Drink?" she added, holding up her glass.

"Gin and tonic, please," said Madeline.

"Well, help yourself. You know where everything is," said Elizabeth, stalking back to Ty. "Tyrone, why don't you show me your gun?"

Dimitri sat at one end of the dining table, his wife at the other end. To no one's surprise, and everyone's embarrassment, she had insisted that Ty sit next to her. Lock was on Dimitri's right, with a good view of the window that faced onto the street. Madeline was the gooseberry in the middle.

It may have been the most awkward dinner party Lock had attended, but he had to admit the food was excellent and plentiful. Unfortunately, so was the wine. Elizabeth had already worked her way through her cocktail and was on her third glass by the time the entree was served by the family's chef.

Ty, tired of being asked suggestive questions, looked down the table at Dimitri who, despite his wife's behavior, seemed to be in a relaxed, expansive mood. Lock guessed that this had been the pattern of their relationship for a while now.

"You mind me asking you something?" Ty said to their host.

"Of course not."

"How come you and the other . . . What do they call them? Oligarchs. How come you guys made all this money?"

To Lock's surprise, the question didn't appear to annoy Dimitri in the slightest.

"I guess that we saw opportunity where others didn't. While everyone around me was panicking about the collapse of the old order, I could see the new one. One like America where there was freedom, and opportunity. If you were prepared to risk everything." He smiled before continuing, "Which is easy when you don't really have anything."

At the far end of the table, Elizabeth held up her hand, rubbing her thumb and the tip of her index finger together. "Here we go. Time to break out the world's smallest violin. My husband loves telling people about how poor he was. In fact, he loves it almost as much as cheating on me."

Dimitri straightened in his chair, ignoring his wife's barbs. "Let me tell you all a joke that explains how things were. And how I was able to do so well. You know I started selling cars, right?"

He looked around the table.

"So back then, even if you had the vouchers, or the money, or a connection in the Communist Party, you had to order your car years ahead. So one day Ivan goes to check on his order. He's already been waiting for four years. Anyway, he goes to the official at the factory and they tell him, 'Ivan, we're very sorry, but you're going to have to wait three more years for your car. But, I promise you, three years from today, it will be ready.'"

Dimitri looked around his guests, pausing for effect. Lock had to give it to him, he was actually a pretty decent storyteller.

"Ivan is disappointed, but he's already waited for four years. Really, what's another three on top of that? But he asks the official, 'And this car, will it be delivered in the morning or the afternoon?' The official's puzzled. 'Why does that matter?'"

Dimitri took a sip of wine.

"'Well,' says Ivan, 'I already have a plumber booked for the afternoon.'"

Everyone laughed politely, apart from Elizabeth.

"What I did," Dimitri went on, "was make sure that if you wanted a car, you could have a car."

"If you had the money," said Elizabeth.

"Of course," said Dimitri. "That's capitalism. Supply and demand."

"You should ask my husband how he got the cars," said Elizabeth. "While you're at it, ask him how he made all this money. He liked to make out he worked for it, but that's a lie."

Dimitri's expression shifted. Now he was getting annoyed. "That's enough, Elizabeth."

Elizabeth Semenov was not for being shut up. Not by anyone, and certainly not by her husband. "He stole it. And when he was caught he got on a plane from Moscow and came here and claimed asylum. Isn't that right, darling?"

"My wife inherited her money," said Dimitri. "She's never had to dirty her hands. Not once."

"That's not true. I was working when you met me."

"Yes, and I'm sure organizing charity events for a non-profit was how you paid for your apartment on Park Avenue and your accounts at Bergdorf and Chanel."

"This meal is absolutely delicious," said Ty, trying to reroute the conversation as Dimitri and Elizabeth drew daggers at each other from opposite ends of the table.

"I'll admit that I was fortunate in my upbringing," said Elizabeth, "but I've never stolen. I've never cheated."

"Never cheated?" said Dimitri. "Come on, Elizabeth. We both know you've had affairs."

"Only after you did."

"So why do you stay?" Dimitri asked her. "If it's so terrible, so awful living with me. You and I both know why."

Elizabeth Semenov slammed her hands down on the table, sending a fork flying. It landed with a rattle on the floor. "Oh, fuck you." She got up, a little unsteady on her feet. "You think I won't leave? Just watch me."

Lock looked down the table at Ty, both men thinking the same thing. If she was even vaguely serious, this could be all kinds of bad. Lock was hoping it was just an idle threat, something people said in the heat of an argument. He wasn't about to intervene in someone else's squabble. Not unless he had no alternative. This was a textbook example of why professional boundaries were so important when it came to close protection. No good ever came from being drawn into a client or principal's dramas.

They watched as Elizabeth stormed out of the dining room. Dimitri pushed back his chair. "She's been under a lot of pressure. Anastasia being sick and then everything else. I'll speak to her."

"Maybe give it a minute. Let her cool down," suggested Lock.

A few seconds later she stormed back in, went to where she'd been sitting and picked up her wine glass, waving it in the air as she launched back into her threat to leave, taking their daughter with her.

"You don't believe me? Well, you just watch me. I'm taking Anastasia and I'm going to the Hamptons, away from all this … all this … toxic bullshit of yours." She took a breath. "Tyrone, come with me. You can help us pack."

Ty didn't move. Lock knew he wouldn't. If there was one thing Ty would like less than some rich white woman thinking he'd be her sex toy, it was being spoken to like Elizabeth Semenov had just spoken to him.

Lock had known his friend long enough to be sure that Ty didn't play those games. He had boundaries. He expected people to respect them. And woe betide anyone who didn't.

Ty stared at her. He didn't move.

"Tyrone," she repeated.

Seconds passed. With glacial slowness Ty got to his feet, but he stayed standing next to his place at the table. "Listen, lady, and this applies to both of you," he said, taking in Dimitri too. "You've got a sick little girl up in that room. Whatever the deal is between you, that's your business, but she doesn't need to be listening to the two people she's counting on to sit down here getting sloppy drunk and tearing each other apart like this."

"Who do you think you're speaking to?" said Elizabeth.

"You don't want me to answer that," said Ty. "Believe me."

Thankfully, Elizabeth Semenov wasn't drunk enough to say anything.

"You take your daughter and leave here, that's your right," continued Ty. "I can't imagine any court, or anyone else, would be able to stop you. But right now everyone is under threat. Not just your husband. So what are you going to do for security? You wanna tell me that?"

"We have people."

"Right now you have half a security team," said Ty. "Less than half. And with this Red Notice, good reinforcements are going to be hard to round up. Yeah, sure, you can go hire a bunch of chumps who look the part. New York's full of guys like that. But they won't keep you safe. So do everyone here a favor and wake up to what's going on."

"Dimitri, are you going to let him speak to me like that?" she said, appealing to her husband.

"It's been a long day, Elizabeth. For everyone."

Her eyes were wet with tears.

Lock noticed that, through all of this, Madeline hadn't said a word. He imagined she'd been party to more than a few of these rows and wanted to keep her job.

"Fine. I'm going to bed," said Elizabeth, turning back around.

Silence descended in the dining room as they listened to her clatter up the stairs.

"I'm sorry about that," said Dimitri, mostly directing his apology to Ty, who had sat down to finish his meal.

Ty stopped chewing and waved his fork. "No offense taken. People have said way worse things to me."

"That's true," said Lock. "Some of them have been true too."

Ty poked his knife at Elizabeth's plate. "Anyone mind if I . . .?"

"Go ahead," said Madeline.

Ty reached over and moved what was left on Elizabeth's plate onto his own and went back to eating like nothing had happened. Rather than shouting, if Elizabeth had wanted to get a reaction from the retired Marine all she'd needed to do was pick up his plate.

"Elizabeth may have a point," said Dimitri. "The beach, the clean air, the open spaces, it might do Anastasia some good. I know you can't cover both residences, but I could work from there, for a while at least. The city can be oppressive at times, especially if you feel like you can't leave."

Lock left to one side the fact that his wife had wanted to go to the Hamptons to get away from him. Instead he focused on the other problem with the idea. "That's true," he said. "I'm sure everyone could benefit from a change of scene. But in the city you're surrounded by people. Cops too. It's a much more secure environment."

"Try telling poor Ruta that," said Dimitri.

"Generally more secure," said Lock. "You go out to the Hamptons, there's a fraction of the number of law enforcement officers there are here. Sure it might be easier to see a threat coming, but so what? Manpower's limited."

"So we stay here?"

"It's your call," said Lock, "but that would be my advice. The Hamptons are not generally considered a defensible position."

"You're right," said Dimitri. "It's safer here."

34

Ninel took off the headphones and placed them on the table in front of Alexei.

"Very good work," she said to the young hacker. "There's less compression on the new phone we gave her. It makes the audio much clearer."

She looked up at him. "You can take a break if you'd like."

"You're sure?" he asked her.

He was reluctant to leave, she could tell. In most ways they had very little in common. But they were both workaholics. When he had been putting together the rig to control the cars she had seen him pull regular twenty-four-hour work sessions, bolstered only by caffeine and sugar.

He might not have been the most brilliant computer and systems hacker that Russia had produced, but he had to be the hardest-working. He was tenacious, never giving up until he had the problem solved. Perhaps that was something else they had in common, although she suspected what drove them was very different.

Alexei seemed to relish the intellectual challenge. Ninel was driven by something much more primitive.

"Yes, go on," she said. "I'll see you tomorrow."

She waited until he had left before walking over to the filing cabinet in the corner of her office, opening the bottom drawer and pulling out two sets of plans.

Laying them on the table, she ran a finger over both. The new bodyguard, Lock, had been correct. So had his partner. Dimitri Semenov and his family were much safer in the city than at their house in the Hamptons.

Both homes had high-level security features. But the property on Surfside Drive was far more exposed. It was low-lying. It faced the ocean. Crucially, as Lock had pointed out, it was quiet. The privacy it offered was also its weakness.

The pressure being applied to Dimitri was working. But not in the way Ninel intended it to.

He wasn't the only one facing pressure. Questions were being asked back home about her methods. Some had deemed them too audacious. Traitors like Semenov were to be punished. Money that had been expropriated was to be recovered. Those had been the instructions from the very top. But there were other voices. Some in the Kremlin were advising caution.

Ninel was a long way from being told to stop what she was doing. But the suggestion had been made that maybe she should pull back a little on the throttle.

She had argued that it would be a fatal mistake. If Dimitri was allowed to regroup, all this chaos would have been for nothing. You needed to force home your advantage when you were winning.

That was what she planned on doing. But she needed to have deniability. If not for her then for her superiors. For this next part she would have to make the same trade-off that she had when she was recruiting Grigor Novak.

She walked back to the filing cabinet. This time she opened the top drawer. She drew out three files, opened them on the table, and studied the photographs of the three men.

35

The three men dressed as if they were back in Moscow in 1990s, not present-day Brooklyn. Stonewashed denim jeans, wife-beater shirts with no sleeves, chunky gold chains and, the trademark of all Russian émigré gangsters, black leather jackets.

Between them they were responsible for hundreds, perhaps thousands of crimes, ranging all the way from theft and burglary to extortion, blackmail and murder. The oldest and brightest of them, although that wasn't saying much, was Viktor, a broken-toothed stripclub owner with a love of violence and, Ninel suspected, a deep-seated hatred of women.

The club was in the still-to-be-gentrified part of Brooklyn, far from the waterfront and the views to the Manhattan skyline. It was midday, and Ninel was running on under five hours' sleep.

The barman studied her with curiosity until she asked for coffee and told him she was there to meet with his boss. He went to get him, came back, told her that Viktor was in the office and would she like to have her coffee in there?

She followed him to the back of the place where Viktor hurriedly concealed the line of coke he'd just finished, shoving the paraphernalia into a desk drawer.

Ninel was starting to have reservations. If time hadn't been a factor she would have held off, found someone else for this particular task. Sadly an early-morning communiqué from Moscow had reinforced her suspicion that certain elements in the Kremlin were calling into question her judgment.

In any case, she didn't need someone who could execute this properly. The opposite was true. Which meant that, however much she disliked and lacked confidence in Viktor and his two friends, who were hustling into the office behind her, they were a good choice.

"I have something for you," she said, pulling the floor plan from her briefcase, and laying it out in front of Viktor, with pictures of the townhouse roof taken from an aerial view on Google Maps.

Over the years, American tech companies, and Google's map function in particular, had saved the FSB millions of rubles and thousands of hours. It had been one of America's great gifts to intelligence services everywhere. Viktor leaned forward in his chair as the other two peered over her shoulder at the floor plan and photographs.

"That's a nice house," said Viktor, king of the obvious.

"With lots of nice art and jewelry. Estimated value of fifty million dollars for the paintings, and ten for the jewelry."

She took another file from her briefcase and handed it to Viktor. Still studying the house details, he put it to one side. "And lots of very expensive security. Alarms. Motion sensors." He glanced up from the plans. "Bodyguards. With guns."

"They won't be there," Ninel lied. "The family who live there are in the Hamptons. The house is empty. Apart from one or two domestic staff, and you're not afraid of a simple cook, are you?" she asked, taking a jab at Viktor's ego.

She pushed the unopened file across the desk to him. He opened it and began sorting through the photographs and itemized lists that Alexei had secured by hacking the household insurance policy that Semenov kept for his properties and their contents. When you had paintings that were worth millions of dollars, every single item was carefully documented before it could be insured. If you were smart that was, and no one had ever accused Dimitri of being stupid.

Viktor got to one photograph and stopped, eyes wide. Ninel had known this particular item would get his attention. It was a painting by the late great Russian painter Ilya Repin.

"This painting, this is here in New York?" he asked, poking a fat finger at the picture. "This one? Not a copy?"

"In the living room. Hung above the fireplace."

That was a lie. It was in the private collection of another oligarch, one who lived in London. But Viktor wasn't to know that. Alexei had even managed to blend the painting with the actual fireplace in Dimitri's home. A detail that would almost certainly not be needed. Ninel would be astonished if Viktor or any of his crew made it that far into the house.

If they did, and they killed Dimitri's security team, all the better. In a fire fight, especially one conducted at close quarters, nothing was ever certain.

The painting had been her ace in the hole. It was hard to believe, but Viktor was something of an art aficionado. Not that he liked to collect them, more that he enjoyed fencing them.

Viktor studied the photograph of the painting. "It's stunning."

Now his interest was established, Ninel directed his attention back to the plans. "Here," she said. "The roof is the best access point. It's the one place they don't have a camera. They have motion sensors here and here," she indicated, "but you can easily skirt round."

"And how do we get up there?" asked Viktor.

One of the other two leaned forward, his nose almost touching the aerial photograph. "The neighbor's house. This one?"

"Exactly," said Ninel. You can access the house here. It's a simple enough lock."

"It's not alarmed?"

"I'll take care of that," said Ninel.

Alexei had already indicated that he would be able to disable the alarm remotely, at least for a short time. The sensors would still pick up any motion, but they wouldn't trigger the alarm.

Viktor stood up, then paced to the door and back. She could tell he was already starting to visualize the burglary in his mind. He stopped at the door. "And what's in this for you?"

It had taken him long enough to ask that, thought Ninel. She already had an answer prepared, one that would satisfy him.

"What do you think? I want half of whatever you make."

It was a lie. It would never get that far. But a lie based on greed was something she knew a man like Viktor would understand.

"Half?" he spluttered. "We take all the risk, do all the work, and you take half?"

"It's my idea," she shot back.

"A finder's fee is usually twenty percent."

"Forty," she countered.

"Twenty-five."

"A third."

"Thirty," said Viktor. "But you supply the weapons."

There was no way she could agree to that. Weapons could be traceable, and she had already taken a huge risk in coming here. This was a black op, completely off the books. She couldn't have it coming back to her.

"Okay, twenty-five then," she said.

"When?" said Viktor.

"Tonight."

"Impossible. Something like this takes time."

"Normally, yes. The preparation takes time. But that's all been done for you. All the information you need is here. If you wait they'll be back from vacation and the chance will be gone. It would be too dangerous."

"No," said Viktor, firmly. "The following night. That's the earliest we could do it."

"Fine. I'll need a time, so we know when to disable the alarm system."

"Okay."

She stood up. The smell of the place was getting to her.

"Oh, there was something I wanted to ask you about," he said.

"Twenty-five. No less than that."

"It's not that. That's agreed. I wanted to ask you about Grigor Novak. No one's seen him in almost a week."

She looked at Viktor. "He's working on something for me. In upstate. He'll be back soon."

36

Lock opened the rear passenger door of the blue Ford Edge and got in. The two men in front didn't say anything. The driver signaled and pulled out into traffic on West 44th Street. As they drove, the passenger scanned the vehicle-mounted cameras for any sign of a tail.

Ten blocks later, satisfied that no one was following them, the SUV pulled to the curb. The driver killed the engine, and the two men turned in their seats to speak with Lock.

"So?" said Lock. "What have you got for me?"

"A big fat nothing," said the driver.

Lock wasn't sure whether to be relieved or disappointed. "Nothing at all?"

The passenger dug into the pocket of his jacket and pulled out a small USB storage device. "It's all here. You can take a look for yourself."

"I'd say whoever did the initial background checks did a solid job."

"What about McLennan?" asked Lock.

McLennan had niggled at Lock since he'd met him. It wasn't that he'd taken an attitude with himself and Ty when they'd arrived to review security arrangements. That part he could understand. Lock might have been the same if the situation had been reversed.

No, what had unsettled Lock was how quickly he had appeared to quit on the job. If you were in the military, especially special forces, seeing your friends being or hurt or possibly dying came with the territory. That didn't mean you weren't allowed to grieve or suffer some kind of psychological reaction. But the job did demand that you compartmentalized that stuff until the mission was completed. You didn't hole up in a side room for a bitching session with your team, as Lock had found McLennan doing at the hospital. Not unless you were feeling the pressure in ways unrelated to the job.

It had made him wonder if something else was going on. If the Russians. or whoever was orchestrating this war against Dimitri, had got to McLennan. After all, McLennan had walked away from the bridge incident completely unscathed. And there was still a question mark in Lock's mind over his role in selecting the shortlisted vehicles, several of which were wholly unsuitable for their intended purpose.

"All his bank accounts are clean. There don't seem to be any unexplained payments. Lifestyle checks out for the money he makes. The day off he had, we had someone surveil him, and nothing. No meets with anyone. Phone records check out too. He talks to family back home, some old army buddies, and that's pretty much it. If he is working for someone else, he's doing a great job of concealing it."

"But he could be compromised in some way?" said Lock.

"Yeah, that's always a possibility. The Russians do love their blackmail," said the driver.

Like most people, Lock was well aware of that. They even had a designated term for it, *Kompromat*. It was so much a part of Russian culture that one former US intelligence officer had even called it a 'blackmail state' because it was all-pervasive.

It usually took one of two basic forms. Either there was evidence of an embarrassing or damaging sexual act, or it was something that could get the person prosecuted, normally an act of corruption.

"What about Madeline, the personal assistant?" Lock asked them.

"Nothing there either," said the driver.

"Bank accounts all checked out," the passenger added. "No secret ones. No unexplained deposits of money. In any case she's extremely well paid and, from what we saw, her lifestyle is pretty basic. She works, she comes home, she may take a run in the park, she does a hot yoga class, doesn't seem to date."

Madeline had made Lock's list because she was the person who had overseen everyone else's background checks for Dimitri. He also suspected that she was party to a lot of information that would have been invaluable to anyone who wanted to get at her boss.

"Boyfriend? Friends?" Lock asked.

The two men exchanged a look. "Actually, we were wondering if she was single."

Lock cut them off with a look.

"Just a little joke," said the driver.

"No, it was kind of weird," said the passenger. "No boyfriend, no close female friends. She had a juice after yoga with some lady in her class but that was about it. Seems like a total career gal. Anyway, it's all on there. You can double-check it all for yourself."

He thumbed at the USB drive that Lock was holding.

"I will. Thanks."

"We ran through everyone else on the list you gave us. More your standard background-check stuff, no surveillance, but nothing popped. You want us to go deeper?"

"Not for now."

"Okay. Well, let us know if you need anything else." The driver dug out an envelope from his jacket. "Invoice. You want us to send it to Mr. Semenov or what?"

Lock reached out and took it. "I'll take care of it."

He planned on covering the cost of the deep review out of his own expenses. He hadn't wanted anyone who worked for Dimitri to know that it was happening. Doing it this way, using an outside agency, one staffed mostly by former FBI and NYPD personnel had been the safest way he knew of ensuring that there was no one close to Dimitri they should be worried about.

"Listen, thank you," said Lock, shaking each man's hand.

"You got it," said the driver, then added, "There was one other thing. It's kind of gossip so we didn't include it in any of the material we gathered."

"Go on."

"Bill here's former NYPD. You know that, right?"

"Okay," said Lock. He hadn't known, but it was hardly a surprise.

"I don't know if this sets your mind at rest any, but word is that the bodyguard in the cupboard was having some mental health problems. That hadn't been his first try, if you know what I mean."

"So he wasn't killed?" said Lock.

"Sure doesn't look like it."

37

"So nothing, then?" said Ty.

Lock stood with him in the front hallway of the townhouse.

"Doesn't look like it." He dug the USB drive from his pocket. "I'll go through everything myself, but there certainly wasn't anything that jumped out at them. No payoffs. No Russian buddies. *Nada*."

"That's good, though, right?" said Ty.

"Yeah, I guess it is. The more we know we can trust the people around us, the better."

They turned to see Elizabeth Semenov walking down the hallway toward them. She had her hair tied back in a ponytail, emphasizing razor-sharp cheekbones, and she was wearing running gear.

"I need to go for my afternoon run. Seeing as I'm not allowed to leave the house on my own at the moment, Ty, can you accompany me?"

Lock stepped in. "I got you. I'll throw on some sneakers and we can go. Do you want to walk over there, or would you like a car to take us?"

Elizabeth cocked her hands onto her hips. "I don't think I asked you, did I?"

"I'm who's available," said Lock.

"Tyrone looks pretty available to me."

Ty tapped Lock on the shoulder. "I'm gonna go check on Anastasia."

He walked past Elizabeth without looking at her. Judging by the look on her face she wasn't used to being thwarted.

"Wait," she said. "I asked for Tyrone to accompany me. Now, as far as I'm aware, you work for my husband, which means you work for me."

Lock straightened. Situations like these were a dime a dozen when dealing with wealthy and entitled clients. The trick was usually to remain polite, but firm. "I'm currently in charge of the security team. A security team that's pretty much a skeleton crew right now. That means I decide who goes where."

She took a step back, studying him. "If this is about the little confusion yesterday when I was getting changed, don't worry, I don't have any designs on your friend."

"Mrs. Semenov, I have no idea what you're talking about," Lock lied. "Now, if you'd still like to go for your run just give me two minutes."

TY KNOCKED GENTLY on the bedroom door. The nurse who had been monitoring Anastasia opened it.

"Good timing," she said, with a smile. "We're almost done here."

"You want me to come back later?"

"No, you're good. Come on in."

Inside he was greeted by the sight of Anastasia, dressed in regular clothes and sitting in a chair by the window.

"Woah!" said Ty, beaming from ear to ear. "You're out of bed."

"That's right," said the nurse. "Anastasia still needs to take it really easy, but she's off the IV, and she's free to move around. Although she still needs to get lots of rest, and I'll be here to make sure she does."

"Me too," said Ty.

Amid all the chaos and death, it was great to have some good news.

"Hey, do your mom and dad know?"

"Yeah, I saw my mom, she was really happy, but she said my dad's probably too busy working to come up here and see me."

"You hold that thought," said Ty. "I'll be right back."

He walked out, pulled the door closed, and stood there for a second, trying to compose himself. If there was one thing he hated to see in situations like this it was adults using kids to get back at their partner. No matter what sins Dimitri had committed, his wife's attempt to undermine his relationship with his daughter was a shitty thing to do.

Ty went downstairs and found Dimitri in his office. He was going over some papers with Madeline. "Sorry to interrupt," he said. "I thought you should know, Anastasia's out of bed."

Dimitri stood straight up. "Is she okay?"

"Yeah, she's fine," said Ty. "I guess the doc cleared it."

"I'll be right back," Dimitri told his assistant, hustling out of the office with Ty to visit his daughter. "Listen, about last night …"

"Don't worry about it."

"My wife's a good woman. A good mother. But I've not always been the best husband."

"It's none of my or Ryan's business. We're here to keep everyone safe and that's what we plan on doing."

"And I appreciate it. We all do."

Dimitri stopped at the bottom of the stairs. "You don't think it's a good idea to move the family to the Hamptons house? I still think the fresh air would do Anastasia the world of good."

"Hey, it's your call, but I agree with Ryan. From a security point of view I'd say you're much better sitting tight here. At least until the cops get a handle on some of this craziness. Something bad happens in the city, you have an army of cops outside. Something goes bad out there …"

"Maybe you're right," said Dimitri.

38

Thankfully, there was no invitation to join the Semenovs that night for dinner. Instead, Lock and Ty spent the rest of the afternoon putting together an updated security rota with McLennan. They were still going to be stretched but having everyone in the same residence made it just about manageable with the numbers they had.

"You think you can get your boss to send some fresh bodies?" Lock asked McLennan.

"I've spoken to him about that already. He thinks he can maybe get us two more guys next week. They're coming off a rotation in Dubai. I should know more on Monday."

"That's good. Thanks," said Lock.

McLennan tapped his pencil against the rota they'd just finished drawing up. "Listen, I owe both of you blokes an apology. I haven't been at my best since, well, you know ..."

"Forget it, man," said Lock.

"Water under the bridge," added Ty, holding up his hand in apology at having mentioned a bridge. "You know what I mean. No apology needed."

McLennan picked up the duty rota. "I'm going to update my guys.

I have Hoyle, who should be able to cover with us tonight, and I can filter in the other two tomorrow."

They watched him walk out of the room.

"Maybe we're finally steadying the ship here, Ryan," said Ty.

"I wouldn't go counting any chickens just yet. We're still light. We're going to have to pick up our share of the grunt work for the foreseeable."

"It'll be like old times," smiled Ty. "Only the coffee's way better here. So the PI firm cleared everyone, huh?"

"As far as they could. There may be stuff going on that we don't know about but, yeah, everyone seems to be above board."

"And no one's been thrown out of a window, or shot themselves in the face in the last twenty-four hours, so that has to be reason for celebration, right? Maybe they've decided to back off."

Lock sighed. "I doubt it. I just wish we had some idea who *they* are. 'The Russians' covers a lot of people."

"Well, Grigor Novak was with the embassy."

"Not according to what the embassy told the FBI. They've denied all knowledge of him. Said they never had someone with that name, or anyone matching his description, working for them."

"You believe them?" Ty asked.

"Hell, no," said Lock. "But you try disproving it."

"Okay," said Ty, yawning loudly. "I'm going to check in on the little Russian princess, then hit the hay for a few hours."

"The princess?"

"Anastasia, not Elizabeth," said Ty.

"Good. You had me worried there for a second. Goodnight."

"Night."

Ty's turn on residential security detail started at two in the morning and would run until mid-afternoon. He would be joined by one of McLennan's team. Until then, Lock was on duty with McLennan.

When drawing up the rota, he and Ty had decided it was better not to work the same shifts. It would help establish their relationship with McLennan's team, and it also served as insurance that everything was being done properly. One man would monitor the camera feeds and alarms in the control room, while the other would patrol. Then they would switch.

Lock had insisted that they use a patrol pattern that shifted over the course of the night rather than taking place at set times. Predictability was the enemy of good residential patrol work. The pattern would vary randomly from night to night. That way, anyone looking to enter the building would have no way of knowing exactly where one of them would be at any given time.

As an additional measure, all four men would be staying in the townhouse, utilizing some of the many spare bedrooms. That way, if there was an issue, four of them would be available immediately to deal with it.

Lock's hope was that once they had everything stabilized, and some fresh personnel added to the team, he and Ty could step down their day-to-day involvement.

But until then, it was a matter of sucking up the twelve-hour shifts.

Ty knocked quietly on Anastasia's bedroom door. She was lying in bed, watching TV.

"Shouldn't you be asleep, young lady?" he said, peering around the door.

"You're not going to be a tattle-tale, are you?"

"Me? No, I ain't no snitch. But, seriously, you should get some rest."

"I haven't had my story."

"You want me to get your mom?" asked Ty.

"Could you read it to me?"

"Sure thing."

He walked across to a small bookcase by the window.

"Any requests?" he asked her, scanning the spines. "Let me see, what do we have that's good? *The Gruffalo*? *Charlie and the Chocolate Factory*? *The Princess Diaries*?"

"*The Princess Diaries*," said Anastasia, propping herself up on one arm.

"You want me to read you *The Princess Diaries*?"

"Yes." She giggled.

"You got it."

"Just at the end there," she said, pointing it out.

He plucked the book off the shelf, went over to the chair by the window that the nurse had been using, and opened to the first chapter.

By the middle of the second, Anastasia was asleep. Ty put the book back on the shelf, switched off the light, and crept to the door.

39

Ty woke by himself at five minutes to two. He got up, dressed quickly in the dark, grabbed his radio, gun and holster, and headed out into the corridor. The house was quiet, everyone else asleep. Everyone apart from him and Lock. Just like old times.

Before he headed downstairs, he checked on the kid. She was fast asleep, limbs stretched out, like a starfish's, not a care in the world. He smiled to himself as he pulled her door closed, vowing he'd do everything he could to make sure she stayed like this, safe, cocooned with her family, and free from the strain of what was happening.

At the bottom of the stairs he made a left, headed for the makeshift control-security room they had set up. Lock was standing, his eyes on the camera monitors as Ty walked in. McLennan was with a member of his team, an Englishman called Hoyle.

"Anything?" asked Ty.

"No. Quiet as the grave," said Lock.

"You know Hoyle, right?" McLennan said to Ty.

"Seen you guys around," said Hoyle.

"Likewise," said Ty, shaking his hand, then turned to Lock and McLennan. "Go get some sleep. We got this."

Lock and Ty bumped fists. Lock grabbed his jacket from the back of the chair picked up his holstered SIG and headed out with McLennan as Ty settled in.

"I'm going to do a quick recon, shouldn't be more than a half-hour," said Hoyle. "Buzz me if you see anything on the cameras."

"Roger that," said Ty.

Hoyle headed out, leaving Ty in the empty control room, which was not much more than a glorified store cupboard.

When Ty had begun working private security this had been his least favorite part of the job. You couldn't watch TV or read a book. You had to stay present, watching the same unchanging view for hours on end. Staying alert wasn't so much an exercise in patience as Zen. You had to be present but detached.

Lock had told him the only way to get through it was to accept it. If you fought against it you were likely to get lax. And if you got lax you screwed up.

A monitor picked up Hoyle, walking along the hallway, headed into the kitchen. Keeping an eye on all eight monitors, Ty watched him move into the kitchen, through a door, and to the rear entrance.

Hoyle opened the back door and stepped outside. The outside camera picked him up as he patrolled the small rear yard, shining his Maglite into the darkest recesses. A rat scurried near some garbage cans, momentarily caught in the beam of light. Hoyle continued to scope out the area, flashlight in hand, his other hand resting on his weapon. Satisfied that all was well, he moved back to the door.

Ty tapped the keyboard that controlled the monitors, switching up a couple of angles. His attention shifted to the front outside camera as a couple walked past, arm in arm, a little drunk. They stopped a few feet from the bottom of the townhouse steps, the man pulling in his female companion for a kiss. His hand moved down to her thigh. She backed off, playfully swatting him away. He took her hand and they moved on, disappearing from Ty's view a few seconds later.

Inside, Hoyle skirted through the dining room, checking windows that had been checked less than an hour before. He kept going silently through the house.

    Minutes ticked by. Outside the city quietened as the small hours ticked by. The odd cab flitted down the street. People hurried past. Ty kept watch, missing nothing.

40

Halfway across the ladder, Viktor froze. Directly beneath him was a sixty-foot sheer drop onto metal railings that separated the rear of the two townhouses.

The gap was nothing, really. Less than fourteen feet. Too far to jump with any certainty.

On the other side, Artur held the ladder in place against the lip of the tar beach roof. He had been first across, his journey more perilous because there had been no one else where he was now to hold it in place.

"Look at me," hissed Artur.

Viktor raised his head. The sudden rush of vertigo passed.

"Come on," said Artur. "You're almost there."

What the hell did he think he was doing? he asked himself. He was too old for this kind of caper. The painting, that was why. Ninel had known exactly what she was doing when she'd shown it to him. It wasn't only the money he could sell it for. It was the prestige of being the man who'd stolen it. The painting was famous and, in Viktor's world of thieves, the glory would reflect directly onto him.

You went out and robbed a bank, or knocked off an armored

truck? Big deal. Money was money. All banknotes looked the same. This was different. Unique. Special.

He moved his hands along the ladder and shimmied forward a few more inches. He kept his eyes on Artur.

"Almost there," said Artur.

"Shut up," hissed Viktor.

Someone would hear them if they weren't careful.

His hands were so cold he could barely feel them. He had gloves, but he didn't want to wear them while crossing. They were slippery and he was worried about losing his grip.

He was almost there. He grabbed the side of the ladder and pulled himself forward one more time. As his hands found the lip of the roof, Artur grabbed him and dragged him towards the roof. Collapsing, he lay there for a moment, sucking air into his lungs. This would have to be his last burglary. It was a young man's game. From now on he would stick to what he was good at: running the club and threatening to break people's legs if they didn't pay what they owed.

Artur grabbed his arm and pulled him to his feet. Now it was Lev's turn. He was already on the ladder, scampering across like a squirrel.

Finally the three of them stood safely on the roof. The hardest part was over.

They dug out their ski masks and put them on. There were cameras inside, and they couldn't count on them being non-operational, even if the alarms had been disabled.

Lev pulled his lock-pick set from inside his jacket, and together they walked to the access door. Once that was open they would be inside.

Ninel had promised that the alarm would be disabled but Viktor wasn't overly concerned. If it tripped his plan was simple. Get downstairs, grab the painting, and whatever else they could carry, and go out through the back door.

By the time the cops got there, they would be long gone.

. . .

Hoyle got up and stretched. He really needed to take a leak, but Ty was out on patrol. Worse, he'd only just left the control room so it would be a good twenty minutes before he'd be back.

Hoyle peered at the screens. They looked exactly as they had all night. Nothing was moving, out there or inside, apart from him and Ty. He looked at the door. There was a bathroom just down the hall. It would take maybe ten seconds to get there, a minute to do what he had to do, another twenty seconds to clean his hands, and ten seconds back.

The protocol was strict. No one stepped away from monitoring at night unless there was someone to cover. But this would take less than two minutes.

No one would even know he was gone.

Putting away his pick set, Lev pushed down on the handle and opened the door. Viktor thumped him heartily on the back. He had been the right choice for this task. No one could pick a lock faster than Lev. He was a craftsman among thieves, a true *vory*, like the old-school men who had come from Russia originally.

Together they walked through the door, down the short set of steps and into the hallway of the top floor of the house. Even a cursory glance told Viktor there was money here.

The carpets were deep and lush, the wall coverings of the finest quality. Everything was clean and polished to a bright luster. The terror of the ladder behind him, Viktor was beginning to feel much more warmly to Ninel.

Ty froze as he walked out of the kitchen. He'd heard something. A footfall, or footfalls. They sounded like they had come from up above.

He stayed where he was and listened. Maybe it was someone going to the bathroom. Or perhaps Elizabeth or Dimitri couldn't sleep and had gone to check on Anastasia.

He listened more keenly. Nothing. If it had been something, Hoyle would have seen it and given him a heads up.

A toilet flushed somewhere in the house. Yeah, he told himself, the noise had to have been someone getting up to take a leak. Maybe McLennan or Lock.

They stopped at the bedroom door. Viktor signaled for Lev to open it. Even though the house was empty, old habits died hard. There was no point making unnecessary noise.

Lev pushed the door open. He half turned. Viktor saw the expression on his face and knew without even looking into the room what it was.

He motioned for Lev to pull the door closed again.

"They're still here," Lev whispered, moving away from the door.

Viktor's jaw tightened. He silently cursed Ninel. But he had come for the painting and he wasn't going to leave without it.

Opening his jacket, he reached down into his waistband and pulled out his pistol. Artur and Lev followed his lead.

They followed him down the hallway, measuring every footstep with care as they made their way to the top of the staircase.

Hoyle walked back into the control room to see two motion sensors blinking. Probably one of the Semenovs going out into the corridor to check on their daughter. There were sensors at either end of the top-floor hallway, and those were the ones that were blinking.

Comfortable now that his bladder was empty, he sank down into his chair and scanned the monitors. Nothing. That particular hallway area was empty. He rolled through all the camera feeds. The only person he picked up was Ty who was making his way to the top of the staircase.

Anastasia Semenov tossed and turned in her bed. It was the same nightmare she'd been having for weeks. She was in a forest. Something was chasing her. She couldn't see what it was. But she could hear it, bearing down on her.

She hurdled a fallen branch, tripped and fell. The thing kept coming. Just as it was almost on top of her, she woke with a start.

She was in her bedroom. At home.

A man was standing over her. She couldn't see his face but knew instantly that it wasn't Ty. Or her father. Or anyone who worked for him.

This was a stranger, and he was wearing a mask.

As she opened her mouth to scream his hand clamped over her mouth, pushing her back down into the pillows.

He wasn't alone.

There were two other masked men with him. Only their eyes were visible.

One held his finger to his lips, ordering her to be quiet.

TY STOPPED at the door that led to the steps up to the rooftop. Something was off, but he couldn't decide what it was. When you'd been in the job as long as he had you developed a sense about things.

He had heard the footsteps. He had heard the toilet flush. Then nothing.

He thought about walking along to where Lock was sleeping and asking if he'd used the can, but he was probably fast asleep again.

He dug out his radio and keyed the mic.

"Hoyle? You there? Over."

As he waited he cranked down the volume on the radio. There was no point waking anyone else over what was likely no more than a rush of late-night paranoia.

It was his first evening patrolling the house. Every place had its own sounds; creaking pipes, wind-rattled windows. He was still adjusting, getting a feel for the place. Maybe that was all this uneasy feeling in the pit of his stomach was.

"I'm here. What's up, Ty? Over."

"I thought I heard someone using the can. You see anyone on camera? Over."

There was a slightly longer silence than he had expected. "Sorry, that was me."

Ty lowered the radio and looked at. He cursed softly under his breath. He'd speak to Hoyle when he got back down to the control room. "Okay, maybe give me a heads up next time. Over."

"Will do. Over."

Goddamn amateurs. Not leaving a control room was basic stuff. He shoved the radio back in his pocket and headed up the steps to the roof.

The access door was unlocked. He looked to see if it had been forced, but the wood and the lock didn't appear to show any damage. Hoyle must have forgotten to lock it when he came back in.

They'd have to speak to McLennan in the morning and tell him Hoyle had to shape up fast or go. The guy was sloppy. In this game, sloppiness got people killed.

Ty wedged the door open and walked the perimeter of the roof, peering over at the front to get a look at the street. A lone cab rolled along slowly, but other than that it was deserted.

He skirted round the rest of the rooftop. As he reached the far side, he saw a long metal ladder stretched between this rooftop and the neighbors.

He ran back for the access door, pulling his radio out as he went. Taking the steps two at a time, he burst through the door into the hallway.

"Hoyle! Check the cameras. Now. Over!"

"What's up?"

"We have a breach is what's up. Over."

"What are you talking about? The cameras are all clear. Over."

"Well, someone put a ladder down connecting our roof to the neighboring property and the rooftop door was unlocked. I'm going to start checking rooms. Over."

"I'll call the cops. Over."

"Yeah, you do that. Over."

Ty's first instinct was to check Anastasia's room, but he kept walking down the hallway to where Lock was sleeping. He rapped on the door, and pushed his way in.

Lock was already out of bed, pulling on his clothes, and slinging on his holster. A notoriously light sleeper he had obviously heard Ty's frantic radio call down to the control room.

"Roof?" said Lock, getting confirmation.

"Yup," said Ty.

"Go wake McLennan," said Lock. "Then check on Dimitri, Elizabeth and the kid. In that order. If they're in their rooms tell them not to worry but get them to go into their bathrooms and lock themselves inside until we come and get them. They're not to open up to anyone but us."

One thing Ty had learned over his years' working with Ryan was to trust him. He had the basics down so cold that he didn't have to think about them. And the basics were always the same. Secure your principal. Secure those closest to them. If you can, call the cavalry. Secure your location. And, if required, faced with a threat, take fast, aggressive, determined action.

Ty jogged down the hall and rapped on McLennan's door. McLennan met him, bleary-eyed and still coming to.

"We have a situation," said Ty, turning for the master bedroom.

He quickly brought McLennan up to speed with what he'd found, jogged back out into the corridor, stopping outside the master bedroom. He knocked quickly and went in. Hell, he had already seen the lady of the house naked, at her insistence, and this was hardly a time for niceties.

Dimitri and Elizabeth were still sound asleep. He called to them from the door, not wishing to startle them more than he had to.

Dimitri was the first to emerge from under the tangle of sheets at the edge of the bed. It was a big bed and, by the look of it, there was a lot of neutral territory in the middle.

"What is it?" he asked, startled.

"We're not sure," said Ty. "But I'm going to need you and your wife to go into the bathroom, lock the door and stay there until one of us comes to give you the all-clear."

Elizabeth was awake now. She threw back the sheets and made straight for the door. "Anastasia! Is she okay?"

"Don't worry. I'm going to her room now."

"What? You haven't checked on her already?" she said, trying to push past him.

He grabbed her by the shoulders. Not tightly enough to leave a bruise but enough to keep hold her. "We have a procedure. We're following it. If you want to be helpful then go into the bathroom, lock the door and stay there. Nothing's going to happen to your daughter. The police are on their way and we don't even know if this is a false alarm or not, so, please, do what I've just asked you to do."

"What's going on? We need to know," protested Elizabeth.

Ty was done. "The longer I stay here, the longer it'll take me to go check on Anastasia. So just do what I'm telling you to do."

"Come on," said Dimitri, shepherding his wife away from the door. "Tyrone knows what he's doing." He looked back at Ty. "The police are coming?"

"They're on their way. I'd guess five minutes top." Ty stepped back into the hallway, and closed their bedroom door behind him as Anastasia's opened and a man wearing a ski mask stepped out.

Without thinking, Ty drew his SIG, and leveled it at the man's chest. As his finger moved to the trigger another masked man appeared in the bedroom doorway. He was holding Anastasia Semenov in front of him, one arm tight around her waist, his right hand holding a gun pointed toward her chest.

Down the hall another door opened, and Lock came out, gun already drawn. McLennan was framed in the doorway behind him, his weapon also in his hand.

For a second no one moved. No one spoke.

A third man, this one larger than the other, appeared from Anastasia's bedroom. He pushed his way past the other two and spoke in a thick Russian accent.

"You," he said, indicating it was Ty he was speaking to. "Black man," he added, in case there was any doubt.

Ty kept his weapon raised, drawing a bead on the man holding Anastasia.

"Hurt her and I'll blow your head clean off," said Ty.

The larger man raised his hands in a gesture of mock surrender. "No one's shooting anyone. We came for something that's downstairs. A painting. We get it, and we leave."

Ty couldn't quite believe what he was hearing. *A painting?* What the hell was that about? "Okay," he said. He had no idea what painting they were referring to. But it didn't matter. If they'd take it and leave, then fine.

"You come with us and get it," said the larger man. "We walk out, and you can have her back."

Ty lowered and holstered his weapon, a show of trust that he hoped would relax the three robbers. Lock and McLennan kept theirs high.

"Let's get this painting, then," said Ty. "Let her go and take me."

The larger man shook his head. "No," he said. "We'll take you both."

"Fine," said Ty, stepping out into the hallway.

The three men stepped out from the doorway of Anastasia's bedroom, one of them lifting her up and carrying her with them. Ty walked ahead, praying they wouldn't change their mind and shoot him in the back, but knowing it was a possibility.

He led the strange procession of the three men and Anastasia down the stairs. At the bottom he stopped, and half turned back.

"Where's this painting then?"

A sharp flash as he took the butt of a gun to his temple. Blacking out from the sudden impact, he felt his legs wobble and fold under him. He fell forward, already unconscious and smashed face first onto the floor.

LOCK STOOD at the top of the stairs, McLennan next to him, and watched Ty face-plant from the pistol whipping. He drew down on the last man with a clear shot of his back but didn't squeeze the trigger.

He was confident in his ability to take the shot. But the man in front still held Anastasia Semenov, the barrel of his gun jabbed painfully under the chin of the now sobbing little girl.

Pushing away the surge of rage from seeing Ty fall to one side, he held position. *Where the hell were the cops?*

He edged down the top step. McLennan followed suit. One of the other men waved his gun toward them. McLennan hunkered down, finding an angle. The man aiming at them backed away, stepping over Ty as he followed the others toward the front of the house.

In the downstairs corridor, Hoyle's head appeared around the edge of a door. He saw the three men and shrank back, hugging cover, only to reappear a split second later, stepping out into the open.

As he dropped to a crouch and took aim, the larger of the men turned and shot him square in the chest. Hoyle fell back into the doorway, blood pooling around him. Blood gurgled from his mouth as he tried to speak.

Lock's eardrums almost exploded as McLennan fired from behind him. McLennan's shot smashed into a wall behind the three men, sending plaster everywhere.

Lock rounded on him. "Ceasefire! Ceasefire!"

The three men scuttled into the living room, taking Anastasia with them.

"Are you nuts?" Lock shouted at McLennan. "They still have the kid."

Lock had zero problem shooting and killing all three of those men, but he wasn't about to risk the life of an innocent child in the process. Not if there was any possible alternative.

Hurrying down the steps, one eye on the entrance to the living room, he made it to the bottom. He knelt next to Ty, who seemed to be coming around. His eyes flickered open and closed. He reached to his head, fingers coming back wet with blood from where he'd taken the blow to his skull.

Inside the living room Lock could hear all three men shouting in Russian.

Ty grabbed for Lock's leg, trying to pull himself up. "You hear sirens?" he asked.

"I can't hear shit after Numb Nuts took that shot right next to my ear."

"I can't hear sirens," said Ty. "They should be here by now."

The two friends looked at each other and then at Hoyle bleeding out on the floor. Lock half crouched, half walked over to him. The shot had caught him dead center in the chest. "Hang in there. We'll get you an ambulance as soon as we can."

He managed to raise his head before it fell back down.

"You called the cops, right?" said Lock.

Hoyle stared at him.

"You called them?"

He shook his head. He tried to speak but all that emerged was blood, spilling through his teeth.

Lock retreated, grabbing Ty and pulling him in out of the hallway. Lock reached into his pocket, pulled out his cell phone, ready to do it himself.

Then he stopped.

VIKTOR STARED up at the painting above the fireplace. It looked to be a Russian landscape, likely from the nineteenth century, but it wasn't by Ilya Repin, that was for sure.

Had Ninel got them mixed up? Had she lied? Right now it hardly mattered. They had minutes to get out of there, at most. For all he knew the cops could be sitting outside now, waiting for them to leave, ready to gun them down like dogs in the street.

It was a mess. He didn't believe Ninel hadn't known there were people here.

They had been used. He was sure of it. But why? What possible reason could she have for sending them to rob a house full of bodyguards?

The other two were freaking out. Artur had his hand so tight around the little girl's neck that Viktor worried he might strangle her without even realizing it. Lev was over by the window scoping out the street for the cops.

As McLennan kept watch on the hallway for any signs of movement, Lock hunkered down next to Ty.

Back in Lock's Royal Military Police days, a wily Scottish instructor had explained the job of the specialist Close Protection Unit as "organized running away." You fought only for long enough to buy yourself the time to get away.

There was no place for ego. Or faux-bravery. That was best left to others. Hoyle had made that mistake and paid the price.

"You not going to make that call?" Ty asked, staring at the cell phone in Lock's hand.

"Cops show up and what happens?"

"They might be on the way in any case. Can't imagine the neighbors are too used to gun shots."

It was a possibility. It was also possible that the neighbors either side of them weren't in residence, and that any sound had been muffled by the reinforced windows and other physical security measures that were in place.

"Come on, Ryan. What you thinking? We're not going to call the cops?"

"They have the kid," said Lock. "Cops show. They panic. Best-case scenario we have a hostage situation that's going to drag on. Worst case they freak out and someone pulls the trigger on her."

"We have to do something," said Ty.

Lock agreed. But the question was what? The immediate knee-jerk reaction wasn't always the correct one. Ninety-nine times out of a hundred he would have already made the call. But something was telling him it could make things worse rather than better.

They already had one dead body in Hoyle. They didn't need another. Especially not if it was going to be Anastasia Semenov.

Procedure had dictated that he and Ty secure Dimitri, but there were other dynamics at play. Human dynamics. Like, would Dimitri and Elizabeth even want to go on living without their beloved daughter?

"They're here to rob the place, right?" Lock said to Ty.

"You think?"

"No one even saw them come in. They knew enough to come in via the roof. What was stopping them going straight to the bedroom and offing Dimitri, or grabbing him instead of the kid?"

"Maybe they messed up. Picked the wrong bedroom. I don't know, it's one hell of a coincidence. I mean, you heard them, right? They sound pretty damn Russian. What are the odds a Russian crew just happen to land here?"

"I dunno," said Lock. "But, listen, we need to get Anastasia back and to do that we have to offer them something."

Ty rubbed at his head. Lock could see him beginning to come back into himself. His eyes were a little cleared and the blood was congealing.

"Agreed."

Lock called to McLennan, who ducked back into the room. "You think you can get back upstairs?"

"Why?"

"Can you?"

"I think so, yeah."

"You know where Elizabeth keeps her jewelry?"

McLennan stared at him like he was the one who'd taken a blow to the head and not Ty. "You're not going to …?"

"Go. Grab what you can. The shinier the better," said Lock, standing up. "I'm going to talk to them."

Ty grabbed for his leg. "Are you crazy?"

"If I get shot then, yes, I'm crazy. But if I don't then I'm just really smart."

"Don't do this, Ryan."

Lock tossed his cell phone to Ty. It clattered onto the parquet floor. Ty picked it up. Lock reached inside his jacket, pulled out his

SIG, ejected the magazine, and replaced it with one pulled from his pocket. Ty watched him do it.

"You know that magazine isn't …"

Lock raised his finger to his lips, silencing his partner.

"They shoot me, make that call," said Lock.

41

Arms out wide, hands extended, palms open, Lock stepped in front of the open door. Two men immediately raised their weapons, and he closed his eyes. When nothing happened, he opened them again.

"No one's called the cops," he said. "But shoot me or harm the girl and they will."

The larger of them, the one Lock took to be the leader, spoke.

"What do you want?" he asked Lock, his gun firmly aimed at the same spot where Hoyle had been shot.

"I want to offer you a way out of this. We give you enough to make this worth your while, I take you out of here, and you give us the girl. That's the deal and, all things considered, it's a pretty damn good one."

"You take us out of here?"

"We have vehicles outside. You can have the keys and take one or I'll drive you myself, wherever you want to go, no questions asked."

Lock felt like he was getting through to the man. On some level anyway. If they were going to shoot him they'd have done it when he'd first appeared in the doorway. That had been the riskiest time.

Anastasia was shaking. He looked at her. "It's all going to be okay,

Anastasia. This is just a problem between grown-ups, but we're solving it. You're going to be tucked up warm in bed in no time. You understand?"

He kept looking at her, maintaining eye contact, ignoring the man who was holding her.

"You understand?" he repeated.

She started to speak but nothing came out. She moved her head.

"Okay, good."

Behind him he could hear McLennan rushing back down the stairs. He hoped he'd grabbed enough to show them this was a serious proposition. In Lock's mind, getting to walk out should have been a good enough deal. But robbery crews like this one weren't exactly noted for their appreciation of a risk-benefit analysis.

To get Anastasia to safety he'd figured the deal needed to be so lavish that there wouldn't be any hesitation on their part.

He motioned for McLennan to slide the jewelry down the hallway to him. It was wrapped up in a red velvet sack.

Lock knelt down, making sure his hands were still visible, and picked it up. His jacket concealed the gun in his shoulder holster. So far they hadn't seemed to notice. That was good. If they got Anastasia to safety and he had a shot at them, he planned on taking it.

Slowly, Lock picked up the sack in his right hand. He walked over to the larger man, who met him halfway, and held it out. The man grabbed it from him with a big, meaty hand. He opened the sack and began rooting around as his compatriot gun-faced Lock.

"Okay," the larger man said. "You drive us. But the girl comes too."

Lock stared at him. "No way. She stays here. That's the deal."

"Maybe I just shoot you right here."

"Then the cops get called," said Lock. "You seriously think you'll be able to go to ground with the entire NYPD after you? Hell, you won't get out of the Upper East Side in one piece. This is your one chance, and you know it, but the girl stays."

The larger man looked to the others. The one holding Anastasia shook his head. "No."

Lock backed off. "Ty, make the call. Tell them we have a home invasion robbery and they've taken a child hostage."

"On it," Ty called out.

Everyone standing there knew what the response to a phone call like that would be. It wouldn't be just a few SWAT members, it would be an army of them. There would be roadblocks and hundreds of cops.

"Okay, okay," said the larger man. "You drive us. When we're in the car we let her go."

"No dice," said Lock. "Ty, hold the call. McLennan, get some keys. What do we have out front?"

"The Suburban's gassed and good to go."

"Perfect," said Lock. "Plenty of room."

"Your friends could call the cops as soon as we're outside," said the larger man. "What's to stop them?"

"You really think I want to get jacked up by the cops while I'm driving you guys?" said Lock. "Use your head, man. All I need is you out of this house. I've got no desire to be a martyr here."

McLennan came back with the key fob for the Suburban. He tossed it down the hallway to Lock who caught it with one hand and dangled it between his fingers.

The larger man motioned Lock over to him. Lock complied. He walked over to him. He could see the man's eyes through the ski mask, beady and darting. He might have come off as cool, but he was as jangled by this whole deal as everyone else.

"Give me your weapon," he said to Lock.

Slowly, Lock opened his jacket, reached up, and plucked his SIG from the holster. He handed it over, grip first, barrel pointed at the floor. The larger man passed it to the free man who grabbed Lock by the collar and jammed Lock's own weapon into the back of his neck.

"The girl," said Lock.

The larger man tilted his chin. The man holding Anastasia released his grip.

"Go on," Lock prompted her. "Run down the hallway to Ty. Don't stop till you get to him."

Sobbing, the little girl took off, her feet slapping on the wood flooring as she ran back down the hallway. Lock allowed himself a moment. The important part had been done. Now came the hard part.

If these bozos believed he was about to drive them off into the night, only to be shot in the head and left for dead when it suited them, they were even dumber than he assumed they looked under their masks.

42

As the echo of the front door slamming filled the front entrance, Elizabeth Semenov pulled her daughter to her, both of them sobbing.

Dimitri put a supportive hand on his wife's shoulder. This time she didn't shake off his touch.

McLennan ran back into the living room and threw a Heckler & Koch MP5 to Ty, who caught it one-handed. Peeking through a gap in the drapes, Ty could see Lock and the three men starting down the townhouse steps. Time was critical now. He turned to Dimitri.

"Take Elizabeth and Anastasia back upstairs. Stay at the rear of the house. Keep away from any windows."

Elizabeth was still lost in a mixture of shock, grief and relief.

"Now!" barked Ty. "Go!"

Dimitri began to shepherd them out, Ty and McLennan moving fast past them and into the hallway, heading for the front door. Ty checked the weapon, making sure the lever was flicked to single shot rather than three-round bursts. This was going to take precision rather than spray and pray.

"You sure about this?" said McLennan, as they hit the door.

"Yeah. You?" said Ty.

"Hundred percent," said McLennan. "Fuck those guys."

Ty liked the math. Three of them with handguns. Him and McLennan with rifles. A narrow New York street. Lock in the middle of the kill zone, the wild card.

Lock stumbled forward as the man escorting him shoved him hard in the small of the back. He'd been slow-rolling his way to the vehicle ever since the front door had closed, trying to give Ty and McLennan time to get into position for what was to come.

On the top step he'd made a show of not having the key fob. That earned him a couple of hard punches, one to the kidneys, and one to the back of the head.

"Hurry up or I'll shoot you," his escort told him.

Yeah, I don't think you will, asshole, thought Lock.

Instead he fished out the key fob and held it up. "Here it is. Relax."

His suggestion earned him a stinging open-handed slap to the side of his face, and the barrel of his own gun jammed painfully into the back of his head.

The Suburban was parked on the other side of the street, about thirty yards to the left of the townhouse entrance. The passenger doors faced the street, and the driver's door was on the side of the townhouses, a crucial detail that Lock had factored in.

He needed one of the two other men, and ideally both, to stay on the passenger side. One man he could deal with. Two or three of them drawing down on him and he'd die. It was that simple.

Ty and McLennan stood at the front door, MP5s in hand. Both men watched the small TV screen that offered a view of the other side of the door and the street beyond.

Lock and the three men exited the top of the frame. McLennan cursed as they lost sight of them walking to the Suburban.

For this to work they needed a visual of Lock. Open the door a fraction too early or a fraction too late and it wouldn't work. Like any other fight, whether it involved fists or firepower, precision trumped power, and timing beat speed.

Ty stood, pressing himself against the door and looking through the door viewer. The fisheye lens distorted what he could see, but if he shifted his eye up and to the left it afforded him a view of the street beyond range of the camera mounted outside.

"You see them?" whispered McLennan.

"Just about. They're almost at it."

"You think this is going to work."

"No idea," said Ty.

LOCK STOPPED as they reached the Suburban. He held out the key fob to the larger man.

"You want to drive, or should I?"

"Funny man," said the big guy.

"I'll drive then, shall I?"

"Open it!" the big guy shouted, reaching for the handle of the rear passenger side door.

Lock hit the button. The Suburban chirped, the lights flashing. He walked round to the driver's door, his escort coming with him, the gun still pressed into his head. The third man had stayed on the street side, ready to get into the front passenger seat.

So far, so good.

TY COULD BARELY SEE THEM. The rear flank of the Suburban was beyond his vision. He could see Lock's legs, but only just. Then, as Lock walked around, stepping onto the opposite sidewalk he lost sight of him entirely.

Now it was down to instinct. Ty focused as hard as he could, internally visualizing his partner's next steps. Moving around to the driver's door, the gunman with him, the SIG still pressed into the back of Lock's head, Lock stretching out one hand to open the door and then ...

LOCK HAD ALREADY REHEARSED the move in his mind half a dozen times on the walk from the door to the vehicle. Click, pivot, level change, then drive back up and take the man behind him to the ground. And pray that Ty and McLennan did their part.

As he reached out his hand to open the door, Lock pressed the button on the key fob, locking the Suburban's doors again.

Click. Chirp.

Bending his knees, Lock dropped down, shifting his weight onto his left leg and pivoting 180 degrees so that he was facing the man holding his weapon.

His escort pulled the trigger.

Click.

The SIG dry-fired, empty.

As he pulled it a second time, Lock drove up as hard as he could, his feet pushing up off the sidewalk, his right shoulder slamming into the man's solar plexus, knocking him off his feet. He brought his hand up, grabbing for the man's right wrist, levering it back at the joint. The gun tumbled from his hand, sliding underneath the vehicle.

As the Russian dove after it, Lock moved around him, wrapping his arms around the man's back, and lifting him from the ground before slamming him down onto the sidewalk. He landed with a thud.

The Russian's hand moved, not under the vehicle this time, but to his waistband, seeking out his own gun. Lock followed him down, diving for his arm again as the man fumbled for the loaded weapon.

AS TY POPPED the door open he heard the chirp of the Suburban and saw Lock make his move, then disappear with the gunman as they struggled on the driver's side of the hulking SUV.

Ty stepped out onto the step as the two other men turned toward him and McLennan.

Dropping down into a squat, McLennan to his immediate left, Ty raised the MP5, caught the larger man in his sights, and squeezed off a single shot. It caught his target a little wide, smashing into his left arm just below the elbow.

Ty re-sighted as the man tried to raise his right arm and take aim at the door. Squeezing off another shot, this one found the larger man's neck, blowing through his throat and sending blood arcing in all directions. His gun fell from his hand as his fingers raked at the hole.

Next to him McLennan fired off two rounds in quick succession, both slamming into the rear panel of the Suburban as his target sprawled to the sidewalk and tried to crawl under the vehicle.

McLennan took his time, scoping out the man's backside and firing anew. This one found its target, burying deep into the top rear of the man's groin.

Next to McLennan, Ty instinctively winced as the man screamed in agony.

Moving down the steps, Ty rushed toward the Suburban as finally in the background he heard the whoop and peal of sirens.

DRAWING BACK HIS FIST, Lock slammed it as hard as he could into the man's face, shattering his nose, twisting the cartilage to one side. The Russian's hand came up with the gun. It went off, the sound deafening. Lock felt the heat from the barrel and saw the flash.

If he'd been shot, he couldn't feel it. But that didn't mean too much. This was no time to look down and see if he was bleeding.

Lock brought back his arm for a second time, this time using his elbow to smash into the Russian's nose for a second time. The man let out a yelp. Lock brought his knee up into the man's sternum, finding the sweet spot, and forcing the air from the man's lungs.

Reaching down with both hands, he went for his gun hand. This time he managed to secure his wrist. Gasping for air, he slowly peeled the man's fingers from the weapon as a shape loomed behind him, and a long barrel appeared over Lock's shoulder, pointing down into the Russian's head.

"Drop it or die," came Ty's familiar, bass-rich voice.

43

The turret lights of a half-dozen NYPD vehicles splashed the block in an undulating red. Yellow and black crime-scene tape was draped at either end. The bodies of the dead Russians still lay where they had fallen. CSU techs moved among them, marking bullet casings and photographing the scene.

It was a rare triple homicide that saw the suspects waiting patiently for the cops to arrive and question them but that was what the first responding officers had found. Weapons made safe, Lock, Ty and McLennan had sat on the bottom steps as the first of many NYPD units rolled in to assess the carnage.

All three men had been cuffed before the cops had gone inside to speak with Dimitri and Elizabeth Semenov. Ty had waved off the first paramedics to arrive, insisting that first they go inside and check on Anastasia. They had come out a few moments later with the news that she was badly shaken but hadn't suffered any injuries.

It was only at that point that a handcuffed Ty had allowed himself to be led into the back of an EMS unit to have himself assessed. He winced as the paramedic shone a light into first one eye and then the other.

"Never mind that," said Ty. "You got any Tylenol in here? My head is killing me."

Satisfied that the three men offered no immediate threat, Lock's cuffs were removed as Dimitri emerged and walked over to him.

"How are the ladies?" Lock asked him.

"Shaken. There's no way Elizabeth's going to stay here for another night. She's already screaming at me about how we should have been at the other house instead of here. Anyway, how are you?"

"Well," said Lock, "my ears are ringing like I just spent a couple of hours with my head in the speaker bins at a Metallica concert. Besides that I'm okay."

"I owe you and Ty my life."

"Don't forget McLennan. He redeemed himself big-time."

"And Neil, of course. Rest assured you'll all have whatever legal support you need."

Lock wasn't overly concerned about that aspect. It would be a very reckless police department that would charge someone for killing three men who had held a ten-year-old girl at gunpoint during a botched home invasion.

New York being as liberal as it was, Lock didn't expect that either Ty or he would be invited to the mayor's mansion for wine and canapés but he doubted they'd be charged. As far as he could see it was justifiable homicide. More than justified. At no point had any of the three men so much as attempted to surrender.

They had got exactly what they'd had coming. Lock wasn't going to shed any tears for them. He doubted many others would either.

Glancing down the block in either direction, he smiled to himself.

"What?" said Dimitri.

"Looks like we got our crowd control barriers back," said Lock.

It was true. The metal barriers and wooden sawhorses had been restored to their previous positions, sealing the block at either end.

"If I wasn't popular with my neighbors before …" Dimitri joked.

"Hell of a block party," said Lock, as a CSU photographer moved around the Russian whose throat had been blown away leaving the ground a mass of blood and gristle.

"Too bad about Hoyle," said Dimitri.

Lock agreed. But this was a job in which you operated on razor-fine margins. It only took one momentary lapse of judgment to pay the ultimate price. Stepping out of the doorway had been one such lapse. It had cost him his life, but it could easily have cost someone else's.

A guy in a suit stopped in front of them. "Mr. Lock?"

Lock knew what was coming. "Where do you want to do this?"

"I'm afraid you're going to have to come with me."

"Fine, but can you guys stagger this? We'd like to have someone with our client here at all times. Unless, of course, the NPYD wants to step up and offer him round-the-clock security."

Lock already knew the answer to that.

"We can post some officers outside the property for a time and make sure there's a presence here, but personal protection is for visiting dignitaries and city employees such as the mayor."

"Good enough," said Lock. "I'll be happy to answer whatever questions you have."

44

It was mid-afternoon by the time Lock, Ty and then McLennan were finally able to return to the residence. To their credit, the NYPD had been as good as their word, posting two uniforms at the door, and keeping the barriers in place at either end of the block.

The bodies had been removed from outside and inside the residence. The street had been washed down. The Suburban had been removed for forensic examination.

Word in the media was that the cops had also identified all three of the home invasion gang, although they weren't yet releasing their names until the families had been contacted and informed. All three came from one of the many Russian émigré neighborhoods close to the city. Rumor was that they were all connected to Russian organized crime.

Lock was starting to think that there was more to this than a Kremlin shakedown. A lot more. He also suspected that Dimitri knew more than he'd shared.

Neither Lock nor Ty was about to walk away. He doubted McLennan was either. Not now. Anastasia had made sure of that. Some jobs weren't about money. They became personal. But Lock needed some answers, and as he walked past the two cops and back into the townhouse, he planned on getting them.

Even though he'd only been gone for a matter of hours, it was an eerie experience to walk through the house again, stepping on the section of floor where a man had bled to death.

Her face pale and drawn, Madeline showed Lock into Dimitri's home office and left them alone.

"You want some coffee?" said Dimitri, lifting the phone to call through to the housekeeper.

"No," said Lock. "I'm going to try to catch a few hours' sleep as soon as I have the chance."

"Of course. Listen, I can't begin to tell you how grateful we are to you for what you did last night. If you hadn't been here who knows what would have happened?"

"Thanks," said Lock. "I appreciate it."

Dimitri leaned back in his chair. "Can I ask you something, Ryan?"

"Go ahead."

"How many people have you killed?"

"A few. Probably more than a few. I don't really keep a tally. It's not something I'm proud of. Any time it's happened it's because I've had no alternative in that moment. Usually because the person was trying to kill me or someone else."

Dimitri didn't say anything to that. He pressed his hands together, as if in prayer. "Is it difficult to carry that with you?" he asked.

"I don't," said Lock. "If I did I couldn't do this job. I try to take each day as it comes." He remembered something. He dug in his pocket and pulled out the tiny USB stick that the private investigation firm had given him. He passed it to Dimitri.

"Take a look at this when you get a moment. I hired an external investigator to go through and take a fresh look at some of the people who work for you."

"And?"

"They didn't seem to think there was anything. Certainly there weren't any unexplained payments or anything that would be a red flag. But they don't know these people as well as you do so maybe have a look through what they gathered."

"Okay," said Dimitri. He took the USB drive and plugged it into the side of his computer. A folder popped up on the screen.

He clicked on it, revealing a series of sub folders. Each sub folder had someone's name.

"Madeline, really?" said Dimitri, clicking on the sub folder with her name. "She's been with me for years, long before any of this became a problem."

"And she's overseen all the background checks. If it makes you feel better they didn't turn anything up on her."

"That's good," said Dimitri, closing her folder. "I'll go through all this later."

He turned his chair back around. "Elizabeth has cleared us moving Anastasia to the Hamptons' house with the doctors. I think they were as keen as she was to get her to somewhere safer."

Lock took a breath. "This might sound crazy and I doubt it'll convince your wife, but right now this house is one of the safest places you could be. They found a loophole in the security with the roof, but that's been closed now. Plus the cops are back outside."

"Elizabeth's adamant. She doesn't want to be here, and she doesn't want Anastasia here either."

"Look at it this way. When was the safest time in this country to get on a commercial flight?"

Dimitri didn't offer an answer.

"Right after Nine/Eleven. Everyone was on high alert, and security was massively heightened. The terrorists knew that. There was no way they could pull a repeat performance, not using that method, or anything even close. They'd taken that shot, and it worked. They were going to ground for a while. That's how I look at this. Last night, whoever is behind all this stuff gave it their best shot." Lock paused. "Assuming it was the same people as everything else."

"But this shot didn't work."

"Correct," said Lock. "It didn't work here last night, which means there is almost zero chance it would work here if they tried again."

"I'm not the person you have to convince," said Dimitri.

"I can speak with your wife."

"If you can talk her round then, by all means, go ahead."

"You know, when the crime scene people were doing their work the word is that those three men had Russian Mafia tattoos," said Lock.

"Why is that surprising? Those are the people they use for their dirty work."

It was time for Lock to be more direct. Dancing around the nature of the threat wasn't getting them anywhere. This would go on until they could work out who was directing this campaign of terror.

"Are you sure this is political and not something else?"

"What do you mean exactly?"

"Well, maybe it's someone in organized crime looking to shake you down and not the Kremlin."

Dimitri smiled. "Are you familiar with the phrase 'a distinction without a difference'?"

"I can follow what it means, but that still doesn't answer my question. I know the Russian state can do some crazy stuff. We all know that. Poisonings. Political assassinations. Openly interfering in other countries. Running assets at the very highest levels of politics and business. Sowing as much confusion as they can."

"And you don't think they're capable of this?" asked Dimitri. "That seems quite a puzzling conclusion you've come to."

"I dunno. It just seems over the top. Even by their standards. One of these incidents. The cars. Or killing that model. Maybe even pulling two stunts like that to up the pressure, but this seems to go way beyond."

Dimitri folded his hands onto his lap and gave a little shrug. "I agree. But how does that help us?"

"You must still have contacts back home," said Lock. "Is there any way you could reach out to them? See if you can't find out who's driving this?"

"I've tried. But to talk to me, especially about this, would mark someone as a traitor. The only reason I'm a free man right now is because I'm here, in a country that respects the rule of law. If I were back home I'd either be dead, or in prison."

45

Lock was waiting for Ty as he returned from his interview with the NYPD. Together they walked through into the kitchen where the housekeeper was speaking with Madeline. From what Lock was hearing, Elizabeth Semenov was still dead set on moving the family out to their house in the Hamptons.

Lock would do his best to talk her out of it, but he wasn't optimistic. His sense was that they'd move out there, for a time anyway. They would have to deal with the security implications and make do as best they could.

"How'd that go?" Lock asked his partner, filling a glass with water from a cooler in one corner of the vast kitchen. He handed it to Ty and filled another for himself.

"Truth be told, I kind of enjoyed it."

"Really?"

"Yeah," said Ty. "I mean, how many times can a black man shoot a white man in this country and not have to lie about it to the cops?"

Lock paused mid-sip, almost spluttering water down his shirt. "I hope you didn't say that to them."

"What you think I am? A fool? No, I gave them the play-by-play as it went down. They seemed kind of excited about the hardware we had, but that was about it. I definitely got an NHI vibe off them when they were talking about us smoking Larry, Curly and Moe."

NHI was shorthand for No Humans Involved, a term often used by law enforcement when people with no respect for human decency lost their lives, either during the commission of a crime or after that. Lock wasn't a fan of the term, but he wasn't a hypocrite either. Faced with the same situation, he would have taken exactly the same actions as he had done in the early hours of that morning.

"Yeah. I don't see the DA being overly keen to do too much. If they hadn't had the kid, and it had just been three assholes looking for a score when they got shot, then maybe, but not the way they went out," said Lock.

"Frontier justice, baby," said Ty, raising his glass.

46

Dimitri couldn't sleep. Every time he closed his eyes he saw a personal horror reel from the last few weeks: the men drowning in shallow water as they tried to claw their way out of a steel tomb; Ruta's broken body lying on the sidewalk like a doll; the haunted look in his daughter's eyes when they had put her back to bed after the home invasion.

It was all too much. The truth was that, if he could, he would happily sign over his vast fortune if he could erase the past few months and weeks. No amount of money was worth this kind of torment.

Elizabeth had taken several sleeping tablets. As she slept next to him, huddled, knees to chest, in a fetal position, he had got up, thrown on a robe and slippers and slipped out into the hallway.

He waved up at the tiny lens of the security camera, making it clear that it was him, and not an intruder, and quietly made his way downstairs to his office.

Work had always been his sanctuary. That hadn't changed.

It had brought his life turbulence, but it was where he had found peace. As he switched on his computer the USB drive that Lock had given him caught his eye. He slid it into the USB port, and clicked open the main folder.

Rows of sub folders opened on the screen in front of him. They were broken down by employee and each employee folder into various categories. The main categories with deep dives were financial, friends, family and lifestyle.

Financial involved looking for unexpected money that could suggest bribery, or lack of money or debt that might suggest someone would be susceptible to a bribe. Friends and family was aimed at seeking out dubious connections. In lifestyle, investigators generally tried to see if someone was involved in anything that might open them up to blackmail. That fell into two categories, something illegal or something immoral or embarrassing.

Curiosity getting the better of him, he clicked on Madeline's folder, and opened up her financial information. There was a pang of guilt he felt at spying on her private financial affairs. He opened a few of her bank statements and scanned quickly through them. He could see why the investigators had drawn the conclusion they had. She was well but not extravagantly paid. Through his company he paid her a salary of just under quarter of a million dollars before tax, and her outgoings were fairly basic.

He stopped halfway down one of the statements and looked at a charge for Victoria's Secret, the lingerie store. Something stirred in him as he studied the date. Long after they had concluded their brief affair. He wondered whom she had bought the lingerie for, if anyone. Maybe it hadn't been lingerie, simply underwear.

Feeling guilt he closed that folder and moved to another. This one seemed to contain pictures taken of Madeline going about her life outside work. At the grocery store. Jogging in a park near her apartment. Eating lunch alone. That one got to him a little. She had never married that he knew of. She didn't have children. He closed the images of her eating by herself.

He clicked on the next set of images. They were taken as she visited a yoga class. She had mentioned it to him a few times. She had even encouraged him to try it. He had found the idea laughable, a man like him sweating among a bunch of women. He couldn't imagine any self-respecting Russian male pursuing such an activity.

As he went to close the picture folder, something in one of the thumbnail images caught his eye. Absentmindedly he opened it.

He looked at it casually. Then he looked again, and froze, his stomach turning over, and his heart racing faster than it had done back on the bridge as he'd watched the vehicles careen out of control.

With his right hand trembling, he moved the computer mouse to the image, and enlarged it so that it filled his computer screen.

No. It couldn't be. It wasn't possible.

He looked at the woman sitting across from Madeline. She was older, a little heavier, but her features were unmistakable. Her eyes were the giveaway. Her eyes and the look they held.

Dimitri swallowed hard. He felt suddenly lightheaded, as if he might just pass out at his desk.

Maybe it was some kind of a mirage, induced by the immense amount of stress he had been under.

That must be it, he told himself. It was the middle of the night. He was exhausted. His mind had reacted by conjuring the image of a nightmare.

He would close his eyes. He would count down from ten, and then when he opened them he would see someone else sitting across from his personal assistant.

He did it. At the count of three he could take it no more. He had to see. He had to be sure.

Opening his eyes, she was still there. A woman he had been sure must be dead by now.

How was this even possible? She wasn't only alive, she was here and, by the look of it, her presence in New York was only one tiny part of the puzzle.

Everything that had happened to him over the past months, all the horror, all the chaos, all the death and destruction, suddenly came into very sharp relief, and settled in front of him. Who would not only want to create this kind of chaos, but be capable of conjuring it?

He had his answer, and it made him sick in his bones.

47

Moscow
September 2000

Vladimir Lenin, the father of the Russian Revolution, had famously said, "There are decades in which nothing happens, and there are weeks in which decades happen."

All through the summer those words had rolled around Ninel's head as she tried desperately to convince Dimitri Semenov to take what was happening seriously.

The problem was that even as things shifted they looked the same. Unless, like Ninel, you knew what you were looking for—or, rather, looking at. She had spent enough time in what was now the FSB to recognize the warning signs.

Dimitri's destiny was now her destiny, and the things that she had admired in him back in Tagliotti—his love of risk, his lack of fear, his ability to take bold action and seize opportunities—now threatened everything. His fortune, his freedom, and their lives.

Wealth had made him reckless, although wealth seemed an inadequate word for the riches he had amassed. In the blink of an eye Dimitri Semenov had gone from a glorified *tsekhoviki* (black marketeer) to minigarch to full-blown oligarch, and one of the richest men in Russia. He owned substantial holdings in Russia's vast natural energy resources as well as a booming import business.

He had also achieved his long-term ambition of owning not one but two banks. He used them to fund his acquisitions, providing his other companies, and by extension himself, with very generous terms. The money he had taken from his businesses ran through a bewildering maze of international companies and trusts that went all the way from Moscow to London and into shell companies in places like the Cayman Islands and Jersey.

In some ways, Ninel believed, Dimitri's fortune, and how it had been acquired, was not the root of their current problems. The Russian attitude to money, and to life in general, was that it could be here today and gone tomorrow, so it was best to enjoy it, which Dimitri most certainly had.

He'd begun by buying, mostly through his tax-shielded trusts, a string of properties. A mansion in Moscow, and a dacha outside the city were followed by trips abroad to buy a house overlooking Hyde Park in London, a condo in Trump Tower in Manhattan, plus apartments in Paris, Vienna, and Zürich, where much of his personal money rested in one of the famed Swiss bank accounts.

Along with the houses and apartments had come, unsurprisingly for a man who had begun by selling cars, a string of high-end vehicles. Everything from Italian sports cars to German sedans and a specially imported armored American Humvee that was used to ferry him around Moscow. The last vehicle was bought partly for show and partly for its utility. The *vory* still circled men like Dimitri, although now the true threat came from Russia's thrusting new leader, Vladimir Putin.

Installed, or at least bolstered by, men like Semenov, the oligarchs had thought Putin would be someone they could control, a man to secure and protect their gains. They had been very, very wrong. Putin had taken power, looked at the nation's accounts and discovered a state in financial free-fall. Someone had to help pay the bills, and who better than the men who had made vast fortunes plundering the country's assets?

Not that Dimitri or the others saw it that way. They hadn't taken the risks they had only to hand it all back to the Kremlin. They were starting to enjoy their new-found riches and the lifestyle it gave them. Dimitri had just purchased a super-yacht, naming the 150-foot craft after his mother, *The Lady Yelena*. He was planning to spend the winter on his new acquisition, sailing around the Caribbean, soaking up the sun with a number of his "girlfriends," whose ages stayed remarkably constant even as Dimitri grew older.

The signs of trouble from Putin had been rumbling in the background for a while. Then had come the infamous meeting in late June where he had summoned the oligarchs to a meeting and laid down the law, telling them to stay out of politics and start paying their fair share, or else.

The reactions inside and outside had varied. For most of the oligarchs the reaction had been one of shock, and no small amount of fear. One or two, the richest ones, had challenged him. They had put him there so they could remove him: that had seemed to be their attitude.

Dimitri had reacted like it was business as usual. He shrugged it off, like it was nothing, as if Putin wasn't being serious. He even told Ninel that it was all an act for the cameras, a piece of theater designed to quell the rumbles of discontent in the country. "Men like me are easy targets," he told her. "Of course people hate us. We have everything while they have nothing. If I was poor I'd hate me too. But where were they when I was facing down the Bitch Killer? I'll tell you where. They were cowering in the shadows, pissing in their pants, too afraid to stand up for themselves."

Ninel had smiled at his little outburst. "The difference between you and him, Dimitri, was that you were a far cleverer thief than he would ever be. If you hadn't been, I never would have saved you."

He'd laughed. A year or two before he might have flown into a rage at what she'd said. But not now. Now he found it amusing. It was another sign to Ninel that they were in dangerous territory, that her partner thought he was somehow untouchable.

"You? Save me?" He smirked.

"I didn't?"

"You certainly warned me, and I appreciated it. But save me? Isn't that a little dramatic, Ninel? You think I wouldn't have been able to deal with that little street thing myself? And, in any case, you have been paid back a hundredfold."

It was a recurring theme in their rare conversations, these days. He resented the fact that Ninel still took her chunk of the profits from many of his deals. He saw it as paying in perpetuity for a one-time piece of work and Ninel saw it as ongoing, which it was, no matter how hard Dimitri denied it.

"And I'm warning you again," she said. "Only this time it's not some small-time thief coming after you but the president."

Dimitri threw up his hands. "He's all bluster. He's playing to the crowd. He can't be seen to be too friendly to people like me, even though we're the ones who put him where he is."

"I wouldn't be so sure, Dimitri."

"Oh?" he said. "And why is that?"

"There's an active investigation into you, that's why."

"Tell me something new. There's always investigations. If there weren't investigations, how would all these petty bureaucrats justify their jobs?"

"This one is serious," said Ninel. "They want your banks. Both of them."

"What do you mean, they want them? I own them. They're private businesses. They can want all they like, but they are my property."

Property. The word that had plagued Russia. What was private? What was public? Who was allowed it? Who wasn't? Was there even such a thing or was it a concept dreamed up by capitalists?

Ninel had always believed that, when you boiled it down, property had cost more people their lives in the Motherland than anything else. It was not something to take lightly. "Things are changing, Dimitri. You need to start taking this seriously."

He sat forward. "So what would you like me to do?"

It was a question to which Ninel had given a lot of thought. She knew he wouldn't like the answer. That was too bad.

"I think you should get out. Gather what you can, sell what you can, leave and don't come back."

She was deadly serious, but Dimitri thought this was even funnier. He started to laugh and couldn't stop. Tears rolled down his cheeks. He laughed so hard he started to cough uncontrollably. "But this is my country," he said.

"You asked me what you should do, and I've told you. If you stay they'll take it anyway and throw you in prison. When you come out, you'll have been stripped clean. If you come out."

"For what? What would they throw me in prison for?" he asked her.

"Now who's being naive?" she said.

He was starting to get annoyed. Ninel was happy to see it. If he was angry, perhaps he might begin to treat this with the seriousness it deserved.

"What do you mean?" he asked.

"You really need me to tell you?"

"Yes, yes, I do."

"You think that every deal you've done has been legal and above board? That bribes haven't been paid, wheels greased, people pushed out of the way even?"

"Of course not," Dimitri scoffed. "You can't do business here without bribes. Any fool knows that."

"And everyone knowing it won't save you," she said.

A WEEK PASSED. Then another. She didn't hear any more from Dimitri. She tried to contact him through the usual channels they had established, but he was dodging her. She knew he was in Moscow, which made it even more galling.

Meanwhile the rumors she was hearing about the coming storm only intensified. The prosecutor general, no doubt under Putin's instructions, had become one of the busiest men in Moscow. Slowly but surely the beast of the state was waking. Some of Russia's richest men were being arrested. Others were fleeing the country. And some, like Dimitri, were carrying on as if nothing had changed.

The problem for Ninel was that if he fell he would drag her down with him. It was inevitable. She had been his roof, more than that in fact. She could be hanged a hundred times over for the things she had done to help him, and the money she had taken. The fact she had passed on most of it might save her and it might not. When the sharks began to circle, people often forgot favors done as they scrambled to get out of the water before they too were eaten.

Ninel was at her desk, working through a stack of surveillance reports on journalists and other dissidents, when her phone rang. The person at the other end gave her a time and a location to meet them. Then they hung up.

She tidied the reports, locked them into a cabinet, grabbed her jacket from the back of the chair, and left.

HER CONTACT WORKED in the office of the prosecutor general. He was former KGB, someone she had cultivated carefully over a period of years. Cultivated for precisely this reason.

They met at a café on Bolshoy Cherkasskiy Lane, near to the Kremlin, old friends bumping into each other. They were both recognizable enough that there would have been no concealing their meeting. Instead they chose a strategy of plausible deniability.

"Ninel, how are you?" he said, giving her a hug, and slipping the envelope into her pocket.

"Very well. I didn't know you came here too."

"It's good to have a change from the old routine sometimes. Anyway, I must be going. We're very busy, these days."

"So I hear," she said, as he hurried back out. Then she slipped off to the ladies' room, found an empty stall, sat down, and ripped open the envelope.

Normally she would have torn up the contents and flushed them. This time she didn't. She would, but only when Dimitri had seen them. Maybe if he saw his actual death warrant with his own eyes he might actually believe her.

She had to find him and fast. The clock was ticking.

48

"Listen to me, you stupid bitch, Mr. Semenov is here. His car is parked outside. Now tell him I'm here."

The bank receptionist stared coolly back at Ninel. "I already spoke with his office. They said he is not available."

Ninel snapped. Didn't this woman understand that, by standing in the reception of a bank that was going to be raided in less than twenty-four hours by the office of the prosecutor general, Ninel was risking everything? Her career, her liberty and, quite possibly, her life.

She had spent the last few hours scouring central Moscow for Dimitri Semenov. She had finally tracked him down by spotting that stupid, overly conspicuous car of his, and now he was refusing to meet her.

She could have walked away. But her fate was enmeshed with his, and it was too late to untangle it. They either rode this out together, or they perished together, and she had worked too hard and sacrificed too much for that to happen.

Reaching over, Ninel grabbed the receptionist by the hair and slammed the woman's face as hard as she could into the edge of the long desk she was sitting behind. The receptionist screamed.

Ninel lifted her head up. She had a gash just below her hairline. Blood poured from it into her eyes. "Do you think this is a game?" Ninel said to her. "Now try again or I swear I'll put you inside Lefortovo myself."

DIMITRI USHERED her hurriedly into the empty boardroom and closed the door.

"What the hell do you think you're doing?" he said.

Ninel reached into her jacket, pulled out the envelope and tossed it onto the table. She watched carefully as Dimitri opened it and read the warrant. His face grew pale.

"I've made some calls. This is just the start. You'll be arrested, and you won't be released until there's a trial."

"This is ridiculous," he protested.

"Maybe. Maybe not. But have you ever paid a bribe? Have you moved money from the country that you can't prove for definite is yours?"

"Have I paid a bribe?" He laughed. "This is Russia. Everyone pays someone."

"Which is illegal, whether everyone does it or not," she said.

He walked to the door and threw it open. "Pasha! Get in here."

A slight, bespectacled man in his early thirties hurried in. He looked nervously at Ninel, who recognized him as one of Dimitri's many lawyers.

Pasha took the warrant from his boss and he, too, paled.

"This is bullshit, right?"

Pasha held up the warrant to the light. "No, I don't think it is."

Dimitri grew more irritated. "I'm not asking if it's genuine. I know it's genuine. I'm asking if they can do this."

In all the years she had known Dimitri she had never imagined that someone as clever as he was, so quick to measure a situation, could pose such a stupid question.

"They're the state," said Pasha. "They can do what they like."

"And I can do nothing?" said Dimitri. "I just have to sit here and take it, accept my fate?"

"No," said Pasha, "you don't, and as your lawyer I would advise you not to accept your fate."

The lawyer walked to the window and looked out over Moscow. Ninel knew what he was going to say, and she knew that that might be enough to get through the hard reality of the situation to Dimitri.

The lawyer held up the warrant. It was pinched between his fingers, as if it was somehow radioactive.

"Apart from the three of us here, no one knows that you have seen this. You have a plane at Vnukovo. You have an important business meeting tomorrow in New York that you must attend. You only this moment found out about it. If you leave in, say," the lawyer checked his watch, "the next four or five hours, you'll be in plenty of time to make the meeting."

Ninel watched Dimitri's face. A slow acceptance seemed to pass over him. She had taken a massive risk in coming here, but it looked like it was about to pay off. "Five hours from now is midnight," she said. "Shall I meet you at the plane?"

Dimitri looked from Pasha to her. "Yes," he said. "Meet me there, Ninel."

His voice was soft, almost affectionate, in a way she had never experienced. They stood there like two comrades in arms who knew that the battle was lost.

She walked over and took the warrant. "I'll make sure this is destroyed. You may want to think which of your papers you don't want anyone to see."

"Thank you," said the lawyer.

At the door, Dimitri caught up to her. He touched her arm. "Thank you. I'm sorry. I should have listened to you."

"Yes," she said. "You should."

49

Vnukovo Airport, Moscow

FLIGHT PLAN FILED and checks complete, Dimitri Semenov's freshly acquired Gulfstream GV sat on the apron, awaiting clearance to taxi. The flight plan showed Kiev as the final destination.

Once they were in the air and out of Russian airspace Dimitri planned on telling the pilot to go to London. The GV had a range of a little under eleven thousand kilometers, or just over six thousand nautical miles, more than enough to get them to London. There they would refuel and go on to New York where Dimitri, on his lawyer's advice, intended to claim political asylum.

Political asylum would muddy the waters in case the Kremlin requested an immediate extradition. America had courts and layers of procedure that would have to be gone through. It would buy him enough time to put together a proper plan.

The money was less of a worry. Most of his cash had been placed outside the reach of the Russian authorities long ago. That was part of the reason this was happening.

He would lose some assets. His two banks for one. He would have to fight to hang on to his gas and oil holdings. Once some time had passed he was confident he could organize some form of settlement, handing them over in return for some payment.

The tricky part was right now. Getting this plane up into the air before someone in the prosecutor general's office got wind of it.

If he was caught now, while he was in the process of fleeing the country, it would be all kinds of bad. He would look guilty, and the prosecution would go to town. Assuming he made it to trial, which was by no means guaranteed.

He unclipped his seatbelt and got up from his plush leather seat. He walked to a window and peered out. He checked his watch for the third time in as many minutes.

Where the hell was Ninel?

She was supposed to have been here a good ten minutes ago. There was only so long they could wait. They should have been getting ready to taxi by now. For someone who had been so uncharacteristically panicked, she was cutting it close.

Unless, of course, there was a reason for her delay. A reason like her having been detained.

If they had her, would she give him up? He knew the answer to that. She would have no other option. He was her bargaining chip. It was him they really wanted, not her. Although now she had warned him, and they were bound to hear about it eventually, that might change.

He was an oligarch. But she was one of them, so her actions would be seen as a betrayal. There was a special kind of justice reserved for traitors. It was the same around the world.

The cabin door opened, and a harried-looking captain appeared.

"Excuse me, Mr. Semenov, if we don't leave soon we'll miss our slot. If that happens we may not be able to leave tonight. There are restrictions. No flights to depart after one o'clock."

"How long do we have?" asked Dimitri.

"Four, maybe five minutes, six at a push."

"Okay. Thank you. Get on your radio, see if you can do something. Maybe swap our slot with someone else."

The captain shook his head. "I've already moved us twice. We're the second to last departure of the evening."

"So swap with the last?"

"I can't."

"Why not?" snapped Dimitri.

The captain sighed. "It's an official flight. The president."

Dimitri closed his eyes. Of course it was. "Very well. Perhaps it would be best not to request that we switch with them."

"I'll delay as long as I can."

Dimitri sank back into his seat. If she didn't get here in the next few minutes he would be left with no alternative. He would have to go without her.

He pulled out his BlackBerry, debating whether to call her. She knew when they were leaving and where from.

But if she had already been detained, and his number flashed up on her cell phone screen, her fate would be sealed.

He threw it onto the polished walnut table and dug out a pack of cigarettes. He would smoke one final cigarette and then, if there was still no sign of her, he would instruct the captain to taxi onto the runway.

THE GUARD FOLDED HIS ARMS, looked down at Ninel from his seat inside the gatehouse, and repeated what he'd just said with a completely blank expression. "No."

Ninel opened her car door, got out, and jammed her official ID right into his face. "I am a colonel of FSB and this is a matter of national security. If you know what's good for you then raise the barrier and allow me through."

"I'm sorry, Colonel, but I have my orders."

"From whom?"

The guard looked around, as if someone might be listening.

"From the office of the president himself. His flight is waiting to leave."

Ninel swallowed the acid bile that rose from her stomach to burn the back of her throat. That was why security was so tight. Putin himself was using the airport. It was a coincidence. It had to be. He wouldn't dirty his hands with someone like Dimitri, no matter how much money was involved. It was beneath the dignity of his office.

But if it was a coincidence it was one hell of a bad one. Bad for her. She had been cutting it fine. She'd had to go to her office and destroy a lot of documents, then go home and swiftly pack, mostly sentimental items, like photographs and letters, things that were irreplaceable.

Still, she had never thought for a second she would be held up here. She could see the airfield. She could hear the roar of the aircraft engines. She was so close to freedom she could almost touch it.

"Why didn't you say that before?" she barked at the guard. "Why do you think I'm here?"

His shoulders lifted and fell. "I have no idea."

She pulled out an envelope from her jacket and held it up. "I have to deliver this."

He went to take it, but she pulled it back. "It's not for the likes of your eyes. Only the president."

Doubt seemed to appear in his eyes. He couldn't risk refusing her entry if this was true. Like so many, he still held the old attitudes, the most important of which was self-preservation. Only ever do something if not doing it might draw the wrath of your superiors.

He withdrew into his little wooden cabin. Turning his back he lifted an old rotary landline phone and began to dial.

Seeing her chance, Ninel grabbed her bag from the passenger seat, ducked under the barrier and took off. The guard shouted after her, but she kept running as fast as she could, beyond the guardhouse and toward the runway.

THE CAPTAIN OPENED the cockpit door and walked down to Dimitri.

"Mr. Semenov, the control tower says that we have to taxi now."

Dimitri checked his watch. They had already gone a minute past the captain's latest estimate. It really was now or never.

"Okay, go ahead," he told the captain. "Let's taxi."

He pulled out his BlackBerry and tapped out the number he had for Ninel on the keyboard. He hit the call button, a last roll of the dice. If she'd already been detained...

She answered. She sounded out of breath.

"Where the hell are you?"

"I'm here. I'm here," she shouted. "Look out of your window."

He scooted over into the next seat and stared out just as the captain dimmed the cabin lights. He didn't see anything apart from a couple of other jets parked at their stands.

"Where?"

"Here. Here. I'm waving."

He saw her then. Running with a bag across open runway.

The engines roared to life. As he grabbed for the seatbelt buckle, ready to run to the cockpit, he saw a military jeep turn the corner behind a hangar. It was heading straight for them. There were soldiers sitting in back, weapons readied.

The jeep bore down on Ninel as she ran toward the Gulfstream. Even if she got to them before the soldiers did they wouldn't have time to stop, lower the steps to let her on, raise them again, and get to the runway.

Unbuckling his seatbelt, the BlackBerry still in his hand, Dimitri ran down the aisle to the cockpit. He muted the call as he threw open the door.

"Get this thing up. Now."

The pilot and co-pilot stared at him, like he was a madman.

"Yes, sir," the captain said, pulling back on the throttle, the aircraft picking up speed.

Losing his balance as the Gulfstream made a sharp turn toward the start of the runway, Dimitri grabbed for the back of a chair. Steadying himself, he put the BlackBerry back to his ear.

"Ninel, I'm sorry. I'll do everything I can for you."

"No!" she screamed down the line. "Wait! Don't leave me here! Not like this!"

Dimitri Semenov threw himself back into his seat, put his seatbelt back on, laid the phone on the table and closed his eyes.

What have I done?

"I'm sorry, Ninel. I truly am."

50

With gray clouds gathering outside, Dimitri hurried down the staircase of the townhouse in shorts, sneakers and a T-shirt. Lock waited for him at the bottom.

It had been an unexpected request. Elizabeth's routine involved a run in nearby Central Park, but Lock had yet to see or hear of her husband being involved in any form of exercise that didn't involve aspiring young models.

"We good?" said Dimitri.

"Yes," said Lock. "All set."

He had already cautioned Dimitri that now might not be the best time for him to take up jogging in such a public place. Dimitri had quickly shot him down, saying he needed to get some fresh air and clear his head. Together the two men headed outside, stepping directly into a Town Car that would drop them at the edge of the park.

In the car, Dimitri was unusually quiet. Lock read it as the residue of shock from the home invasion.

The car dropped them off in a relatively quiet spot on Fifth Avenue and the low 100s. Dimitri managed to jog for a hundred yards before stopping, hands on knees.

"You okay?" Lock asked him.

He straightened up. "I don't want to run, or jog. Let's just walk."

"Okay," said Lock, puzzled, but scanning the smattering of people walking or running past them for any sign of a potential threat.

They walked on for another hundred yards, Dimitri sucking in big gulps of air. Finally, when he had caught his breath, he stopped. "I needed to get out of the house so we could talk. Last night, I couldn't sleep."

Lock was hardly surprised.

"I looked at the material the outside agency you hired had gathered."

"And?"

"There was something. No one apart from me could possibly have noticed it, or realized its significance, but there it was."

Dimitri looked around as if some masked assassin might spring from behind a tree at any moment. It was strange: even among all the mayhem, Lock hadn't seen him quite this rattled. Or paranoid.

"So what was it?"

"I'll get to that in a moment. But it's serious, Ryan. You know how I told you this is all being orchestrated back in Moscow?"

"I do."

"Well, that's only half the story, and to understand, you need to hear all of it."

"Well," said Lock, "if we're going to have a big heart-to-heart, maybe we should find somewhere that's a little less exposed."

THEY HEADED for the quietest part of the park, which was the Conservatory Garden. Lock used to come here when he lived in New York with his fiancée Carrie Delaney and they needed a break from everything but didn't have time for a weekend escape. He selected a spot that gave him the best view of people coming and going. He would have preferred to be back in the townhouse, with the two cops posted outside the front door, but Dimitri obviously didn't trust that he wouldn't be overheard there.

"I'll organize a fresh anti-surveillance sweep of the house for tomorrow," said Lock, "in case you need to talk. Being out here is risky."

"I'm not sure that'll help," said Dimitri. "They have someone on the inside."

"Who?" asked Lock. He was still wondering what could have been thrown up by what had seemed a fairly innocuous background check.

"Madeline."

Lock was taken aback. Not completely shocked. Very little shocked him when it came to people who could be compromised or bought. And if he'd chosen someone to target he couldn't think of a better person than the one closest to Dimitri, outside his immediate family. "How do you know? They didn't catch any unusual payments." Casting his mind back to Madeline's file he couldn't think of anything that had struck him as out of the ordinary.

"There was a photograph, at her yoga class. She was with someone, a woman called Ninel Tarasov."

"Obviously you know her."

"Oh, I know her, and she knows me, probably better than anyone."

"Old flame?" asked Lock.

A rueful smile crossed Dimitri's face. "Business partner, of a kind anyway. It's hard for Americans to understand what life was like when I was born. Everything you did, everything you said could get you or your parents or the people you loved the most killed. Then one day things changed. Suddenly there was all this freedom."

He paused, seemingly gathering his thoughts.

"Have you ever seen an animal that's lived its entire life in a cage when someone leaves the door open? They don't rush out. Not straight anyway. They're scared. The cage is all they know. It's safety. It takes time for them to gather their courage. That's what it was like back then. I was one of the first to step out of the cage, me and the others they called oligarchs."

"So what's this got to do with Ninel Tarasov?"

"Well," Dimitri smiled, "what I discovered when I stepped out of the cage was that there were people who'd been living outside all those years we were inside. Those were the *vory*, the thieves in law. They didn't take too kindly to people like me, and then Ninel came along. It was the first time I'd met someone who understood my world, and their world, and her world, and could navigate all of them."

"Her world being?"

"Her world being the KGB, then the FSB. She was the person who smoothed the way for me. More than smoothed, made the impossible possible. At first she kept me and my businesses safe from the vultures. The criminals, the others like her, the politicians. Believe me, the politicians were the most dangerous of them all. Then she began to introduce me to people in Moscow."

"I take it this wasn't something she did out of the goodness of her heart," said Lock.

"No, it wasn't, but she was worth every ruble I paid her."

"Until?" asked Lock.

"When Putin came in, things changed. It wasn't even the money the oligarchs had. I don't think he cared about that as much as everyone believed. It was the power it brought. He wanted to put us in our place. Ninel warned me. She risked her life doing it. We were supposed to leave Russia together. But she never made it. I got out and she was left behind to face the consequences."

He stared at Lock. "I'd always assumed she was dead. The last I'd heard of her she had been charged and convicted, sent to prison. But now she's here. In New York."

"You think she's freelance? Or working for the government?" Lock had his own hunch, but he wanted Dimitri's take. He didn't see how a private individual could possibly engineer the mayhem that had consumed Dimitri's life without the help of a state.

"I don't know."

"Look, I know you're shaken up, but at least now you know who you're up against."

"What do we do about Madeline?" Dimitri asked him.

It was a good question with no obvious answer. Not that Lock could see anyway.

"For now, I'd say nothing. Have you mentioned any of this to anyone else?" Lock asked.

"No, just you."

"Let's keep it that way for now. I want to bring Ty up to speed, if that's okay with you?"

Dimitri nodded.

Lock exhaled loudly. "Is there any way you can figure out what Ninel's deal is without tipping her off that you know?"

"Perhaps, but it's risky. I can make some general inquiries without mentioning her name."

"You do that, and let's keep being careful here."

They began to walk back in the direction of where the car would pick them up.

"When you got out and left her behind, how bad was it?" asked Lock.

"As bad as it could get."

"But she survived?" said Lock.

"More than survived by the look of it."

51

Lock angled his phone so that Ty could see the picture of the woman they now knew to be Ninel Tarasov sitting at the table with Madeline Marshowsky.

"And you're telling me they weren't, you know, doing the dirty?"

"Nope. Purely business. Although I suspect Madeline was a different story."

"That would explain why she's helping without any money changing hands," said Ty.

"Exactly," said Lock. "The question now is what we do about it. I mean, she may have breached her employment contract or an NDA, but I'm not sure Madeline sharing information on Dimitri is a criminal matter."

"Depends on the information," said Ty.

"True."

"So what does he want to do with Madeline?"

"I told him to take his time deciding. The way I see it she's the best asset we have right now."

"All this cloak-and-dagger shit makes me nervous," said Ty. "Why doesn't he just go to the cops or the FBI?"

"And say what exactly? There's no evidence to tie Ninel to

anything that's happened. If she's FSB, I'd imagine she's been pretty careful about covering her tracks."

"What about putting those guys you used to get this on her tail?" said Ty, tapping at her face on the picture.

"Good idea," said Lock. "But risky. Right now our biggest edge, maybe our only edge, is that we know about her and she has no idea."

"See, that's why I hate all this cloak-and-dagger BS, Ryan. Can't we just track her down? Tell her to back off."

"The direct approach?" said Lock.

"Yeah, the direct approach."

"And what happens when she tells us to get lost? Here's the thing that Dimitri's scared of. This woman was basically screwed when he left her back on that runway. She was in it up to her neck, and yet, somehow, she not only survived, she's in a position where she's looking for revenge. That's not someone you want to mess with. Not lightly anyway."

"Well, we can't just sit here and wait for her to throw the next load of crazy shit at us. We have a crew that's bare bones as it is," said Ty.

"Maybe that's it."

"What is?"

"We give her an opportunity that she can't pass up."

"Yeah, but that's the problem, isn't it?" said Ty. "She doesn't want to straight up kill him. If she did, she'd have done it back on that bridge. There was nothing stopping her. They could have done to Dimitri's car what they did to the others. Hell, when those guys broke into the house, they could have smoked him in his bed."

Ty had a point. It wasn't going to be as simple as offering her a gilt-edged opportunity to take her revenge. They would have to prime the pumps first. If Dimitri was right, and she wanted him ruined, they had to find a way to remove that option first, make it so that killing him was the only avenue left open to her.

It was a problem that came in two parts. The second, offering Ninel an opportunity to murder Dimitri Semenov could be engineered. Lock was confident of it. The first, giving her the motivation to do it was trickier. But there had to be a way.

Ty snapped his questions. "I just remembered something."

"What?" asked Lock.

"Do we have any tech guys we can trust? You know, electronic surveillance, bugs, keystroke recorders, phones, that sort of shit."

"Yeah," said Lock. "We have the guys McLennan was using for the house and Dimitri's office. They're solid. What's the problem?"

"Did you notice Madeline's rocking a brand new iPhone? Like a few days ago. It's the very latest model. I only know because I was thinking about getting one. When I asked her about it she got kinda cagey. It seemed weird to me at the time, but I didn't think too much about it."

"Can't say I noticed," said Lock. "But if she's an asset, then a dime to a dollar, they have something installed on it."

52

Lock knocked on the office door, Ty behind him. Madeline opened it. Dimitri was at his desk.

"Car's outside, Mr. Semenov."

"The car?" said Dimitri, puzzled.

"Your run? You said you wanted to go running in the park this morning."

"Oh, yeah, of course," said Dimitri, catching on.

"I have your gear. You can change in the car," said Lock.

"Great," said Dimitri, hustling past Madeline as Ty appeared, escorting a slim, neatly dressed Asian man who was carrying a gray metal flight case. Lock followed Dimitri out, all business.

"Lance here just needs to do a quick sweep of the office," Ty said to Madeline, who was busy sorting through some papers.

"Oh, of course," said Madeline. "I'll leave you to it."

Ty put out his hand. "We're checking everyone's phones too. Just a standard check. We won't be looking at anything personal. We just want to make sure that no one's downloaded any trojans, stuff like that."

"Of course," said Madeline. "No problem. Feel free to look at whatever you need to."

She crossed to where her bag was sitting, opened it and faked surprise.

"This is so embarrassing."

"What?" said Ty.

"I must have left it in my apartment this morning. No wonder I haven't been getting any calls. Should I go get it?" she asked, thumbing toward the door.

Ty looked at the tech guy.

"It's no biggie. Whenever."

"Don't worry about it," said Ty.

"Okay," said Madeline. "I was going to get some tea. Either of you want anything from the kitchen?"

"I'm good. You?"

The tech guy shook his head, laying the flight case down and clicking open the fasteners.

Madeline walked out. They gave it a few seconds before trading a look.

"There's your answer," the tech guy said to Ty, removing a small black RF scanner from the gray foam inside the case.

Light rain spattered off a park bench as Dimitri Semenov bent down to tie the laces of his sneakers. Lock stood with his back to him, scoping out the immediate area for any sign of a threat.

"Are you crazy?" said Dimitri.

"Why is it crazy?"

"Because I'd be giving those assholes exactly what they want," said Dimitri.

"Yes, but you could structure it how you like. Keep the houses, the cars, some of the toys. Place the rest in trust for the family, and establish a charitable foundation for the rest. Make sure a good proportion of it is targeted at projects and charities in Russia. See how they try to spin that in the press back home when they're painting you as an enemy of the state."

Dimitri looked up, exasperated, and still apparently out of breath from a two-hundred-yard jog. "Why can't you just find her and kill her?"

Lock's focus jumped to a nearby stand of trees. A couple of kids appeared, a boy chasing after a girl who wasn't trying that hard to get away. Lock switched his attention back to his principal. "Maybe because the idea of spending the rest of my life in prison isn't all that appealing. And, you know, the rule of law, which was the reason you moved to this great nation."

"So what?" said Dimitri. "I have to just sit here like a fool while she destroys my life?"

"No, that's not what I'm saying."

"Okay, so if I give all my money away, that will save me."

"I didn't say all your money, and I'm assuming there would be a gap between you announcing that kind of move and it happening."

Dimitri eyed him with a little more interest.

"I'm assuming that with a hedge fund it's not a matter of rolling down to the local savings and loan, taking it all out in bags and closing the account," said Lock.

"So I could announce it, and then not do it?"

"Not my area, but that might not exactly endear you to people, especially these days. All I'm saying is, structure it how you like, but this might be a way of outflanking them. If they're genuine and they're making it about the money they believe you took out of the country unlawfully, well, this removes some of that pressure, doesn't it?"

"You honestly think that will stop her?"

"Let me ask you something, Dimitri."

"Go ahead."

"Do you honestly think any government is going sit back and allow this kind of mayhem to unfold on foreign shores unless there's something directly in it for them? No matter how smart this woman is, she'll have had to sell this to someone near the top. Repatriating billions, that's a good reason to let someone have their head. Personal revenge, maybe not so much."

He could see Dimitri chewing it over. He didn't respond. Seconds rolled by, extending into an uncomfortable silence.

"Let me think about it."

53

One week later

Lock had to hand it to Dimitri Semenov. When he committed to a course of action, the Russian didn't half-ass it. He went all in, balls to the wall.

The Grand Ballroom of the Plaza Hotel on Fifth Avenue was a cavernous space. It hosted many of bluestocking Manhattan's most decadent charity balls. But according to the glossy hundred-page press packs sitting on the five hundred red velvet seats this was to be the most charitable event of all: a one-off, one-time giveaway.

Dimitri's hedge-fund billions had drawn the financial press corps, from a Bloomberg TV crew to the *Wall Street Journal* and London's *Financial Times*. The more scandalous aspects of his private life, especially the murder of Ruta, had drawn media from the other end of the spectrum including the *New York Post* all the way to supermarket tabloids.

There was also a healthy turnout from the international media, mostly European, but also Russian. Lock had ensured that anyone sporting Russian or Eastern European media credentials had undergone additional security screening, although he assumed any damage they'd do would be by way of editorial spin.

For the past week, Madeline Marshowsky had been on vacation. Playing the role of concerned employer, Dimitri had insisted she have some time to herself. He didn't want her burning out.

Lock had no idea if she'd bought the reasoning. He doubted it. But it would have served to keep her handlers, Ninel included, on their toes. They'd know something was up.

All attempts to track, or gather intelligence on, Ninel Tarasov had run into a series of dead ends. As far as they could tell there was no record of her working at the Russian Embassy or any of its consular offices. Apart from the snatched photographs of her with Madeline, she didn't appear to exist. She hadn't shown up to that week's hot yoga class. Madeline had attended alone.

Maybe Ninel knew they were on to her. Maybe she didn't.

They had, however, managed to gather, via Dimitri's contacts back in Russia, who included any number of political dissidents, some intelligence on Ninel's fate.

Following her detention at the airport, she had been prosecuted and imprisoned. For five long years she had felt the full force of the state, shuttled from one bleak jail to another. From October through March she was in Siberia. Then from April through September she was moved back to Moscow where she would receive regular visits from her former colleagues.

Somehow, though, she had used these visits, slowly but surely, to improve her position. Whatever she had said must have worked because early in the sixth year of her sentence she was suddenly and inexplicably released by way of a pardon granted at the highest level of government. Not only was she released, she resumed her duties in the FSB, assisting, in a covert role, an anti-corruption task force. The poacher was now the gamekeeper.

Then, two years before she had popped up in New York to direct the operation against Dimitri, she had, the rumors went, disappeared off the radar completely. No one knew where she was, or what she'd been doing.

Lock did a final check of the dais where Dimitri was due to speak. He and McLennan were down front, earpieced up and scanning the reporters. Lock walked back into the wings to find Dimitri pacing back and forth with a team of PR advisers.

"You ready?" Lock asked him.

Dimitri steered him off to one side. "Tell me something."

"What's that?"

"Am I really crazy?"

"Crazy like a fox, maybe," said Lock.

That drew a smile. "I like that. That's good."

"Maybe don't use it in your speech, though," said Lock.

THE QUESTION of Dimitri's sanity came into sharp relief as he strode manically back and forth across the stage. About two minutes into his opening remarks he had abandoned the dais, as well as the carefully crafted announcement put together by his highly paid team of PR and media consultants, for an off-the-cuff, higher-energy and apparently improvised version.

What was supposed to have been, from Lock's earlier view of the teleprompter during rehearsals, a sober and somber announcement of hedge-fund billions being moved into a charitable trust to help the poor and unfortunate was becoming something else.

To the delight of the tabloid elements and apparent horror of the likes of Bloomberg and the more mainstream Wall Street news outlets, Dimitri roamed back and forth, like some kind of demented Russian Oprah Winfrey. Lock was half expecting that he'd ask every member of the media to check under their seat to see what they'd just won.

"As you'll see outlined in the press pack you have all received, over half of the first billion dollars I am giving away will go directly to help the poor and disadvantaged in Russia. In particular, money will go to help children suffering from cancer and other life-threatening conditions. My own family has been touched by such an event, and while my daughter is recovering, her convalescence hasn't been helped by the way in which my family has been targeted by shadowy forces."

A sea of hands shot up from the first three rows of reporters. The home invasion was in the public domain and the media knew that his daughter had been present, but her recovery from cancer had been kept private.

Dimitri waved off the questions that had begun to come at him. He had just thrown a big bucket of chum into shark-infested waters, and Lock didn't believe for a second that his revelation was an accident.

Going after some Russian billionaire was hardly likely to elicit public sympathy. Targeting the family of a child with cancer was something else. It wasn't just that the public would find it abhorrent, they would. It was that their abhorrence would force the hand of politicians and law enforcement.

Onstage, Dimitri Semenov was starting to fight back, and it looked like he was only getting started.

"As you are all aware, I and people close to me have been the subject of intimidation and violent attacks. Some have paid for their loyalty to me with their lives. I hope in making this announcement today, that I will be liquidating my fortune and giving it away to others less fortunate, that the people behind these attacks will come to their senses."

He took a theatrical pause.

"But if they do not then I say this to them."

He made sure that he was looking at the section of the ballroom holding the members of the Russian media. "Intimidate me all you want. Hurt me. Murder me even. But do so knowing that you will never receive a cent of my fortune. I owe my enemies nothing. Not a single ruble."

He stopped again, redirecting his attention back to the front of the ballroom.

"Now, if anyone has any questions..."

Lock moved out onto the stage, closer to Dimitri, as the place exploded with noise.

54

Alexei hunched over his laptop as Ninel paced back and forth. She was waiting on a call from Moscow, and as Alexei's communications were more secure than anyone else's, she had pitched up at his place to wait for it.

He had never seen her like this before. She was agitated, unable to settle.

Finally, his screen lit up. She almost shoved him out of his seat in her haste to take the call. She grabbed the headset and put it on. "Yes?" said Ninel. "I'm here."

Alexei toggled a switch on the laptop keyboard, switching on his earpiece so that he could listen in.

The caller spoke in Russian with a deep, tobacco-heavy voice. Alexei had no idea of his name, only that he was important enough to make Ninel very nervous.

"Are you safe?" said the caller.

"Yes, I am," said Ninel.

"Good. You're important to us."

"Is there a decision?" Ninel asked.

"Yes," said the caller. "We cannot tolerate this kind of open dissent. You can proceed to termination."

At that word all the tension seemed to melt from Ninel. Her shoulders rolled back, and she sighed.

"Termination?" she repeated.

"Correct," said the caller.

"It's the right decision," she began, as the caller disconnected.

Alexei looked at her as she walked to the apartment window. From what he knew this must have been like Christmas, New Year and her birthday rolled into one. She had finally been given official clearance to take out Dimitri Semenov.

There was only one problem. Before she'd arrived Alexei had also received a call from Moscow. It had spoken of a termination, but Dimitri's name hadn't been mentioned.

55

Bridgehampton, New York
One week later

LOCK OPENED the French windows and walked onto the vast wooden deck that looked out over the sand dunes. Steps led down to a wooden dock where Dimitri Semenov was puttering around on a small boat, one of several pleasure craft he kept at the house.

They had moved out to the estate on Surfside Drive four days ago, Elizabeth Semenov finally getting her way, as Lock had always known she would.

Along with McLennan and what remained of his crew, Lock and Ty had spent the time identifying as many possible weak spots in the property's security as they could.

Lock had concluded that with good surveillance they could make the more isolated location work to their favor. At least out in the Hamptons you had a better shot at spotting a threat as it approached.

New cameras had swiftly been installed around the perimeter. A new control center had been established in a crow's nest room to monitor the cameras and the existing alarm system.

Better still, a replacement close protection team had been sourced: eleven men and one woman from a small but highly regarded company based in Denver. They were arriving in a week's time.

When the new team arrived, Lock would work with McLennan on a three-day handover. Then he and Ty were heading back to Los Angeles, much to Carmen's relief.

Ty was a different matter. He'd formed a strong bond with Anastasia, and he was reluctant to leave her side. It was going to be a wrench when he left for LA with Lock.

Dimitri waved Lock down to the dock. He set down his mug of freshly brewed coffee on the railing and walked the short distance to the Russian. "You need help with something?"

"No," said Dimitri. "Could use some company, though."

"Sure," said Lock, jumping onto the narrow deck.

"I just wanted to thank you for everything. I know this wasn't what either of you signed up for."

"Hey," said Lock. "It's never been a nine-to-five gig. You do what's required. We were never going to abandon you, not with Anastasia being ill."

"I should have told you about that, shouldn't I?" said Dimitri.

"So why didn't you?"

"Because I needed you. I knew that if you saw her, you'd stay. Not just stay but do everything in your power to keep my family safe."

Lock didn't say anything to that. You didn't get to accumulate the kind of money Dimitri had without being able to get people to do what you needed them to do.

Dimitri reached into the pocket of his gray cashmere hoodie and took out a piece of paper. He handed it to Lock.

It was a check, made out to Lock's company. "That's a lot of zeros," he said to Dimitri.

"I figured that while I was giving away my fortune, I might as well take care of the people who had my back when I really needed them."

Lock was still looking at the check.

"Go on," said Dimitri. "Take it."

"Maybe I'll frame it. Put it on my wall as a keepsake."

"That's up to you," said Dimitri.

"Can I ask you something?" said Lock. "The last few days you've seemed very . . . relaxed. Like you know something we don't."

"You're good, Ryan. You can read people."

"Lots of experience," said Lock.

"You're right. I am feeling a little more relaxed. It's amazing what clarity comes from telling people you're happy to give everything away."

"The Russians?" said Lock.

"They opened a channel of communication shortly after my press conference. They weren't happy that I would offer money to people back home without them having any involvement in how it was spent."

"They want to decide who you give it to?" said Lock.

"And maybe take their cut," said Dimitri. "Not that it was presented like that, of course. But some things never change. We have a word for it in Russian. It's called the *obschak*. The *vory* used it. It's like a big pot of money, a slush fund, that the people in the gang have access to. Only this gang are in the Kremlin, and you need to put a lot of money into their *obschak* if you want them to leave you alone."

"They mention your number one fangirl?"

"Indeed they did. They are painting her as . . . What's the phrase in English? Oh, yes, a rogue element. They've assured me she won't pose any further threat."

He finished tying the bowline knot he'd been working on, holding up the rope to check his work. "I suspect she overplayed her hand and that may also have helped my cause."

"So, that's it?" said Lock. "You're in the clear?"

"I would never assume that, but certainly things are more favorable than they were. Of course, I have to finalize all the details, and perhaps I won't be quite as generous as some of the media have reported. Don't get me wrong. I'll still be contributing a significant proportion of my wealth, but I'll have enough left to keep everyone in the lifestyle to which they've become accustomed."

The wind was picking up. The boat rolled a little in the water, choppy waves slapping up against the dock pilings.

"So everything's worked out?" Lock asked him.

"It usually does," said Dimitri. "One way or the other."

56

Never return to the scene of a crime. Wasn't that the saying? Yet here he was with Ninel, speeding through the Midtown Tunnel on their way to Bridgehampton. Ninel on a mission to wreak her revenge against Dimitri Semenov, Alexei in the passenger side to make sure she never got there.

Alexei dug his laptop out of his backpack as they came up on their exit off the Long Island Expressway. Ninel gave him a quizzical look. "Everything okay?"

"Just some last-minute tweaks," he said, completely truthfully.

There was no way Ninel would have stepped into a Level 2 vehicle. This, like most modern cars, was a Level 1. But if you had physical access to the vehicle they were easy enough to rig by installing additional hardware.

Of course, he could have just tampered with the brakes, but that offered far less control and Alexei didn't want to take any chances while he was a passenger. He dug out his phone and checked that it was synced and working with the laptop. Jamming the laptop back into the backpack, he placed the backpack in the footwell, keeping one hand on the strap.

There was a stop light about five miles from the house. Immediately beyond it there was a turn-off that led down to a bridge. He would jump out at the light, take control of the vehicle from his phone, lock the doors and pilot the vehicle off the edge of the bridge, at speed.

Even if, by some miracle, she survived the impact, which was unlikely, given that he had also disabled the driver's air bag, she would be in no shape to do anything to Dimitri.

THE LAST EMBERS of sunset gave way to darkness. When you'd lived in the city for as long as Ninel had it was easy to forget just how black the night could be, even with a half-moon and an ocean for it to glimmer off.

They were almost there. Ninel took a moment to appreciate the young man next to her as they came up on a stop light that was showing red when there was no other traffic within a half-mile of them.

He was quite brilliant, Alexei. A rare and precious talent. But, sadly, no amount of technical expertise could offset her understanding of the human mind.

She eased off the gas pedal. Then, a few hundred yards short of the stop light, she jammed hard on the brakes, bracing one hand on the steering wheel.

Alexei startled.

She let go of the steering wheel and came up with her gun. "Time for you to leave," she said, opening the driver's door.

"What?" said Alexei, not moving.

She stayed where she was, looking through the open door at him.

"You don't want to be here for this, do you?"

He was frightened. He knew something was up, but he was hoping to ride it out. But the fear came off him in waves.

"What do you mean?"

"Well," she said, still leaning into the cabin, the gun pointed at him now, "you don't like to kill up close. That's not your thing. You like it remote. Computer-controlled. I, on the other hand, don't mind it. I'm happy to look someone in the eye when I do it."

She waved the gun. "Get out."

"Why? Get out? Why?"

He was disintegrating in front of her. She didn't want to have to shoot him here, but she would if she had to.

She raised the gun, two-handed, finger on the trigger. "Out. We're going to take a walk. Just you and me."

Hands shaking, he opened his door and climbed out, still holding that beloved backpack of his.

"Step away from the car," she instructed him.

She didn't want him climbing back in and taking off on her as she walked around to his side.

"Further," she said, as he backed away.

He took six more steps back. She closed the driver's door and walked quickly around.

"Down there," she said, motioning toward the side road leading down to the bridge.

"No," he said, standing his ground.

He knew what was coming. If he'd been smart he would have walked, maybe picked up the pace a little, got some distance and taken off. She would have shot him in the back, but there was always a small chance she might miss.

"Fine," she said with a sigh. "Goodbye, Alexei."

She pulled the trigger, catching him high in the chest. He fell backward, still holding on to the backpack. She pulled the trigger twice more, taking her time.

Bending down, she retrieved the backpack, walked back to the car and threw it inside. She went back to him, stripped out his wallet, phone and keys and put them into her pockets.

Finally, she rolled his body off the side of the road and down a shallow slope. It would be discovered. But not in time to make any difference.

Tonight, she had one advantage and it was a good one. Ninel had neither the intention nor the expectation that she wouldn't be caught. As long as it came after she had settled her score with Dimitri, it wouldn't matter to her. She was already a dead woman walking.

57

Ninel abandoned the car in an unused overflow beach parking area about a quarter-mile from the house on Surfside Drive. She and Alexei had assessed the security. It had been ramped up since the family had relocated. There was no way that one person would be able to dodge the alarms and bodyguards and make it inside the property without being caught.

Given the remoteness, a full-on armed assault would have worked. That, however, wasn't an option open to her. She was good with a gun, but so were the three men inside.

Thankfully, there was another option. She couldn't be certain it would work but her instinct told her it would.

Perhaps the greatest weakness in any man was his ego. And Dimitri Semenov was no ordinary man. Not anymore. He was a billionaire, and had the ego to go with it. Like the other oligarchs he had labored under the delusion that he was somehow self-made. That the vast fortune he had accumulated had come from his own abilities. That somehow he was unique, an intellectual king among peasants.

That was his weakness, and she would use it against him. Why go to all the trouble of disabling alarm systems and picking locks when there was a much simpler, more elegant way?

She came to the driveway that led down a shallow slope to Glasnost. Stepping off before she was picked up by the security cameras mounted at the entrance, she hunkered down, out of sight, and settled in to wait.

DIMITRI CLINKED the crystal tumbler with his salad fork. He sat at the head of the table in the dining room, Anastasia to his right, Lock to his left, and Elizabeth at the other end. They had been joined by a family who also had a vacation home nearby and a daughter close to Anastasia's age.

The atmosphere between Dimitri and his wife was the best Lock had seen. He had no idea whether it would last, but the arguments and petty sniping appeared to have fallen away since they'd left the city. It was good to see, if for no other reason than that their daughter already had enough on her plate without adding warring parents to the mix.

"So, I would like to propose a toast." He signaled to the housekeeper to fill shot glasses with Russian vodka. "You and you can have lemonade." Dimitri pointed to Anastasia and her friend's glasses as everyone laughed.

"Lemonade for me too," said Lock. "I'm on duty later."

"Very good," said Dimitri. "Three lemonades and vodka for everyone else. Now, the toast."

He stood up and raised his glass, looking at Anastasia.

"We," he began, "are a family of fighters, and there is no greater fighter at this table than my daughter, Anastasia. Not even Mr. Lock here."

Lock raised his freshly filled tumbler of lemonade. "No argument from me."

"Today, we received some very good news from Anastasia's oncologist at Mount-Sinai," said Dimitri.

Lock was watching Elizabeth, tearing up at the end of the table. She reached across and rubbed her daughter's arm.

"Our beautiful brave daughter is in remission. A toast! To Anastasia!"

Everyone raised their glasses as Anastasia beamed.

"Anastasia!" they all toasted.

Lock sat back, enjoying the perfect family moment. He looked from Dimitri to Elizabeth and then to Anastasia, happy for them and relieved that they'd come through what they had.

Bodyguarding rarely offered such clear moments, but when it did they were to be treasured. He excused himself and went to find Ty to share the news.

58

Dimitri woke to a chirp and the glow of his phone on the nightstand next to his bed. It was flashing with an incoming call. He looked at the time. A little after two in the morning. The number showed as withheld.

Rubbing at his eyes, he looked over at Elizabeth, fast asleep next to him.

He got out of bed, grabbed the phone and stumbled into the bathroom, keeping the light off so as not to wake his wife.

"Yes, hello?"

"If you want to talk to me, I'm outside. Down at your dock."

Even now, all these years later, he recognized the voice.

"Unless, of course, you want to hide behind your wife's skirt, or your bodyguards, like the coward I've always known you are. And don't worry, I'm alone. You've made sure of that. You have five minutes."

"Wait," he said, into the silence, but she was gone.

He paced to the toilet and took a leak. His mouth was dry from the vodka and wine at dinner and his head was fuzzy from a joint he'd smoked out on the deck before he'd come to bed around midnight.

He should inform his security and call the cops. He walked out of the bathroom and into his dressing room. He pulled on a pair of jeans, a T-shirt, a hoodie, and threw on some deck shoes.

He grabbed a step stool and used it to reach a safe he had installed above the top shelf. He pressed his index finger against it. It popped open. He reached in and pulled out his own personal protection weapon, a single stack Glock 43. It was ready to go, no round in the chamber but with a fresh magazine.

Dimitri moved back through the bedroom as quietly as he could, not wanting to wake his wife. He walked down the hallway to the stairs, the gun tucked out of sight.

As he reached the stairs, the control room door opened, and Lock appeared.

"You okay?" he asked him.

"Fine, Ryan, thank you. Couldn't sleep. Thought I'd get some air."

Lock eyed him, like maybe he didn't buy it. Or maybe Dimitri was being paranoid. His heart was beating out of his chest. Part of him wanted to tell Lock about the phone call. And another part of him knew that if he did that Ninel would have been correct when she'd called him a coward.

He would go downstairs, see if he could spot her and then decide. If he saw anyone else, or any sign she wasn't alone, he would raise the alarm.

"Good news about Anastasia. I told Ty—he was delighted," said Lock.

Dimitri turned back. "Thank you. She's going to miss you guys."

"Okay, well, holler if you need me. I'll cancel the alarm so you don't set it off when you go outside but let me know when you come back so I can reset it."

"Will do. Thank you."

Dimitri kept going, moving down the stairs and walking to the rear of the house. He turned the key and opened the French windows. Sea fog obscured the dock and the Atlantic beyond. He stepped out onto the deck.

This was crazy. For all he knew she could be at the side of the house, a gun aimed at him.

A figure appeared down by the dock, the lower half of the body shrouded in fog. Ninel Tarasov. A spectral figure from his past made flesh. Until now she had been almost an abstract figure, even as she'd sown mayhem all around him.

Now she was real again, and he couldn't help but remember leaving her on the runway back in Moscow. What if the tables had been turned? Would he have sought revenge? He knew the answer. Of course he would.

Down on the dock, she stood there, arms folded, apparently waiting for him to decide. He reached down, lifting the bottom of his hoodie and felt the Glock tucked in at his waist.

He should go back inside. He should raise the alarm. No good could come of this.

Dimitri knew all of those things. But, as at so many other points in his life, he ignored the voice of caution in his head, and headed down toward the dock.

Lock watched as Dimitri stepped out onto the deck. He seemed to hesitate, as if he wasn't sure where he wanted to go. Something was off. Lock had spent enough time around the man to know that. He'd been so happy at dinner, but when he'd met him in the hallway, it had seemed like the weight of the world was back on the Russian's shoulders.

He saw Dimitri reach down to his side. Lock tapped the camera controller, pulling back the video stream of what he'd just seen. He hit the freeze-frame button, stopping just before Dimitri's hand moved, then placing it in slow motion.

It was what he'd thought he'd seen, the grip of a Glock. Switching back, Lock saw Dimitri step out of the bottom of the frame, headed for the dock.

His P226 already in its holster, Lock grabbed his radio from the desk and took off out of the control room.

. . .

DIMITRI STEPPED ONTO THE DOCK, hand by his side, ready to draw the Glock. Ninel was standing almost at the very end, arms crossed. He couldn't see anyone else with her.

At first neither of them said anything. Finally, she tilted her head up toward the house. "It's very nice," she said.

"Thank you."

"I would ask you how you've been, but I already know."

"What do you want, Ninel?" he asked her.

"What? Can't two old friends catch up without one of them wanting something?"

He laughed. "I always admired your sense of humor. It was very un-Soviet."

"I was sorry to hear about your daughter."

She sounded strangely sincere. It could have come off like a threat, or gloating, but he detected neither of those in her tone. "She's in remission."

"That's good."

"Listen, I can't stay down here too long. Why don't you and I go for a little jaunt on my boat?" he said, looking down at the deck boat. "Catch up properly without any worries about someone listening in."

He'd thought it through on the way down here. There was no way he was allowing her to leave alive. She was way too dangerous and she knew far too much. And experience told him he couldn't count on the Kremlin getting rid of her.

Some things were better handled directly, and this was one of them. He couldn't shoot her. Even with all of his money he doubted he would get away with cold-blooded murder. Back home in Russia maybe, but not here.

He would take her out and he would force her off the boat and she would drown. It would be hard to prove anything. He could claim it was an accident.

"A late-night boat trip?" said Ninel. "Why not?"

. . .

Lock stood on the dock with Ty and McLennan and looked at the lapping water where Dimitri's deck boat was usually tied up. McLennan raised his flashlight, the beam pushed back by the sea fog.

"He can't have gone far," said Ty. "When did you see him walking down here?"

"Five minutes," said Lock. "Six tops."

"We can take this one," said McLennan pointing a toe at the small engine-propelled wooden runabout tied up on the other side of the dock.

"You know how to use it?" Lock asked him.

"Yeah, I've had the family out on it before," said McLennan.

"Ty, you good to hold the fort here?"

"Yeah, I got it."

"Good," said Lock. "Call local law enforcement and the Coast Guard and shut the place down until they get here."

Dimitri let the boat drift, the current taking it out. Ninel on a bench seat, one hand dangling over the edge.

"You know, I had no choice back in Moscow. If I'd delayed the flight we both would have been arrested," he said, studying her.

He knew she was armed. There was no way she would have confronted him if she wasn't. But she had yet to produce her weapon. He had studied the folds of her jacket and the area around her waist and come to the conclusion that whatever gun she was carrying was similarly compact to his, and secreted either at her ankle, or more likely in the small of her back.

All he had to do was make sure to keep a close eye on her hands. As soon as she reached down or around, he would do what he had to, although he was hoping he wouldn't have to shoot her.

"And what about after I was arrested?" she asked him.

"What about it? I paid for a lawyer."

"As if a lawyer was going to help me. You knew I'd never be allowed to get off."

"So what would you have had me do?"

"What we always did," said Ninel. "Pay someone. Give someone money to look the other way while I got out. Bribe someone to drive me to a border. There were a thousand ways I could have escaped. If you'd helped me."

She was right. He knew it. He could have done more. But the truth was that, with each day he had spent in New York, the country he'd fled had seemed more and more like a part of his past he was eager to forget. That also went for Ninel.

There had been enough questions to face in America without getting further dragged into the mire back home. The Americans had been willing to accept him as a businessman, a thrusting young entrepreneur, someone who'd fought the old hated system of Communism. Ninel, with all her baggage, didn't fit into that image.

"And what now?" he said. "What do you want?"

"I did want you dead. But now I need you alive so you can help me. Repay your debt to me, Dimitri. Make up for all the years I lost when you left."

Dimitri took his time thinking it over.

"Okay," he said. "I can do that. But first I need you to show me some trust."

"Of course."

He produced his Glock and leveled it at her.

"I need to trust you, but you point a gun at me? That's a nice kind of trust. I thought it was a two-way street."

"Give me your gun," he said. "Then we can talk."

"Okay," she said. "Fine."

THE RUNABOUT BOAT eased slowly through the water. The fog made seeing anything at further than a few hundred yards close to impossible, but the ocean was as smooth as it got.

Lock stood at the bow and arced a high-beam marine searchlight back and forth. There was no sign of the deck boat. "Maybe we should head out a little further," he suggested.

They had stayed close to shore, sweeping up and down in either direction, setting out to the east then passing the dock again as they came back west.

"Okay," said McLennan, opening up the throttle.

Lock stayed where he was, sweeping the searchlight beam against open water that revealed nothing.

DIMITRI TURNED Ninel's gun over in his hand. As he suspected she'd hidden it in the small of her back.

The boat was still drifting, moving into a channel close to where the current would take someone out into the Atlantic.

The water was cold. Not so cold that you would freeze to death. But it didn't need to be. Fatigue would take care of anyone unfortunate enough to end up outside the boat.

Turning over her gun in his hand, he drew his arm back and threw it overboard. The splash barely registered over the sound of the boat's engine.

"Here's my proposal," he said. "I can't be seen to be bringing a fugitive to shore on my boat."

"So drop me off."

"That's what I'm doing," he said.

She looked around, incredulous. "Here?"

"Yes," said Dimitri. "Here. You can't see for the fog, but we're not that far out. Maybe a half-mile. Probably less. Nothing for a strong swimmer. The tide will be in our favor."

He reached down, opened a bench seat, and pulled out an orange life preserver. He threw it to her.

She eyed him, seemingly unsure whether to believe his story or not.

"Aren't there sharks in these waters?" she said.

"Don't worry. They'd never eat one of their own," said Dimitri.

"And once I get back to shore. Then what?" she said.

"Contact me. Use a different name obviously. Say you're a reporter from the *Washington Post*. I can arrange things from there."

"Money?"

"Money. A new identity. Whatever you need."

"You must think I'm stupid. I go in that water, and I'll never come out again. And if by some miracle I did survive, you're not going to help me, you're going to bury me."

She started to walk toward him. He held the pistol grip tight, his finger on the trigger.

"Don't make me do this, Ninel."

"You just don't want a body with bullet holes washing up, do you?"

She kept coming forward, slowly but inexorably.

"I'm giving you a chance. Take it," he said, raising the gun up high.

ELIZABETH SEMENOV PACED THE KITCHEN.

"Where the hell is he?"

"We think he went out on his boat," said Ty. "He went down to the dock and it's gone."

"In the middle of the night?"

"Ryan and Neil are out looking for him now. I've contacted the Coast Guard and the Southampton PD are on their way now. I don't mean to pry, Mrs. Semenov, but did you guys argue?"

"No, I was fast asleep. But I can make a decent stab at why he's done a disappearing act."

"You can?" said Ty.

"It's probably something to do with a woman. That's usually the reason for him disappearing on me when he should be home."

LOCK WAS up near the bow, McLennan at the stern. They were out in deep water now. The fog had lifted a little, but the swell of the ocean had picked up.

"You hear that?" said Lock.

McLennan listened. "Nope."

"Cut the engine, would you?"

"Okay," said McLennan. "But it's on you if we can't get it restarted. This thing is a piece of junk, and it's not really a boat that should be out this far."

With the engine noise gone, Lock listened to see if he could hear what he'd thought had been someone shouting.

Nothing.

He looked down the boat to McLennan. "I don't hear anything," said McLennan.

"There. You hear that?" said Lock.

It was muffled, distant, but it was a human voice. Maybe the Coast Guard, maybe Dimitri, but someone was out there.

It came again. It sounded like "Help," but Lock couldn't be certain. "Over there somewhere," he said pointing to the starboard side.

"Okay, let's go see," said McLennan, the engine sputtering a couple of times before it kicked back into gear.

They moved slowly through the fog. The voice came again. A little louder. It sounded to Lock like a woman's voice, but he couldn't be certain. He sat at the side of the stern and scoured the water. Then he saw it, a flash of orange that rose on a swell and disappeared.

"Over there," said Lock. "Someone's in the water."

"Dimitri?"

"I don't know. Sounded like a woman."

McLennan maneuvered the boat around, circling the person in the water, and coming up behind them. Lock leaned over the edge, ready to grab them and haul them up, not sure he could do it without capsizing their craft.

As they closed in, the shape in the water took form. They were floating, head tilting back. McLennan steered them in close. Lock reached down. He'd been right. It was a woman.

"Here, give me your hand."

As he leaned out, and the woman reached up to grab him, he saw blood on the back of her head.

He turned back to McLennan. "I'm going to need some help here."

McLennan let the engine idle, walked down to Lock, and together they managed to haul her over the side and into the boat.

The two men looked at each other, both recognizing her in the same instant.

59

With a barely conscious Ninel propped up close to the stern, Lock huddled down near the bow with McLennan as he piloted the small boat back to the shore. A wind had picked up from the south-west and the water was choppier.

It looked like Ninel had taken one hell of a whack to the back of her head before she'd gone into the water. Lock had searched her for weapons and found nothing. He'd given her his jacket in an attempt to keep her warm. They'd asked her what she was doing drifting out into the Atlantic, and about Dimitri, only to be met with stony silence.

Hardly surprising, given what Lock knew of her. She would tell them only what she decided to. Right now that was nothing.

"How far out are we?" Lock asked McLennan.

"Twenty minutes. Maybe a half-hour. I tell you what, Ryan, she was lucky we found her when we did. That tide was taking her right out."

Lock took in the trembling figure at the stern. "I'm not sure she feels all that lucky."

McLennan straightened up. "Okay, let me put it another way.

She's lucky you were in the boat with me. I might have left her. In fact, there's no might about it, I would have."

Lock didn't feel the need to ask why. Ninel had been behind the death of a number of McLennan's colleagues.

"No, you wouldn't," said Lock.

"You wanna bet?" said McLennan, coming off as deadly serious.

"There are rules of engagement," said Lock. "We both know that."

"Yeah, well, you didn't watch some of your best mates drown in front of you." It was an emotion Lock was familiar with. It was understandable. Human. But it didn't change the fact that when they'd found Ninel in the water she wasn't offering any threat. They would take her back in, hand her over and let the justice system deal with her.

If Dimitri was correct, and the Russians wanted her dead, Lock very much doubted she would make it to trial. The Kremlin had a long reach and a jail, even a women's facility in New York, was a very easy place to organize an assassination.

Lock checked his phone for a signal. A single tiny bar showed at the top of the screen. They must have been closer to land than McLennan's estimation, or maybe there was a cell tower on the water's edge.

His battery was good. He tried Ty. The call dropped before it could connect. McLennan threw him his radio.

"Here, give this a shot."

There was no luck with the radio either. Meanwhile, he could see McLennan eyeing Ninel, the cogs turning.

The sooner they got back to land, the better. He knew exactly what was on McLennan's mind. The same thing he'd have been thinking about if she'd killed Ty. Payback.

And payback in the world that Lock, and McLennan inhabited tended to be a final arbitration with one man serving as judge, jury and, ultimately, executioner.

60

The fog was lifting, the shoreline visible. Lock pulled out his phone and tried Ty again. This time it connected.

"Ryan, where are you?"

"Heading back in. What's the word?"

"We're all good. The Coast Guard found Dimitri. He's here now talking with cops."

"If you can, get him for me. Make an excuse if you have to, but I need to speak with him, and keep it on the down-low that it's me. I don't want law enforcement overhearing any of this."

"Okay, hang on," said Ty.

There was some muffled conversation in the background. As Lock waited, he kept an eye on Ninel. She wasn't moving, but she seemed to be shaking off whatever concussion she'd suffered from the blow to her head.

"I got him for you. Here he is," said Ty. "Dimitri, it's Lock."

"Yes, I'm here," said Dimitri. "I'm sorry I had everyone worried, I decided to take a little—"

Lock didn't have the time or the patience for whatever nonsensical story he was about to be spun. If the cops bought it that was on them. "Listen," he said, "we're not coming back in alone. We picked up some driftwood floating out here. I'm assuming you may know something about it."

"Hang on," said Dimitri.

The voices in the background faded. Lock guessed he was making sure he was well away from the local cops.

He came back on the line. "I can't explain right this second, but I will. I'm sorry I put you in this position. Now, is McLennan with you?"

Without all the details, Lock knew enough to sketch in what might have gone down. The only part that surprised him was them having to fish Ninel out of the drink, not Dimitri.

Lock turned to McLennan. "Someone wants to speak to you."

He stepped down the boat to McLennan, passed him the phone and walked back to keep an eye on Ninel, who was watching all this unfold with increasing interest.

For his part, Lock didn't want to have any knowledge of what Dimitri was saying to his original bodyguard. He could take a guess at what it might be, and it was unlikely to be anything good.

McLennan had a hurried whispered conversation that wrapped up quickly and handed the phone back to Lock.

"So?" said Lock. "We're taking her back in, right?" There was only going to be one acceptable answer, but it seemed polite to pose the question.

"Of course. Take her back in, hand her over. What else would we do?"

The way McLennan said it offered scant consolation. A slow feeling of dread crept over Lock. He was going to need some extra insurance to make sure they didn't suddenly head back out into the ocean and return Ninel to where they'd found her, which he imagined was McLennan and Dimitri's preferred option.

He called Ty back.

"What's up?"

"Ty, we have a woman on board. Early fifties. Russian. I think it's Ninel Tarasov."

"No shit?"

McLennan had abandoned his duties and was walking up to Lock.

"Ryan, we may not want to," he said, reaching for the phone.

Lock gave him a one-handed shove, pushing him back. "Don't," he said to McLennan. "You don't want me as a problem. Believe me."

"Lock? You okay?" said Ty.

McLennan retreated, muttering something under his breath.

"I'm fine. Anyway, she has a head injury and she's going to need medical attention. I'm guessing local law enforcement are going to want to meet us at the dock, so make sure they don't leave."

"Roger that," said Ty.

Lock stared hard at McLennan. "We'll be there soon."

"You shouldn't have done that," said McLennan.

"Oh, yeah, why is that?"

McLennan didn't respond.

"Just so I'm clear," said Lock. "This isn't Iraq or Afghanistan. There are rules."

"Yes," said McLennan. "There certainly are."

61

At the dock, a heavyweight reception committee awaited their arrival. Lock counted six uniforms, including the local chief of police. An ambulance had driven down, parking as close as it could to the dock, and a little further back sat a fire truck. He could also see Ty, standing on the deck at the rear of the property.

It was a fairly impressive turnout. Lock guessed that a multimillion-dollar property, and the high property taxes that came with it, pretty much guaranteed this kind of response.

They were maybe a thousand meters out from the dock. McLennan was at the stern, and Lock was up near the bow, guarding Ninel, who studied him with weary eyes. "I'll make sure they look at that head wound before they take you in, okay?" he said.

She glared at him and kept her own counsel.

He dug out his phone and called Ty. "Hey, do me a favor. Make sure Dimitri stays inside until our cargo is safely out of the way. I don't want any more excitement."

"You got it," said Ty. "Everything good your end?"

Lock swept the boat from Ninel to McLennan. "Yeah, all good."

"Okay, see you in a few."

Lock killed the call as McLennan eased up on the engine, the boat slowing as they began to cruise slowly into the dock.

"Hey, Ryan," said McLennan. "Can you take this for a second? I just need to grab a rope so we can tie up."

"Sure, I got you," said Lock, stepping gingerly down the boat, half an eye still on Ninel, not that she had anywhere left to go.

Lock and McLennan squeezed past each other on the narrow craft, Ninel studying them with apparent disinterest. Lock took control of the craft, not that there was much to do other than maintain the present course.

Near the bow, McLennan grabbed a rope, and hunkered down close to Ninel, making a show of tying a loop. He shifted his weight and crouched.

He was close to Ninel. Too close for Lock's liking. And something about the way he was behaving set off alarm bells. He didn't know what he was up to, but whatever it was he didn't like it.

McLennan dropped the rope and rubbed his hands together as if forcing the cold out of them. He was crouched down, side on to Lock. He inched a little closer to Ninel and then it happened in a tumbling rush of motion.

Ninel's hand shot out, snatching at McLennan's waist and coming up with his weapon. At the same time, she half stood, kicking into the back of McLennan's knee and sending him tumbling over.

McLennan fell towards Lock, his hands splaying out to catch himself as her hand came up with McLennan's gun. She aimed it at McLennan's back.

Lock had already drawn his own weapon, his SIG pointed over the top of the fallen McLennan at Ninel.

Shouts came from the dockside. They were close, but not close enough for any of the cops standing there to have a clear shot at Ninel. Not without risking taking out Lock in the process.

There were two clear lines of fire, Ninel on McLennan, and Lock on Ninel, although a fractional adjustment and she could as easily shoot Lock.

At the bottom of his vision, he could see McLennan. He was staying stock still, legs and arms splayed.

"What the hell was that?" Lock asked him.

"I don't know. She just grabbed it," said McLennan.

In one sense, he was right. She had grabbed it. But he'd let her. No one in their right mind, and certainly not someone with McLennan's experience, allowed an unsecured prisoner that kind of easy access to their weapon. Not unless they were a complete idiot, or they meant to.

Even as she'd reached for it, McLennan hadn't reacted. He was lucky not to have been shot. Then again, maybe he'd factored in that Ninel wasn't dumb enough to take him out and risk Lock immediately shooting her.

It seemed to Lock like McLennan had manufactured this. But if he wanted rid of Ninel before they reached dry land, why hadn't he shot her himself?

Lock suspected he knew the answer and he didn't like it. McLennan wanted rid of Ninel, but he didn't want to face the consequences of doing it himself. Not with a bunch of cops standing on the dock as witnesses.

"Like hell she did," said Lock.

McLennan twisted his torso so he could look up at Lock.

"What? You think I let her have it?"

"I don't know. Did you?" said Lock, his gun never leaving Ninel's chest. "So what's it going to be, Ninel?"

He could tell that she was thinking. She'd been handed a lifeline that wasn't one. Even if they dove overboard and let her have the small craft, she'd be picked up in no time. She didn't have an escape route so much as the appearance of one.

Escape.

Was this how McLennan had done it last time? Back when he'd been in the military? Had he engineered a situation where he could kill someone in such a way that his hands were clean?

If it was, if this was some kind of replay, Lock didn't plan on being his patsy. Not if he could avoid it.

"Put down the gun," Lock ordered Ninel. "There's no way out of this for you. Even if you shoot both of us, look at all those cops. You really think they're going to let you get away?"

She didn't move.

"Look, if something happened out there," continued Lock, "if Dimitri left you in the water, and you want to get your own back, make his life difficult, then this is your chance."

Something shifted in her expression. It was small. Almost imperceptible. But Lock caught it. It flickered across her face for a second. A look that suggested revenge might still be on her mind.

She nodded in the direction of the dock. "They'd believe me?"

Lock shook his head. "I can't say. But it's not like back home. You'd get a hearing. People would listen."

She started to lower the gun. Lock's shoulders slumped with relief.

As she brought it down, McLennan made his move, launching himself across the boat to low-tackle her.

Ninel's gun came back up, pointing at Lock.

Instinct kicking in, Lock fired. His shot hitting her flush in the middle of the chest. He fired again, this one punching through the ribcage and finding her heart.

She fell back, her shot going high and wide. Slumping to one side, her arm fell into the water, her hand trailing through the waves.

Lock lowered his weapon, pointing it at McLennan, giving his next move some serious consideration. Part of him, the dark part, told him to squeeze the trigger one more time. McLennan had almost got him killed.

Lying flat on his back, McLennan stared up at him.

"I thought she was going to …"

Lock pointed the SIG straight at McLennan's head. He stopped talking. He could hear Ty calling to him from the dock.

"Ryan, you okay?"

Lock held up his free hand to indicate he was. He stared into McLennan's eyes and saw nothing. No humanity. Only cold calculation. If it was a look intended to chill him, it failed. It sickened him. That was all.

Refusing to break McLennan's gaze, Lock removed his index finger from the trigger and pointed the barrel of the gun into the bottom of the boat.

"You and me, we'll talk," Lock told him. "But not here and not now."

62

Declining the opportunity to get some sleep, Lock accompanied the local cops back to Headquarters and gave them a statement. In terms of Lock shooting and killing Ninel Tarasov, it was, on the surface, straightforward.

It helped that the local cops, including the chief of police, had stood on the dock and watched it play out. Lock could tell that they had no appetite to give him a hard time. The Hamptons relied on their wealthy visitors, and the local cops wanted this squared away as quickly as possible.

After giving a bare-bones rundown on finding Ninel, and what had happened during the final approach, Lock had submitted to questions.

"And you've no idea why your colleague got so close that this individual was able to grab his weapon?" the detective in charge asked him.

Lock absolutely did, but he wasn't about to share his suspicion in this forum. Instead, he settled for an attorney-like, "You'd have to ask him what he was thinking. I couldn't tell you."

As he sat there in an uncomfortable chair that squeaked every time he shifted his weight and drank bad coffee, his resentment built. It was one thing to sit there and defend a decision you had taken yourself. It was quite another to defend killing someone when the decision had been taken for you.

After another period of going around in circles, they finally wrapped things up. Lock stood, stretched, and shook the detective's hand. He walked out of the building into a hazy early-morning sunrise.

He thought about calling the house to have someone pick him up but decided against it. Ten minutes later an Uber driver pulled up to take him back.

On the way, he called Ty.

"You good?" Ty asked.

"Yeah, I'm good. How about everyone there?"

"Still sleeping," said Ty.

"Perfect. What about McLennan? Is he back?"

McLennan had been brought in by the local PD. Lock imagined the statement he'd given would have been the same BS he'd tried to palm him off with in the boat. He couldn't imagine the cops would have bought it either. The man had all but handed over his weapon.

"He's here," said Ty.

"I'll be there in ten," said Lock. "Ask him to meet me out front. Make sure he's not carrying. One accident is plenty."

"You got it," said Ty.

The Marine knew the drill.

TWENTY-FIVE MINUTES LATER, Lock pulled up in his Uber. He thanked the driver and got out.

McLennan was standing close to the gate, arms folded, Ty a few feet from him.

Lock waited until the Uber driver had left and walked slowly down to confront McLennan.

"Listen, Ryan, I did what I had to do," said McLennan.

Lock's reply came in the shape of an arcing-over slap that caught the left side of McLennan's head. Cup your hand, catch someone flush on the ear, with sufficient force, you could burst their ear drum.

McLennan staggered back a few steps, caught off guard. He put up his hands, falling into a boxer's stance, side on, left foot forward, right foot back. Unfortunately for McLennan this wasn't a Marquess of Queensberry type contest. Lock wanted to hurt him, bad.

Circling to the outside, Lock bided his time. As McLennan moved in with a snapping jab, Lock's right foot came up, then down, the sole snapping hard on McLennan's shin.

Angered, McLennan lunged forward, all rage, no technique. Lock reached up, grabbing the back of McLennan's neck and pulling him forward. Only rather than falling into a boxer's clinch, Lock snapped his knee up hard into McLennan's face, breaking his nose before pushing him away.

McLennan swiped at the blood running down his face with the back of his sleeve. "What's your problem, eh?" he said. "You're not exactly a choirboy."

Lock circled him again. "True, but there's one difference between us."

"Oh, yeah, and what's that?"

"I do my own dirty work," said Lock, aiming a fresh kick into McLennan's chest.

McLennan staggered back again and Lock followed in, underhooking both of the other man's arms and linking his hands before tripping McLennan, and sending them both to the ground.

Lock landed on top. McLennan tried to kick at him as he landed, but Lock rolled to one side. McLennan's hand came up, open, and he jabbed a finger hard into Lock's left eye.

His vision blurred, Lock climbed on top of McLennan and began to rain elbows down onto the face as McLennan did his best to cover it.

Lock kept going, alternating punches and elbows, smashing them as hard as he could into McLennan's face until he struggled to catch his breath.

Finally, he felt Ty grab him from behind.

"That's it, dude. Much more and you'll kill him."

Exhausted, he allowed Ty to pull him back to his feet. He looked down at the bloodied mess of McLennan's face. He was barely conscious, bleeding from his nose and several cuts around his eyes.

As Ty ushered Lock away, he shook himself free, and circled back to deliver a final kick straight into McLennan's side. He groaned with pain. Lock held up his hands, signaling that now he was done, and walked away.

Looking up, he saw Dimitri standing in the doorway, watching. Lock had expected to feel better, but in truth he felt worse. He hadn't quite fallen to McLennan's level, but he had lost it.

It wasn't just what McLennan had done on the boat, or the position Lock had been placed in. That was just a symptom of a wider malaise. It wasn't why he did his job. To protect wealthy men who saw everything as a game.

Dimitri Semenov had used all of them, even his own daughter, knowing that he and Ty would never turn their back on a sick child. Lock was sick of it, the whole thing.

Along with Ty, he pushed past Dimitri and into the house, McLennan still writhing around outside.

"You're fired. Both of you," said Dimitri.

Lock turned back to him.

"Good. Saves me quitting," said Lock.

"I can take care of the handover to the new guys," said Ty. "I can't leave the kid with no security."

That was fair, thought Lock. He didn't have the stomach for a second more of this, but Ty was right: Anastasia was an innocent in this, and even with Ninel dead, there was no guarantee that her father wouldn't come under a renewed threat.

"Okay," said Lock. "But I'm done."

"Done? As in this gig?" asked Ty.

"No," said Lock. "With the whole deal. I'm finished. I'll go find something else I can do."

"Come on, man," said Ty. "Look, it's been a rough few weeks, that's all."

"No, I mean it, Ty. I'm sick of doing rich assholes' dirty work for them. I'm out."

EPILOGUE

Marina del Rey, California
One month later

EVEN IN A CROWDED bar on a Friday evening, Ty knew exactly how to scope out his partner. All he had to do was find the corner table nearest to the kitchen. The corner because that meant Lock had a view of the place, and no one could sneak up on him. Near the kitchen because that offered an exit point.

Pushing his way through the crush, Ty pulled out a chair and sat down across from Lock, who looked tanned and relaxed.

"This how you're going to spend retirement, huh?" said Ty. "Hanging out in bars?"

Lock smiled. "I'm meeting Carmen and we're going to dinner."

Ty nodded and the two men lapsed into silence.

"You want a drink?" asked Lock.

"Sure. I'll take a beer."

Lock held up two fingers and signaled to a passing waitress to bring him a fresh beer and one for his buddy.

"So how have you been?" asked Ty.

Apart from the occasional text or email related to business, they hadn't spoken in several weeks. Ty had figured that Lock needed space, and a chance to decompress after the mayhem back east. Lock had been lucky not to face any significant legal problems. So had Ty to a degree. Dimitri Semenov's money had made sure of that.

"I'm good," said Lock. "I'm enjoying life."

Ty shrugged. "Yeah, good. Happy to be back in LA."

The waitress returned with their beers. Ty raised his and they clinked bottles.

"So?" said Ty.

Lock smiled. "So?"

"Come on, Ryan. You know why I'm here."

Lock tilted back his beer and took a sip. "You want to know if I really meant what I said back there. About quitting."

"And did you?"

Lock sighed, like he'd been anticipating this conversation, but not exactly relishing it. "Yes, I meant it. I'm done."

"So that's it?"

"Ty, come on, it's not like you're going to be unemployed. You still have a ton of security review work. You'll be able to pick up other stuff too, including close protection gigs. You don't need me."

"I'm not worried about me, Ryan. I'm worried about you."

"Well don't be. There's no need."

Ty took a long drink. He known coming here that he wasn't going to talk Lock out of quitting. But he'd wanted to know if his partner was serious, or whether he'd just gotten caught up in the moment.

"So what are you going to do with yourself?" Ty asked. "Take up fishing?"

"Carmen's office always needs investigators. I might do that for a while. Or I might not. I don't know. I've not really had a long break since I came out of the military."

Ty tilted his beer and took another drink. "You'll be back."

"You think?" said Lock.

"Come on, you're an adrenalin junkie, just like me. You really think you're going to get your fix chasing down people cheating their insurance or whatever it is you'll be investigating?"

"You want to know what it is?" asked Lock. "I'm tired of working for rich assholes who think they can behave how they want and not face the consequences because they know they can pay people like us to come along and clean up their mess."

"I get that," said Ty. "I really do. I just don't think it's a good enough reason to walk away."

"And maybe I'm tired," said Lock. "How many people can you watch get killed before you stop caring? And I don't want to stop caring."

Ty watched Lock drain the last of his beer.

"You want another?" Ty asked.

"No, I'd better not," said Lock, reaching into his pocket and pulling out his phone to read a text. "That's Carmen, she's outside."

"Okay, man," said Ty as Lock stood up.

"You know we can still hang, right?" said Lock.

Ty stood, the two men embracing.

"If you change your mind," said Ty.

Lock broke from Ty's embrace and took a step back. "You'll be the first to know."

"I'd better be."

THANK YOU FOR READING

I hope you enjoyed reading Avenue of Thieves. This is the eleventh novel featuring Ryan Lock and Ty Johnson that I've written since 2008.

Book number twelve in the series, The Last Bodyguard, will be out in early 2021, but you can pre-order it now by clicking on the title.

If you enjoyed this book and you have a moment it helps me hugely if you leave a brief review. Positive reader reviews are the number one way to help readers find the series.

You can post a review on your relevant Amazon, or other store, by following these links:

Amazon USA
Amazon UK
Amazon Canada
Amazon Australia
Barnes & Noble
Apple Books

If you have any thoughts, comments, or even complaints, feel free to contact me via my website.

Thanks again for reading
Sean Black

ALSO BY SEAN BLACK

The Ryan Lock & Ty Johnson series (in order)

Lockdown (US/Canada) Lockdown (UK/ Commonwealth)

Deadlock (US/Canada) Deadlock (UK/Commonwealth)

Gridlock (US/Canada) Gridlock (UK/Commonwealth)

The Devil's Bounty (US/Canada) The Devil's Bounty (UK/Commonwealth)

The Innocent

Fire Point

The Edge of Alone

Second Chance

The Red Tiger

The Deep Abiding

Avenue of Thieves

The Last Bodyguard (January, 2021)

Ryan Lock Boxsets

Ryan Lock Boxset One: Lockdown; Deadlock; Gridlock (Ryan Lock Series Boxset Book 1) - (US & Canada only)

Ryan Lock Boxset Two: The Innocent; Fire Point; Second Chance

Ryan Lock Boxset Three: Second Chance; Red Tiger; The Deep Abiding

The Byron Tibor Series

Post

Blood Country

Winter's Rage

~

Sign up to Sean Black's VIP mailing list for a free e-book and updates about new releases

Your email will be kept confidential. You will not be spammed. You can unsubscribe at any time.

Click the link below to sign up:

http://seanblackauthor.com/subscribe/

ABOUT THE AUTHOR

To research his books, Sean Black has trained as a bodyguard in the UK and Eastern Europe, spent time inside America's most dangerous Supermax prison, Pelican Bay in California, undergone desert survival training in Arizona, and ventured into the tunnels under Las Vegas.

A graduate of Oxford University, England and Columbia University in New York, Sean lives in Dublin, Ireland.

When he's not writing, Sean trains in Brazilian Jiu Jitsu. In 2019 he became the first amputee in Ireland to be awarded his blue belt. He competes regularly, including at the 2020 European Championships in Lisbon.

His Ryan Lock and Byron Tibor thrillers have been translated into Dutch, French, German, Italian, Portugese, Russian, Spanish, and Turkish.